LOST STAR

WINGS OF ARTEMIS 11

REBECCA ROYCE

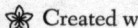

INTRODUCTION

Dearest Reader,

Thank you so much for taking the time to follow me to this point. *Lost Star* (Wings of Artemis 11) is the first part of the final arc of this series. There will just be one more book after this one. If you've read all of them from Melissa through Amber leading up to this book, I can't thank you enough. If you've jumped around, that's okay too, and I am just as happy to have you reading. That dratted black hole messes with the timeline anyway.

Sienna and her guys are newcomers to the universe. Somewhat literally. Those Super Soldiers don't have a lot of experience at living and neither do Sienna, Wade, or Trenton. I love these guys, and I hope you'll agree with me that they were the perfect people to end these stories. They need each other in a way that is hard for me to articulate, except to ask you to follow them on the page with me.

Hugs,
RR

If you haven't already please find me online, particularly on Facebook in my reader's room, Rebecca's Randomness.

1 / STRANGER ON A STRANGE SHIP

A BRIGHT LIGHT assaulted my eyes, and I swatted at it as though I could make it go away. It was instinct more than conscious thought. I knew, intellectually, I couldn't stop light by waving at it, but oh, the pain it caused in my head. I'd do anything to make that cease. The light, thankfully, moved, and I sighed from the relief.

What was happening? Where was I?

"Sienna?" A low scratchy voice that I didn't know said my name. "Can you hear me?"

Several low beeps from a machine followed his question. Where was I that there were electronic devices nearby? We didn't have any at home. They went against the rules of the ancestors. We weren't to have these things at home. Was I...not home?

"Sienna?" The voice again. I wanted to answer, but it was like my mouth wouldn't work. It was glued shut, or maybe it was my throat. When was the last time I had spoken? Why was this so hard?

The sound of footsteps approached. I couldn't turn to look. With the bright light gone, all I could make out were blurry shapes, the outlines of things. Nausea rolled through me. If I moved, even an inch, I was going to puke. There was nothing I hated more than throwing up. Was there anything worse?

"I don't think she's hearing you." A new voice. Also male. This one even lower.

There were two men here. Two? How were there two men in the room with me? Maybe one of the bishops might be around, but never more than that. They weren't allowed near the trainees. What was happening?

A sigh. Not one of tiredness, but exasperation. "This is a process. She probably hears me, Blaze. But she's been in cryogenic sleep for a very long time, and she's been sick. It's going to take a little while for her to be okay." Anxiety rushed through my veins. I'd been sick? What? Was I going to be okay? What was happening? A gentle hand stroked the hair off my forehead, soothing me. "Not all of us are Super Soldiers." What was a Super Soldier? "Sienna, rest. You're safe here. I'm taking care of you."

He had a kind voice, even if it was male. I could count on one hand the number of men I'd heard speak before him. There was something familiar about it, too, as though I'd heard him from a distance. Blaze, which seemed a strange name, or at least, not one I'd heard before, was recognizable, yet not as clear as the nameless one. Still, I closed my eyes, trusting the voice that I was safe where I was.

Something was wrong, but maybe I...

The next time I opened my eyes, there wasn't a bright light. I looked around, able to make out my surroundings. A man stood with his back to me, reading something on a screen in front of him. He turned slightly, and I studied him, as he hadn't yet noticed me. Was he the owner of the voice that had encouraged me to rest, or was he someone new? Where was I? What was happening?

I fought for clarity, but none presented itself. Okay. I had to figure things out and quickly. I knew one thing for sure—I didn't know this place. It was a medical bay of some kind. The machines surrounding me were unfamiliar. Understanding technology wasn't on the list of the things expected of me as a trainee. When I'd been selected as an initiate to spend my life in the temple at the age of five, I'd been removed from all things modern.

We knew that these things existed, but not what they did or how they worked. Others kept that knowledge for us.

Something must have happened to me, and I'd been brought for help. That made sense. He'd said I'd been sick. Was I now better? With my mind settled on this as the most likely scenario, I stared at my companion again, who had yet to notice me. I didn't know what was on that tablet, but he furrowed his brow as he stared at it.

He was what my fellow trainee Christiana would have called handsome. She was very preoccupied with things like that. If she ever had a husband, she was sure he would be very good looking as a qualification. I didn't expect to ever have one, since it had been all but decided I would be chosen. I wouldn't have a family of my own, the whole universe could be called my children.

But Christiana, had she made the remark about this man, would have been correct. He was handsome.

He had a long, angular face with tired eyes. What gave me that impression? His blue depths were exhausted. Add to that the dark smudges beneath them, and tired was absolutely the first impression he gave me. My heart clenched. This man had seen pain. My fingers tingled to do something about that. I swallowed. I couldn't soothe his hurts by petting him like a dog. His hair was a combination of blond and brown, streaks of it looking one color and then the next. It fell slightly in his eyes. His beard was mostly brown, which made me wonder if the blond in his hair had been dyed to look that way and then left to grow out.

The stranger appeared neat, put together, like he took time to do so. His pants were light colored, but he wore a black sweater that frayed slightly at the waist. It had seen better days. Someone wasn't taking care of this man.

He jolted all of a sudden, like he came back to awareness, and swung around to look at me. His tired blue eyes widened. "Sienna? Are you awake?"

I tried to clear my throat, suddenly aware it was dry and scratchy. It hurt to clear it. "I think so."

He crossed to a machine, pressed a button that put water in a cup, and then quickly carried it over to me. "This will help. Cryogenic sleep takes a lot out of a person."

I sipped the cool goodness. Talking still hurt, but I managed it, given that I absolutely had to get some information before my head exploded. "I'm afraid you have me at a disadvantage. You know my name, and I don't know yours. And I don't know what cryogenic sleep is."

He stared at me for a long second. "Okay. Sorry. I'm Wade." He pressed his hands to his chest as he said his name. "I'm your doctor. You've been sick. Well, technically you're still sick, but now we've got that mostly managed. And your people put you in cryogenic sleep—a kind of deep sleep during which the body is stored at a very cold temperature to keep the person from getting sicker. It can also delay aging, but that was not the purpose of it for you."

Dizziness suddenly assaulted me. He must have noticed because he laid me back down. "Easy. Baby steps. Okay? Don't try to do anything too fast for a while."

"It's... Wade, why are you taking care of me? What do you mean I was cold? This doesn't...it doesn't..."

He pressed a cool hand on my cheek. I don't know why it calmed me, but it did. "I'm a doctor. You're my patient. You have been for about six months now. You're on a ship called Artemis. You're not alone." The calmness of his voice, the easy nature of his tone, helped me slow my heart rate, which had to be skyrocketing. "There are five other people on this vessel with us, all of them dedicated to keeping you safe."

I digested this information. "You said I was sick. Are they all doctors like you?"

"No." He shook his head. "I'm the only doctor. I have so much to tell you, so much to explain, but why don't we just start with what I've told you. Okay? Bits and pieces." He held up my arms, and I looked where he indicated. There on my pale skin—I always burned in the sun—was a device I'd never seen before. A clear tube with pink liquid flowing inside of it was attached to my skin. I stared at it, my mouth falling open.

Wade—the doctor—spoke again. "This is going to keep you healthy. I made it for you. I mean, I did this so you could stay healthy. But the idea for it was someone else's. A much better doctor than me. Her name is Amber Chen. Anyway, you've got me, so I did it. I'm only pointing it out because I want you to not touch it. Leave it. This is why we could wake you up." He moved the pillow behind me. "Lie back on this. I don't want to feed you for a few hours, and I doubt you're hungry. But I want you to stay right here and just relax. I promise, you'll get all the answers I have soon. Plus, I have some questions for you. Later."

He had questions for me? Wade turned like he was going to leave, and I grabbed his arm, stopping him. There was one very pressing question. I had to know right now. "Am I going to die?"

My voice broke as I vocalized that thought. His blue gaze softened as he looked at me for a second before it hardened once again to a tired, withdrawn appearance. "No. I won't allow it."

I let go of his arm. If nothing else, I believed him. That was something.

My sickness must have taken more out of me than I could have imagined. Never in my life could I have fallen asleep with so much anxiety rushing through me, but that was just what I'd done. I woke up to a blaring alarm. Immediately, my heart was in my throat. What was going on? I jumped off the table where I lay, looking around. The ship —I was on a ship!—shimmied before it keeled left. I almost fell, but grabbed on to the table just in time.

I was alone. Where was Wade?

What was happening?

"Hello?" I called out, terror becoming a palpable entity in the room. I couldn't remember if I'd ever really been afraid before today. It was like my mind had gone entirely blank.

The door flew open, but it wasn't Wade who walked in. No, it was a huge, nearly shirtless man. I tried to make sense of my own thoughts even as I registered them. His shirt was...well, it was nearly gone. Torn, burned. He was covered in a black substance that coated part of his exposed, muscular torso area.

"You are frightened, female." He strode toward me completely unconcerned and unaffected by the fact that the ship was darting around beneath our feet as though we were on waves. How was this even possible? What was going on?

I backed up into the table. I'd never seen anyone as

big as him. Besides his nearly gone shirt, he had on camouflaged pants that were rolled at the waist like they might actually belong to someone larger. His hair was brown, cut short, and his face clean shaven. His eyes were dark brown and currently staring into mine like he might...

Well, I had no idea, none, what he might do.

"I am...I am frightened. Yes. Very frightened." To my utter horror, tears sprung to my eyes. I sucked them back. Crying was a waste of time and energy. That was one of the first things I'd learned as a trainee, and I wouldn't forget it now.

Tears were fruitless. But I'd never been this afraid before. He had a weapon strapped to his back. A very large gun. Oh wow. It was a day of firsts. I had a tube in my arm, I was aboard a spaceship, the man was shirtless, and now a gun. Where was the quiet temple? Where were my pastoral views? Had there really been a time I'd thought life dull and longed for adventure?

"I take it back." I spoke aloud so the universe would hear me. "I didn't mean it."

The man tilted his head just slightly before he picked me up. I yelped before I outright shouted. "What are you doing?"

"Taking you from this room."

He was what? No. I wasn't going anywhere with him. Shirtless strangers who had weapons couldn't just haul me around. What was going to happen to me? "Where is Wade? He...he told me to stay on the table."

"He is busy." The man put me over his shoulder.

Okay. Enough. I kicked him as hard as I could just as he strode out of the room, barely missing the door itself in my effort. It seemed to make no difference. In fact, I wasn't sure he even noticed. I tried again. No reaction. How could that be? Surely that must have hurt.

Out of the medical bay, I scanned quickly, trying to take in my surroundings as the brute hauled me quickly down the long corridor. The walls had peeling paint, like no one had taken care of the ship in a long while, because there was evidence that it had been, at one point or another, covered in neat strokes of color.

The hallways were wide, and we passed multiple doors on our way before we arrived wherever we were going. Oh... was he going to put me out the airlock? I'd heard about that from some of the girls. That was a thing that could happen. Or maybe that was just fiction.

He stormed through a door that led into a room with even more computers everywhere. A man sat in a chair, swinging around to stare at us for a long second before he jumped to his feet. "Anders? What the fuck, man?"

"She's frightened. I need you to fix it." Anders—I now knew his name—set me on the chair the new man had vacated. I'd never seen so many males in my life in one space. They stayed away from us. Three in the course of one day, and Anders was shirtless. I rubbed my arms, bumping my hand against the new device there, which made me wince.

What had happened to my life?

The new man had long, multi-colored hair. The bottom half was bleached blond and the top a dark black. It looked like he needed a haircut and hadn't gotten one. Was this a thing? Wade had multiple colors in his hair, too. Did men just do that in space?

And it was the least of my issues.

"You're Sienna." Multi-colored man knelt to my level. "And this alarm that Anders should be turning off instead of hauling you around has to be terrifying you. Where is Wade?" He asked that last question over his shoulder.

"When the equalizer exploded, it burned Corbin pretty badly. But he's refusing to get in the med machine until after the equalizer is fixed. So Wade is treating him." He pointed at me. "She's scared. Fix it."

The new multi-colored haired man placed a gentle hand on my knee. "I'm Trenton. I fly this old lady we're all on right now. She needs a little repair, but we're all going to be fine. How much has Wade told you about what's going on?"

He held my gaze, and the feeling of sadness rushed over me. Wade had been tired. Anders confusing. And now Trenton was sad. My empathic abilities were not serving me well at the moment. I wished for the first time in my life I didn't have them. It would be nice to just concentrate on me.

I found my voice. "He said I'd been sick."

"You're still sick," Anders spoke over Trenton's shoulder. "It's just controlled."

I was still sick? Anders pointed at me, speaking to Trenton again. "She's scared again. Fix it."

Trenton shot up and swung around. "I get that you don't like fear. You're allergic to it. I mean, I get it in the sense that I sort of understand, not that I have the same problem. But this woman has been ill for a very long time. We don't even know how long. And add Evander to the mix. She has big problems. We're strangers. There is an alarm blazing. She's going to be frightened."

"I can't think through her fear." Anders ran a hand through his hair. "Her heartbeat racing is all I can hear."

He sounded frantic, and I couldn't stand it. If I'd really been letting my empathic abilities out, I'd have known for sure how he felt, but I wasn't going to do that right now. I stumbled out of the chair, but managed to keep my feet despite the rocking of the ship, which didn't seem to be bothering either Trenton or Anders. It must not be that big of a deal. I placed my hand on Ander's arm. "I'm...I'm not sure exactly how my heartbeat is bothering you, but I'm sorry that's happening."

Anders stared at my hand like it was a foreign object on his skin. Dread shook me. Had I done wrong in touching him? He'd carried me into the room, I'd been pressed against his bare chest. Was this...not okay?

"Anders has better hearing than most people. In fact, four of our fellow shipmates do. As much as it sounds insane, it is possible that he can hear your heartbeat over the alarm that he should be working on turning off." Trenton walked over to one of the computers and entered something into a tablet he picked up off a console.

Lifting his eyebrows as he spoke, Anders didn't take his gaze off my hand on his arm. His skin was warm, and I wondered if my hands were cold and bothering him. "Yes. What he said is true."

"I can't really apologize for being scared. I'm terrified. I'm not going to be able to control that. If it helps, I'm not sure how long we'll be together, but I am very rarely scared. I can't remember the last time it happened." We were all shouting to be heard over the alarm. "Would you like me to stop touching you? I...I have the need to touch people. It's just something I do because I tend to... Well, never mind. Are you worried I'm going to make you sick? Wade said this device in my arm would keep me okay, but maybe I shouldn't." In fact, that had to be it, I pulled my arm back. Germs were a real thing. If I was still unwell, then...

Anders took my hand in his, squeezing it. "No one touches me."

I let that sink in. How strange a statement. Almost everyone I knew reached out to make that kind of contact with me all the time. It was a given for a person who ended up on my path. "Why not?"

"Anders," Trenton whirled around. "The alarm. For the love of the universe, shut off the alarm."

Dropping my hand, Anders nodded. "I'll get on that. Fix the scared, Trenton. Sienna." He furrowed his brow and strode out of the room as fast as we'd entered.

Now alone with me, Trenton shook his head. He indicated toward the chair. "You get used to them. They're very intense. Super Soldiers. Would you sit down? I can't imagine Wade wanted you up and running around just yet."

It did sound nice to sit, so I did. My head pounded. It might be the alarm blaring. It might be...all of this.

"How did I come to be here?"

Trenton sat across from me. "One of our colleagues named Amber Chen was on a space station finding out about a new strain of virus when you were given to her by a doctor there. He told her that Evander Corporation was after you and asked her to keep you safe. You stayed with her, on Earth, in cryogenic sleep for a long time, but then we got word Evander had located you and was coming to get you. We arrived and took you with us. They've been chasing you ever since, but we've managed to avoid them. Does any of that sound familiar to you? Do you know about Evander? About what's been happening?"

The name darted around in my head like a flopping fish that I couldn't quite catch. Still, there was something. They'd come...two men demanding entrance to the Temple.

We hadn't let them in. They wanted to see me... Then there had been heat. Why was there heat?

"Sienna?" Trenton's voice called me back to the present, and I blinked, trying to clear my head. The alarm stopped. How long had I been sitting there not speaking?

I rubbed my eyes. "I have some recollection of Evander. There's a war, right? A big one. They came. Wanted me. That's all I really remember. Then heat..."

He scrunched up his face. "You got sick. Maybe that's the heat? They gave you something to make you sick. We're not sure why. Perhaps to compel you to do something for them. What would they want you to do?"

The door opened and closed, an out of breath Wade rushing into the room. "Fuck. Sorry. Trenton, Anders said he put her in here with you. Sienna, I'm so sorry you were alone to deal with this. There was an emergency." He waved his hand in the air. "We're all fine now."

Trenton sat back in his chair. "I was just getting some information from our guest."

"What did you tell her? I wanted her to rest, to take in bits and pieces. Not overwhelm her with everything."

Trenton laughed. "We don't do gentle in this world. You know that. She's fixed as best she will ever be, short of Evander handing over a cure to the hundreds of things they injected her with. At this point, I think we need to know what she knows if we're going to keep her, and us, alive long enough to beat the shit out of them."

The language they used was so course, so different from the few men I knew. My cheeks heated up. Fuck. Shit. They were forbidden words. It was actually kind of fun to hear them. I shook my head. Focus. I needed to keep with the moment.

Breathe. Stay present. My heart rate was slowing. That

was good. There were things to be afraid of, but other than Anders hauling me around, nothing too untoward had happened here. I wasn't in immediate danger.

"She's my patient, Trenton. I say when and how she gets delivered information right now."

Trenton shrugged. "Then I guess you should have been there with her and not had her dropped off in my command center. I don't take orders from you."

"No, you take them from Blaze, and he put me in charge of her. So..."

Their argument ceased as the door opened and four others entered the room in a straight line. Anders, I recognized, and although he'd been gone a brief time, I smiled when he came in. "I'm calming down."

He nodded at me. "I can hear that. We all can, actually."

Trenton ignored Wade to turn to the four guys who entered. "You know Anders because of before. That's Blaze. Corbin. And Kellan."

I swallowed. That was a lot to remember. They were supposed to be like Anders. Super Soldiers. What made them super, I didn't know.

"Blaze is in charge." Anders moved to stand next to me. I looked around. Was there a reason he'd picked that spot on my left? It had seemed a deliberate move. Or maybe I was overthinking things? "But Corbin and Kellan are also like me. We can hear things, do things you might not expect."

Blaze shot him a look I couldn't decipher as I quickly tried to pick up emotions from the new people in the room. Blaze was the tallest, biggest of them all. He looked like a giant muscle. His hair was blond, shaved tight to his head. His face was all angles and slopes. And he was...focused.

What a strange sense to get. Focus? I couldn't say I'd ever read that on someone before.

Corbin by contrast was the smallest of the Super Soldiers, putting him more in line with Trent and Wade's height. I wondered if they'd consider him small. His hair was long, halfway down his back and dark. It fell in waves. His shirt was also off, like Ander's, and he had cream applied all over him. That was right. Anders had said Corbin was burned. Was he in pain? I picked up nothing but annoyance and disappointment in himself.

Finally, Kellan, with his neatly trimmed black hair and equally dark eyes, stared at me like I might be his enemy. I didn't have to do much reading on him to immediately get that. He was the predator and I was the prey.

Actually, I was suddenly glad for Anders standing right where he had.

I gulped. Everyone's attention was on me. I was used to that, it tended to be when I was in the room. I nodded toward Blaze. "You're in charge?"

"That's right. So why don't you tell me why Evander wants to kill you so badly? Let's start with that and work from there."

Fair enough. I took a long breath. "It might be better if I just showed you."

Some of my fog cleared. The reason Evander wanted me was the reason everyone did. And it was the bane of my existence.

"DOES it have to do with the fact that you can talk in people's minds?" All four Super Soldiers and Trenton stared at Wade at his question.

Kellan shook his head. "Dr. Bryant may be suffering from post-traumatic stress disorder. Or he may have just lost his mind. None of us actually believe you were talking in his mind. That's not possible."

Unfortunately, it absolutely was. "We've spent a lot of time together, haven't we?" I rose from the chair, speaking to Wade. "More than I did with anyone else? That must have been the case, right? You're my doctor, and I'm...I'm sick." That still didn't feel real. I needed an explanation on what that was exactly, but they seemed to want answers, and in my experience, things went easier if I pacified before I charged. That was my way at least.

I was lost in space with strangers, but things didn't change.

Wade nodded fast. "Yes, a lot of time. It was my job to make sure you were okay."

Trenton spun his chair in a circle. "I'm sure that's why you spent so much time in there."

What did that mean? Wade punched him hard in the arm, which made Trenton grin. I didn't understand what had just gone on, but it was fascinating. How did hitting him make Trenton happy? This was confusing.

"I do have the ability to speak in someone's mind if I know them, if I've spent a lot of time with them."

Wade grinned. "I knew I wasn't crazy. Amber heard her, too. I told you all it happened."

Kellan shook his head fast. "It's impossible. Human brains can't do that. If such a thing were possible, I'd be able to do that."

This made the others all smile like he'd been joking. He narrowed his eyes, a muscle ticking in his jaw. He was already intimidating, and like that... No, I didn't care for that at all. Not in the least.

Blaze furrowed his brow, obviously missing the look he was being shot by Anders or not caring about it at all. Weren't they scared of Kellan? He was... A hand pressed on my shoulder. Anders? Was he being comforting? I squeezed it back for a second before every other eye in the room felt like they bore into me. Kellan's look they ignored, but a hand squeeze garnered that much attention?

Nothing made sense here.

"Is this why Evander wants you? Because you can talk in someone's mind?"

I wished that was it. "No."

"It can't be because that's impossible. That isn't something she can do, and if she says she can, she is lying."

Lying? Anders let go of my hand even as he widened his stance. "I never lie. Sometimes I keep things to myself for privacy or respect, but I never lie. You've all been taking care of me. I would certainly never lie to you."

Kellan took a step toward me. Just one. He wasn't in my personal space, but that didn't matter. If he wanted to, I was sure he could grab me. Trenton adjusted until he was slightly in between the two of us. There was so much going on in this room, but one thing I knew, even in the short minutes I'd been here, was that they could hear my fear. That meant I either had to have none, learn to control it, or own it.

"Then someone has lied to you." Kellan sounded so smug, so sure of himself. And his leader, Blaze, was doing nothing to stop it. I didn't know what was going on with Corbin, but so far, my impression of the three of them wasn't as favorable as Wade and Trenton. Or even Anders— who had hauled me over his shoulder like a piece of luggage, showing just how low the bar was at this point for me liking someone.

I was going with option three—own it. "I think you mean to be frightening. I am already there. I'm scared, so you can back off. But no, I'm not lying, and I resent the implication. Where I'm from, people don't talk to me like that, they don't accuse me of fabrication. The reason for that? Well, I can do this."

Normally, I'd ask permission for my act. I even knew it was inappropriate as I did it. My temper was a wicked master, and it was better that I didn't reach the point where I lost it to begin with. But there was Kellan, with his accusations, aggressive eyes, and clear distaste for me when I'd done nothing to him.

It was always a matter of tuning in to a person's frequency. His was right there for me to tap. I could hear it like a zing in my eardrums. Always there but easily ignorable, unless I needed it. There it was, and all I had to do was zap him.

I pushed the electricity in my field toward him, targeting his head. His eyes widened for a second before he hit the ground, his knees taking the fall. I'd barely touched him. I could kill like that if I wanted to. I never had, but the ability was there.

Kellan grabbed his head, rocking back and forth. The effects would wear off momentarily, although if he really was as sensitive as they seemed to be, it might burn him for a minute or two.

"That's why Evander wants me. The women on my planet, we're all pretty much born weapons. But I'm the worst of them all. I can be lethal. With my mind."

The room exploded in action. Wade rushed past me, his eyes wide as he put his hand on Kellan's back. I sank back into my chair. Blaze stared at me, panting like he'd run a race, even though he'd been standing still.

Corbin laughed, which seemed a little off considering the circumstances, before he covered his mouth with his hand like he could stop the sound.

Anders touched my shoulder again. "You okay? Does it hurt you to do that?"

"Not now. Usually later. Too much, and it knocks me out in a few hours." I stared at him. "Aren't you scared?"

He shook his head. "Oh no. You wouldn't do that unless you had to. Kellan baited you. He won't do that again. It's not a bad idea to knock him around. Trust me on that. There's a pecking order with him. And..."

"Okay." Trenton walked toward me. "Anders, fly the ship. Come on, I'm going to feed you, Sienna. I'm not sure what you just did, but we're going to let the Super Soldiers digest that they might not be the most dangerous people on this ship. That's going to take them a hot moment. Then I'll show you to your room. My guess? We're pointing this ship toward the Farm any second and going to report in about you. Someone like you? Evander's never letting you go."

He held out his hand, and I took it. If the ship was going to start shaking again, then I would take the help. Corbin stepped in front of us. "Really glad you're here, Sienna. Welcome to Artemis."

I nodded. "Thank you."

He winked at me before he got out of my way, and Trenton groaned, leading me from the room. "Don't mind him. He probably watched a stream on flirting. They're all trying so hard to be human. They just don't know how. Some days, I feel like I'm babysitting, and oh they can hear us by the way. They can hear everything we say on this ship. Never say anything that you don't want everyone to know. They haven't quite figured out privacy. The other night... you know, never mind. Sienna, you're on a ship with a bunch of men who can kill in a heartbeat without pause. Yet something, or someone, one day made them pause. Now keeping you from Evander is our cause."

At some point, he'd added the word *our* and included himself in that phrasing. "Who are you to them? They're all different...okay, I'll figure that out. And Wade is a doctor." Exhausted to boot. "Who are you, and why are you here?"

"I'm a lost cause." He took me through a doorway that led to a kitchen. "But I can cook, so that is something. Anything you don't eat?"

My stomach grumbled. "How long since I ate anything?"

"We have no idea."

Now that was a concept that was going to take some getting used to. "I'll eat anything."

"Great. That works for me."

My stomach pained me, and I sat down. Trenton wasn't the doctor, but he seemed to be more readily willing to tell me the truth. "Do you know what's wrong with me?"

The spot on my arm hurt where the tube stuck out, showing me the liquid moving through my body. Was it some kind of machine delivering the stuff?

He looked over his shoulder as he placed bread on a plate. "I'm going to make French toast. An old Earth recipe. Breakfast for dinner works in crisis situations, which means I eat it a lot lately. And I don't know the names of what Evander gave you, Sienna. But they made you sick. Presumably so that you'd have to turn to them for the cure. Then they'd have you, and that thing you did with your brain. I actually heard you zap Kellan. That was something. Your people sent you away rather than give you to them, and eventually, you made it to us."

The adrenaline was wearing off. I'd just zapped a man I didn't know, who hadn't physically harmed me, just to show I could because he accused me of being a liar. I put my forehead on my knees and closed my eyes. I was sick, I'd been frozen, I was on a ship. Oh, I missed my people. I hadn't let myself think of them since I'd woken up, but now? I wanted them.

Marla. Kate. Janice. Framje. The whole set of instructors who made me nuts most of the time. I wanted them. All of them. My mother and father. I didn't see them much, but I'd do anything to spot them in the distance.

I swiped at my silent tears but not before Trenton noticed them.

He placed what looked like gooey deliciousness in front of me. I almost never got sugar unless it was honey, because it was so scarce on our planet. And even honey came and went with shipments depending on the current state of the pirates in the sky. They took most things from us that were worth anything. Sweet was always a treat for me.

I wiped my eyes again. "Thanks."

He handed me a napkin, and I dabbed at the evidence of my tears. "Sorry. I'm not a crier. It doesn't help, doesn't fix."

"No, it doesn't." He cut into his food, and I did the same. "That doesn't mean that sometimes we don't do it. You've had a huge upset. I don't think any of us were thinking about how odd this would be for you when you woke up. More focused on wanting answers as to what Evander wanted, how to keep you safe." He tilted his head. "Not that the Soldiers would think about emotions. They almost never do. And that's normal for them, I'm discovering, and it's worked for me, because I'd rather not go around feeling everything all the time either. Better to just do. Still, Wade should probably have realized. Here." He reached forward and dabbed at the corner of my mouth where I must have had a little syrup.

That was sweet. No one had done that for me in years. I'd been taking care of myself for at least a decade. When I turned thirteen, I was pretty much considered grown, if not fully matured yet. "Thank you."

He nodded. "You're welcome. Good?"

"Crazy good. I've never had this before." I chewed and swallowed. "Thank you."

"You've already thanked me. There's no need to—"

I wasn't sure what he would have said, because Wade tore into the room. I looked up. The poor man seemed like he did a lot of running around. "Are you okay?"

Still practically running, he slid into the chair next to me, scooting it over so he was close. "Don't eat too much of that. We're not sure how long you were in cryogenic sleep, but it was certainly long enough that you're going to want to take that slow."

I set down my fork. He was right, I was already really full. I wiped at my lips. "I'm...I'm fine." I would be at least, once I had some answers. "What's wrong with me?"

He visibly swallowed. "A lot of things. Our best guess is that Evander injected you with a lot of different engineered viruses to try to force you to work with them. Now we understand why. They want to exploit your abilities."

I pointed to my arm. I hadn't asked enough questions earlier, but my head was clearer now. "This will fix me?"

He shook his head. "This will keep the virus numbers low. Look." Wade had soft hands, and when he touched my arm, warmth flooded me. "See right here?" He ran his finger over the side of the strange device in my arm. I looked down where he indicated. "There are three sets of numbers. The first two are really for me, or whoever is doing your medical care. It tells us various things about the viruses you're fighting. The drug dosages. But here, this third one? That's for you to see."

There was a number 1 indicated where he pointed. "What does it mean?"

"That's your virus number, simplified, so you can see it and monitor yourself, if you want to. Basically, one is a very good place for you to be. Zero would be better. That would mean you were cured. Wouldn't we love that? But one is the lowest number I can see here without it being zero, so I'm very happy with one. You are safe to be around, and relatively healthy, at one. The lower the number the better."

I caught my breath. "I might not be safe to be around for others?"

"There is a threshold where some of the viruses in your

body become contagious to others. Yes. In that case, we have to get the numbers down again or place you in a quarantine situation."

"Or it kills her, right?" Trenton had his back to us as he washed dishes at the sink. "Don't sugarcoat it, Wade. She's a grown up. She gets to know the current state of her life. That number goes up too high, and she is also at risk for dying."

I'd already worked that out myself. I'd spent my life in what a lot of people called The Dark Planets section of the universe. We got very little help, almost no medical care. People died from illness all the time. More times than not, in fact, if someone got very sick, they didn't come back from it.

"What's the number where I...where I'm at risk either personally or against others?" That was key to know. I didn't know what was going to happen to me, but I wouldn't—couldn't—let anyone else have to go through this because of me.

Wade squeezed my wrist before he let go. "Ten. You're good as long as you're under ten. But if it starts to rise, like one day you're at one and then next at five, and then the next eight, we need to know that. So make sure you tell me. There could be variants. Like you might be at two tomorrow and then back to one the same day. That's fine." Wade touched my forehead. "When you do that thing you did with the zapping, does it hurt? Are you okay?"

I sighed. "I need to apologize to Kellan."

"No." Corbin leaned in the doorway, watching us. How long had he been there? "Don't do that. He won't know what to do with an apology, particularly because he was being such an asshole." He strode into the room.

"Besides, he just heard you say that, I guarantee it, so yeah, you made your apology. Now, what is this that you're eating in here?"

Trenton groaned. "No."

"I haven't asked yet." Corbin nudged Trenton. "And you know you want to make it for me. You know you do. You have this skill set, and you are just refusing to share it with me? Why? I would never deny you something like this if it was mine to give."

Trenton leaned his head back, a smirk showing on his face as he turned around. "You want French toast, Corbin?"

"I do." He pulled up a chair and sat down. "I really, really need to know what this French toast is and how it tastes."

Trenton nodded. "And you'll do what for me in return?"

Corbin drummed his fingers on the table. "Not tell Blaze how..."

"Okay," Trenton cut him off. "Fine. French toast it is. Now of course Blaze knows there's something he doesn't know. He's going to be like a dog with a bone about this."

Corbin winked at me. "Yep. Oh, don't worry about the numbers, Sienna. Wade won't let you die. He's a lot smarter than he thinks he is and good at this."

"Thanks." Wade rolled his eyes.

"I...I need to thank all of you for keeping me safe after what's happened. You don't know me. You're under no obligation and..." I sighed. "When do you think I can go home?"

Corbin furrowed his brow. "Probably not anytime soon. That's very bad strategy. The Dark Planets have no real military to speak of. Outdated ships worse than this one." He shrugged. "Bringing you home would get all those people killed, since Evander isn't going to rest until they've acquired you. Yep, you're not going home."

My heart sank. Not going home? My breath caught in my throat. "I have to go back. I'm important there. They need me. And that's my family…"

"Because you can zap people?" Corbin asked as Trenton set his French toast in front of him with a thunk.

I shook my head. "No, the thing is that—"

Kellan stormed into the room, grabbed a chair, and sat down right next to me. "Do it again."

I blinked. "What?"

"Do it again." He pointed at his head. "Zap me."

Was it getting hot in here? I'd never been around so many men and rarely this many people at the same time. I'd always hated the solitary nature of my existence, the amount of time I spent alone, but right now, I wasn't sure what I had been complaining about.

"I'm sorry that I did that. It goes against my nature to do that, and it won't happen again."

Corbin groaned, closing his eyes. "I told you not to apologize to him. It's only going to confuse him. And fuck, this is good."

Wade whacked him in the arm. "Don't curse in front of our guest."

"You don't understand the intricacies of human behavior any more than I do," Kellan shot back at Corbin. "What are you eating? Never mind. Sienna," he leaned forward, "do it again."

Blaze entered looking left and right. "If you do that again, I'm locking you in your room for the remainder of the time you're on this ship."

His declaration shut the room up. Everyone fell quiet.

"I just apologized. It isn't something that I do, ever. I'm

not myself." I didn't want to be locked in a room. And for some reason, I absolutely believed that this man would do that and that no one in here would stop him. Blaze was in charge.

And I was at his—and all of these strange men's—mercy. Not just to keep me safe on this ship, but to keep me alive because I was sick and totally dependent on them making sure I didn't die.

This wasn't...okay.

I knew nothing about any of them. Trenton had been nice and cooked for me. Wade certainly seemed to have my best health intentions at heart, but I couldn't understand the others. Just that they were foreign. Somehow different. What did they mean they didn't understand human ways?

Corbin lifted his gaze to look at Blaze. "You've frightened her." He threw down his fork. "And ruined my appetite."

"She should be afraid," Blaze countered, staying exactly where he was. "There are a lot of reasons for her to be frightened. Not to mention the fact that she is probably terrifying for people to have around. That little zap she gave you, Kellan? How much worse could that have been?"

Next to me, he nodded. "That's what I'm hoping to find out. Do it again. I liked it. You'd be doing me a favor."

I ignored that, for now. Rising slowly, I decided the best thing for me to do was not to be in this room when I had a meltdown, even if they would be able to hear me have it whether I was with them or not.

Blaze met my gaze. "I don't know if your people scurried you away in cryogenic sleep because they wanted to save you, or because it was a relief to have someone who can do what you do off the planet. I personally can't wait to get you off this ship. I have enough to worry about tracking down and beating Evander to submission without having to worry that my own men are going to be attacked from within. So I'm taking you to the people who should be in charge of you and getting you out of my hair. You want to go home? Take it up with the Chens. Or the Sandlers. Or Diana Mallory and her mother Melissa. I don't care. One of them. We are not equipped for you."

Trenton slammed down his dish in the sink. "That's enough, Blaze. She didn't ask for this or to be with us when it happened. Don't talk to her like that."

Blaze ignored him. "Do we understand each other, Sienna?"

His anger hit me hard, but it was only part of what I felt right now. My natural shields that I'd harnessed over the years to protect me were holding, or the second emotion that Blaze threw off would have been the harder one to take. He was pissed, but he was also overwhelmed.

I certainly understood what that was like, and even though his words burned at my own insecurities like they might break me apart, I wouldn't lose it in front of him.

"If I was who you think I am, I'd zap you right now. Straight into oblivion. But I'm not. So if someone could point me to my room, I will stay in there until I can speak to someone who might be willing to let me go home. I really... don't want to be any trouble."

Trenton opened his mouth, but it was Corbin who stood up first. "I will. Come with me. This whole day is fucked."

"Language," Trenton and Wade called out almost simultaneously.

I sighed. This would be funny if it wasn't so... completely unamusing.

3 / PLAYING GAMES

I'D SPENT most of my life walking the same five-mile stretch of land. I'd even been born within those five miles; my mother and father lived in the town closest to the temple where they'd worked as tailors. It had been amazing that my father had gotten my mother, considering the female shortage in the universe. I was told that on places like Earth, you had to be rich to get a wife. But on our planet, it had to do with what the temple elders decided. They'd decided he would have her.

And I was lucky that they had.

Not that I particularly knew them. The day they'd left me in the temple was really the last time I'd spent any real time with them outside of lunches and visits. They tried. I could see that. They'd never had more children. Maybe it had been too hard to lose me.

As I walked through the room with Corbin, I felt like I'd woken up in a different existence. I didn't know what any of the buttons on the wall did, or even how to turn off the lights. I wandered into the bathroom. The shower looked the same. There were knobs. That I was sure I could figure out.

My shoulders felt too heavy. Had my numbers already gone up? I stared down. No, it still read number one.

Corbin leaned in the doorway, watching me. "Everything look okay? We're going to have to get you some clothes. But I think this is exactly the same room the rest of us have. We've all slowly acquired stuff, which is weird because I never had any, so there are some differences, but not much."

I sighed. They didn't have stuff? "At some point, maybe you could explain to me how you guys are as you are. I don't really understand it. But then again, I don't really understand anything. I feel like a baby. I don't know how anything works. The place where I grew up was sort of allergic to most electronics. We had most basic things. Don't imagine us without a stove. But I don't know any of this."

He nodded. "I actually one hundred percent understand how off putting that is. When I first woke up on a ship far from here and traveled to this side of the galaxy, following Blaze into the unknown, everything was new, everything was strange."

Maybe he did understand. "So...um, which one controls the lights?"

He touched a button by the side of the door, and they went off. Although I couldn't see it, he must have hit it again because the lights came back. He strode farther into the room. "Are you tired? I ask you because you don't sound tired. I can usually tell because...never mind, I can just tell. It has to do with heart rates. Anyway, you don't sound tired."

Now that was interesting. "You guys hear fear. You hear

tired. You hear hearts. Must be exhausting to be so constantly surrounded by other people's noises."

His smile was huge. "Well, we learned how to tune it out when needed, or to keep quiet about it when we were young or they put us down."

"Which one did you do? Tune it out or shut up about it?" I don't know why I asked, except that I was so used to people telling me their stories, it seemed odd to not be given information like that. I looked down at the floor. Truth was, it was rude to ask questions of strangers. I had enough manners to understand that.

Corbin stayed so quiet that eventually I had to lift my gaze to see what he was doing.

He smiled, flipping some of his long hair over his shoulder. Had he been waiting for me to look up to answer? "Depends on the day. I can tune it out when I have to. I'm one of the greatest killers ever produced by Evander Corporation. When I'm doing that, I don't hear anything. The world goes silent. But when I'm not—and lately I'm not—then it is hard for me to not be fully aware of every noise I can hear, every sound anyone makes. Internally or externally. And I have the good sense, most of the time, to not mention it. Except that with you, I'd like to understand things I don't, so I mentioned it." He paused. "Does that make sense?"

I shook my head. "No. But that's probably more me than you. I don't think I've ever spent time with a killer before. Not that I knew, anyway."

"Well, you're on a ship with six of us. Yes, even Wade." His smile fell. "But you're perfectly safe. Maybe the most you've ever been. If you're not tired, take a shower. And I'll bring you some clothes you can change into. Then, maybe we can play a game."

Some of the anxiety in my chest loosened. Yes, a shower sounded wonderful. "A game?"

"You'll see. One of the benefits of being out of Evander is that we can do things like have fun. Although none of the rest of them seem to realize that, and no one will play with me. I get the feeling you might?"

This might have been among the strangest conversations of my life. "I guess it depends on the game."

"You'll like this." He nodded toward me. "See you in a bit."

When he closed the door, leaving me in the room alone —the first time I'd been so since I'd woken up—I was almost not sure what to do. A brown blanket covered the bed. The sheets were white, as were the pillowcases.

Otherwise, the walls were white, the floor was tan, and all of it felt like it might swallow me whole. I had to...I had to get it together. This was happening. Somehow, I was going to have to deal. I rushed toward the bathroom.

The ship moved beneath my feet, and I stumbled, grabbing onto the bathroom counter. Okay. Other than when the ship had been darting around in space, I hadn't been particularly cognizant of it moving. But now...oh yes. I could.

My feet buzzed, and there was a constant sway. My stomach turned, and I breathed through my nose. No, I was not going to throw up all the food Trenton had fed me. That couldn't be good for me, not in my current state. I turned on the water. It worked, and I thanked my luck for that. Laughing seemed like a strange thing to do, and yet I couldn't help myself.

This was my fault. I'd had so many bad thoughts over the years, so many times I'd wished for more than I had. It was vile and low when I had so much more than everyone else. I'd had a future guaranteed to me.

And now this.

I took off my clothes. Where had I even gotten them? They were pants I'd never worn and a black shirt I'd never seen before. They weren't the temple robes and certainly not any of my regular clothing. Who had dressed me in them?

Wade? My cheeks heated up thinking of him seeing me naked. Had Corbin really meant it when he said Wade was a killer? Were they all that way?

Kellan, yes. He had calculating eyes. Blaze, for sure. He'd practically murdered me with his words. But Anders seemed gentle. Corbin had a fun spirit. Trenton was helpful and kind. Wade was a healer. But then again, I knew we were all many, many things. Look at me. I was incredibly ungrateful and messed up.

I turned on the water, and it was instantly hot. At home, it took minutes, sometimes up to twenty, to get to the point of hot water. I stepped under the water. My body instantly relaxed. There was nothing I liked better than warmth under the spray of water. I'd forgotten to ask Corbin how long I could stand under here, because surely there would be a shortage of this on the ship with seven of us having to use it.

That just meant I couldn't overindulge. I closed my eyes and counted to ten. Most things could be solved if I just counted to ten. Sometimes a few times. This was one of those times that it was going to take a few times.

I had to get my bearings. I was on a ship called Artemis. There were six men with me. Blaze, he was in charge, and he didn't like me because I'd zapped Kellan, who had challenged me, and I'd had no patience. Wade was a doctor;

he'd told me I was sick. I had medicine on my arm, and I had to watch numbers and make sure they didn't get above ten. Trenton with his kind manners but short temper with the others seemed a contrast. It seemed like he was hiding things. And Wade, who had put this medicine in my arm, who I had reached out to in my sleep, had the most tired eyes I'd ever seen.

They wouldn't—or couldn't—take me home. I was headed somewhere to become someone else's problem. I fisted my hands and opened my eyes. At this moment, I wasn't in any capacity to take control of my life, but I would. So help me, I would. No way no how was I going to be a passive observer in my life. I never had been. Yes, my destiny had been decided for me in a lot of ways, but I always found a way to have a say.

That wasn't going to change.

Somehow.

Evander wanted me for my psychic abilities. I wasn't giving them anything. I'd said as much when I'd discussed it with the caretaker at the temple. I could still picture him. He was the only man I regularly saw before now. Older, he watched all of us while we worked on ourselves, while we honed our special gifts.

Kind. Generous if pushy, and in some ways unyielding.

"No," I'd told him. "They couldn't have me. I wouldn't agree to it."

I used the soap that was in the shower. They both had a clean smell that wasn't too overwhelming. In any case, I had to smell better than I had been. Being in cryogenic sleep—that was what I thought it was called—probably didn't lend itself to being clean. Unless someone had bathed me. I shuddered at that thought. Even if it had been handsome Wade. I didn't like the thought of being that vulnerable, that out of it. I shut off the water as the memory of my insistence to the caretaker fled. What had happened next?

I didn't know. Had I agreed to this, or had it been done to me?

Why couldn't I remember? I wrapped myself in a towel and came out into the room. Nothing had changed. It was still like I had stepped into another universe that I had no idea how to navigate. Corbin had said he'd bring me clothes. Was he going to do that?

A beep sounded in the room. I stood there. What was that? Looking left and right, I couldn't figure out where it had come from or what I would do with it if I did locate the sound. Whatever it was beeped again.

I sat down on the edge of the bed. I was going to lose my mind by the end of the night.

The door opened, and Corbin stood in the archway. "You okay?" He stepped into the room. "I debated waiting, but I could hear you were getting more and more upset, so I came in. Breaks protocol. I know that. Manners and all that, but..."

I sighed. "Something was beeping."

Forget the fact that I was half-covered in front of a man —a really good looking one, not that appearance mattered— for the first time in my life, it was the beeping that was going to make me lose my cool any second.

He blinked. "The door." He pointed at it. "That was me. Asking you if I could come in. The beep is a signal that someone wants to enter."

"Oh." I threw my head back, laughter catching me by surprise for the second time in however many minutes it had been, and I nearly dropped my towel. "Like a doorbell. It was beep...and I am totally like a baby on this ship. I have no idea what anything is."

He handed me a brown bag, and I tried to ignore that he was shirtless and still covered in cream. "There are clothes in here. We don't have any that would currently fit you perfectly on board, but these will, I think, be good enough until we get where we're going. Or stop to get you some. Go take a look. I have an idea. Can you read?"

Could I read? That seemed like a sharp left turn away from what we'd been discussing. "Ah...yes, I can read. Since I was four years old. I read the common tongue."

"I ask because the brief research I did on the Dark Planets—and there isn't much out there—says that not all the planets have literate populations."

And now we were into the type of conversation I regularly had. "Yes, that's true. That's because after the planets were created and terraformed, they were left to languish as basically the providers of all things Earth's empire needed with little care of the people there. If they lived, if they didn't. Who cared as long as things got taken care of?" I shut my mouth. Now really wasn't the time. "Yes, I read."

He nodded. "There's always empires everywhere we go. Always people who will use others for their means. Earth didn't seem so bad to me when I was there, but I was mostly with the Chens and...I don't know. You know more on this subject than I do. Check out the clothes. I'll be here when you get out."

"Thanks, Corbin." I rose to head back into the bathroom, pausing right before I went in. "I'm not the kind of person who did what I did today when I zapped your friend."

He shook his head. "He's not my friend. He's my brother in all things but blood. I'd walk through fire for him. Take down planets for him. And today? He baited you. Talked down to you. You pushed back. I get what you did.

Don't worry too much on it. We are violent people. We respond to violence. Maybe you just read that? I don't know. I barely understand how anything works when it comes to emotions or motivations. None of it."

I swallowed, the effort of doing so seeming so hard, because I was so completely focused on what he'd said to me. "I...I think that you may understand things better than you think you do."

His smile was huge. "Nah. I'm full of shit. Oh sorry, language. Or whatever."

I did as he said, heading into the bathroom. They were all men's clothing. Were they Corbin's? Or one of the other guys? He seemed to have torn off sleeves and rolled pants. I smiled. They'd probably stay up on me, even if I was going to look like a child wearing my parent's clothing because of how huge they were.

Not that I'd complain, I was glad to have them and grateful. Everything being done for me by these strangers I had just met were not things they had to do. I guessed they could have left me frozen. They could have let me die. Or given me to Evander. Or any number of things.

Instead, I was being treated with kindness, pretty much. And if some not nice things had been said, I had probably earned those moments. I splashed warm water on my face and put on my clothes. A black t-shirt and a pair of loose sweatpants. I could wear them in or out of the room.

Coming back out, I stopped immediately. There were small signs all over the room, taped to the wall next to the buttons. Corbin waited by the door, silently watching me. The one by the lights said lights, and next to that further to the left read the word temperature. I covered my mouth. Okay. That made sense. I could...adjust the temp in the room that way. I whirled around. Intercom—calling out for assistance. Yes. I'd never done that through a machine, but I could manage it.

Exhaust fan to filter the air. Connection to Artemis' mainframe. I had no idea what that was. Door lock. That was right near the bed, which seemed counterintuitive, but who was I to judge?

When I found my voice, I turned to Corbin. "Thank you. You have made this...so much better."

He nodded. "Most of these things you don't need the buttons or knobs for at all if you have a tablet." He held up a small device in his hands. "But we'll start with that since you've lived a pretty mechanical free life, it seems. And you don't have a tablet, and we don't have one to give you at this point. This was simple enough. I wish all problems could be solved this easily."

"Well, it may have been easy, but it's life changing. I feel...I feel like I can breathe in here now."

He rocked back on his feet. "Breathing is good. Pivotal. All living creatures have to do it. The clothes fit, good. Why didn't you ask me why?"

There he was again with the sharp left turns. "What?"

"When I asked you if you could read, it seems to be that the logical question would have been for you to ask me why I was asking. You didn't do that. Why didn't you?"

I didn't try to hold back my smile. "Why are you asking?"

He blinked. "You're joking?"

"I am."

His smile widened. "I love joking. I mean...we don't do that. But I love it."

They didn't do it? "You asked me why I didn't say why, so I said why. Um, I'd love to hear your background some-time if you want to tell me. As for your question. Why I didn't ask why you wanted to know if I could read?" I sighed. "I wasn't sure I wanted to hear your answer. The general impression you all have of the Dark Planets and everything." I waved my hand. "You asked because you wanted to know so you could leave me the notes. That turned out to be incredible."

He ran a hand through his hair. "Didn't want to hear the answer to why, so you didn't ask. I understand." He walked over to a small table. "Come on. Let's play a game."

Corbin seemed really motivated to play whatever this game was. I followed him over and sat across from him. He placed the device he'd called a tablet in between us. "I should warn you that I don't play a lot of games. I'd like to learn though."

He waved his hand. "This one isn't hard."

Turned out that was correct. It wasn't hard. I had to press certain things on the device to roll a dice and move a piece. It was possible to crash the whole game or lose in one move. I did that several times. But then I got the hang of it. I had to get a piece to move. Corbin laughed a lot, and it was infectious.

I couldn't believe he was really enjoying the actual game. Clearly, he could get the little virtual piece to move around the board with his eyes closed. "Did you do this to teach me how to use the tablet?"

He leaned on his hand. "I find that people learn things better when they don't know they're being taught. That being said, I wanted to spend time with you, see how your mind worked. And not be so serious for an entire evening. Everything is always dour. Everything is always hard. You've been through hell, even if you slept through it."

I snorted before I outright laughed. Oh forget it. I'd lost

again. I leaned back in my chair as he pointed at me. "See? I made you laugh."

"You did." I shook my head. "Where did you come from?"

He moved his piece, starting the game again. "I was born on the other side of the galaxy. Kellan. Blaze. Anders. We all were. But we weren't born like you were born, or like Trenton. Or Wade—who is pacing around the med bay, trying to figure out if he should come check on you or leave you alone."

I'd forgotten for a second that he could hear everything. "Should we contact him?"

"No, he'll figure it out." He shrugged. "And he won't like that I told you what I could hear. Calls it invasive. Anyway, we were made in a lab. Hundreds upon hundreds of us. Most of us were killed at birth. We were designed to be Super Soldiers for the purpose of helping Evander Corporation do whatever it is that they want to do." He shook his head. "And that seemed to basically be the purpose of life. Go. Fight. Kill. Steal. Break. Whatever it was. Then get back on a ship, get knocked out into cryogenic sleep, and do it again. But then we woke up, and there was a woman's voice, turned out her name was Waverly, and she suggested to us that we could stop. We could help them fight Evander instead. Most of our fellow soldiers scoffed at that, but not Blaze."

I wasn't sure what to say, if there was anything to be said. It didn't seem like it could be real. How was it possible? "You said yes. You said that you wanted to stop and fight back, too."

"Well, I follow Blaze. I always have. And I liked the idea that there could be something more." He set down the tablet. "Even if I still have no idea what this life is going to look like or what it could even be. Most of what goes on makes no sense to me. You and me? We're the same that way."

He was a Super Soldier, and I was a girl who grew up in a temple in the Dark Planets. I'd never have thought it possible he could have uttered those words. But yes, it seemed we really did have more that we shared than we didn't.

I PLAYED another three rounds with him before I gave up. Shaking my head, I stared at him. "I am terrible at this."

He smiled at me. "You really are, but it's fun playing with you. Could come up with something else if you want. This is the most fun night I've had."

I didn't think I had any more strategy games in me for a bit. "What would you normally be doing right now?"

"Reading or watching something, maybe streaming a movie. Most of them I just don't understand. Irritating Trenton and Kellan for fun." He tilted his head to look at me. "Not very exciting."

"I don't know. A movie would be novel for me. I've heard of them, never seen them. We can't get them where I'm from. That much technology I know about." I shrugged. "Where do you watch movies? On the tablet?"

He shook his head. "I could do that, but no, I watch them in this room that I think was designed for things like socializing." He yawned, which seemed to surprise him because he widened his eyes. I managed to withhold my grin. Did Super Soldiers not yawn?

I cleared my throat. "Tired?"

"No. We almost never sleep." He rose and walked to the small window that must show space outside. "Space travel is not natural. I've spent almost my entire life on one ship or another. I like this one. It's comfortable, and the old lady survives. Battle after battle, she makes it through, keeps us safe. Wins somehow. But I can sort of understand why Evander perpetually knocked us out."

I quickly looked away from where he watched the outside. "I can't look where you are. It's too much. I'm barely hanging on feeling the ship beneath my feet. I can't look out there and see nothing."

He turned around. "First time you're conscious on the ship. Yes, I can see how it would be weird."

"To say the least." I walked over to the bed and sat down. "I think we should probably both try to go to bed. I know I've been asleep for a huge amount of time, but that's not real rest, is it? It's somehow different, maybe?"

Corbin stretched his hands over his head. Although he now wore a white shirt, and I'd seen him shirtless earlier, the motion showed a distinct V where his shirt went up. He was really beautiful. I sat forward, a mark on him catching my attention. "You got burned. Are you okay?"

He rubbed the back of his head. "I heal quickly. In a few days, it'll be nothing at all."

"Aren't there med machines here to fix that? We even had them. You've been in pain this whole time." Guilt washed over me. Granted, I'd just met him, but I knew he'd been injured. I should have thought about it earlier. "Can I do anything for you? Help?"

"Well..." He pulled a tube out of his pocket. "Wade gave me this. Told me if I won't go in the machine, I need to rub this into the burns. I can't do my back. I guess I could ask Anders, or I may not bother. But if you wouldn't mind, he's not likely to do more than just laugh at me. We don't do medical treatment if we can avoid it. As a Super Soldier, it's a bad idea to look like you need anything at all in terms of help. We get killed for seeming weak. We may have all brought some of that with us when we left Evander. I...I was just going to ignore it."

I shook my head. "Come here. Where I come from, ignoring something like burns is how you get infections and die." The thought made me look down at my arm. Still reading as one. Okay. Was I going to do this all day, every day? Worry about that number?

He walked over to the bed and took off his shirt before he sat down and handed me the tube. Our hands touched for a second, and a jolt of awareness rushed through me. I sighed. He was warm, and that was a really nice feeling. "What happened to you?" His back was covered in burns, red, raw. He should absolutely be in a med machine. "How did this take place?"

"The regulator blew up. I was tinkering with it. My fault. I shouldn't be trying to push the old machines to do so much. I knew it was risky. I did it anyway, just to see if I could. And it blew."

I winced. That sounded painful. "I guess next time, don't do that."

He laughed; it was a rich sound. I'd liked it every time he'd done it, and sitting this close to him, even more so. "The sad truth is I probably will do it again. It's really bugging me. That should be working better than it is."

I squeezed some of the cream on my hand and gently placed it on one of the burns. He sucked in his breath, and I winced. "I'm sorry. Does that hurt worse when I touch it?"

"No. Don't worry. Even if it did, I'm used to pain. I always live with a little bit of it. We all do."

Well...I hated that. As carefully as I could, I rubbed the cream in all the places I could see, then got off the bed to go do his chest. Even though he could do his chest himself if he wanted, I needed to help. If I was this injured, I'd really want someone to do this for me. In fact, Wade had. I'd be dead without him and the others.

Corbin's shoulders slumped. Despite what he said, I wasn't at all convinced that he wasn't tired. "Healing takes a lot out of people."

His smile was small. "Maybe. I should go back to my room."

Still, he made no move to do that. I chewed on my lip. What was the right thing to do here? I'd never been around men like I had today, and certainly never touched one like I just did with Corbin. His skin where he wasn't burned was soft. He was strong like I'd never seen anyone before, and yet, right now he seemed...needy.

I made a decision I hoped I wouldn't regret. "Do you want to stay in here with me? I'm new to this space travel thing, and it might be nice to have company who could explain to me if there are any weird noises or jolts in the air or something."

What I didn't say, because it would embarrass us both, was that I needed a friend and it seemed to me that he needed one, too. As happy as he was, as jovial as he seemed to be compared to the others, my senses were telling me he wasn't happy. Lonely, perhaps. Sad. Whatever he'd been through, the transition from the life he'd been living to this one had to be jolting. It was for me, and I hadn't been made in a lab.

How did they make babies in a lab?

I wasn't going to ask that right now.

He hadn't answered, so I spoke really quickly. "I've never spent so much time with men as I have with you. Ever. And I've never asked anyone to stay over in my room. This isn't a thing I do. Just so you know. Plus, you should feel completely fine with the idea of saying no."

"I'm not going to say no." He grabbed his shirt and put it on. "Thank you. I grew up in a nursery with one hundred other boys. But I haven't had a roommate of any kind since we decided to defect, so to speak."

He rose from the bed and lay down on the floor. It took me a moment to realize his intent. "Oh, don't sleep on the floor." That had to be particularly uncomfortable with the burns. "This bed is huge." I hadn't even thought about how big it was, but the truth was it was gigantic. Why was it so big? I shook my head. Everything was just different here. "We can share."

Corbin sat up straight. "Really?"

"Really. I've never shared a bed, but look how big this is. We can both sleep in it."

He finally got to his feet and walked over. "I'm sure we can."

I walked to the wall where he'd labeled the switch for the lights before I remembered there was also one by the bed. Eventually, I'd get the hang of this. I hoped. "Do you want light or dark?"

"Whatever you'd like." He smiled at me, the same one he'd given me earlier before he winked at me. This time, he didn't follow up with the wink, but it warmed me like he had. I flipped off the light. The ship rumbled beneath my feet. I was never going to get used to it, and I couldn't say as I cared for the feeling.

There wasn't much to bump into, and I managed to

climb into the bed without too much fuss. Corbin did the same, rolling just slightly until he adjusted on the other side of the bed. I turned on my side, the natural way that I slept, meaning I wouldn't be facing him, which was probably best. It had to be weird to have someone sort of looking at you while they fell asleep.

I'd never given it any thought before. It was a day of that. "Are all the beds this big?"

"They are." He moved just slightly. "The rooms are all the same. Huge right? And that's me saying that. Super Soldiers are all huge. It's a requirement of our genes, I think. If we were scrawny, we'd probably have been put down."

I turned slightly so that I could reach out to touch his side. I was a toucher. It was part of how I connected in the temple. And I couldn't be overthinking these things all the time. If he didn't like it, he could tell me not to and I'd respect that.

"You're not an animal. Where I'm from, we put down animals who are sick and in pain." I'd been particularly heartsick over a horse I'd once loved. But I wasn't going to think about that just now. "You're humans, whatever your start was. It's not putting you down. It's murdering you."

He scooted closer, still leaving plenty of distance between us, but making it easier for me to keep my hand on his arm where it was. "Sometimes, I don't feel human."

It was truth time. "Sometimes, I always feel human, but I also always feel so...other. Hard to explain. Like I don't quite fit, and now, being hunted and sick? Even more so."

"Nothing is going to happen to you, Sienna." His voice was low. "We've taken care of you all of these long months, and we will continue to do so."

I almost reminded him that Blaze was turning me over to be someone else's responsibility just as soon as he could, but thought better of it. They were also unwilling to take me home. I needed to see my people, to remember what happened. Surely there had to be a way to do that safely, without risking anyone's lives. If Blaze and this crew weren't the people to do that, and I believed them that they thought they weren't, then maybe it was the next group who would help me. Eventually, I needed to be able to take care of myself. That might be the key. Figure out how to get a job, earn some credits, hide from Evander, and take myself home.

I didn't expect to go to sleep. But that must have been what I did, plowing forward on a ship I couldn't have anticipated, taking me who knew where. And a Super Soldier with sad eyes lying in the bed next to me.

"There's someone here to see you." My caretaker, Otto, the only man ever around for any length of time, spoke to me with his eyes averted. He'd never looked at me straight once in my whole life, and lately, it had been grating on my nerves.

I set down my pencil where I'd been calculating exactly how much we could give to the needy and have enough to not be starving all winter. It wasn't an easy decision. Left to my own devices, I didn't care how much I ate. I'd do with less. But it wasn't just me I had to feed. If only the pirates weren't stealing so much of our grain before it ever made it through space. If I ever had the chance to speak my mind to one of those space faring thieves...

I got to my feet. I wasn't even technically in charge yet. If they wanted me to do this, they should go ahead and appoint me as such. Do the ceremony. Let me live my life inside this box where I would forever be everyone's mother and no one's just the same.

Okay. I had to get out of my own head. "It's not visiting hours for me. Can whoever this is please go see one of the other trainees?"

They didn't have my natural abilities and never would, but they were good women and excellent counsel, traits that would serve them well when they got to have husbands and families. Things I was going to be denied without my consent, since no one had ever asked me if I wanted to do this to begin with.

Okay...not helpful.

Otto shook his head. "They are here specifically to see you. I should have turned them away. But they frightened me."

They scared him? Well, I didn't like that at all. Otto was a kind-hearted, simple person, who had devoted his life to the idea of the temple and the notion that what we did here mattered. From the time I was a child, he'd acted as though I had some eternal abilities granted to me because I was special, instead of just one of many who could do things a lot of women on this planet could do. I wasn't special. But he'd never believe that.

Sometime around my fifteenth birthday, I'd started taking care of him instead of the other way around. The last time my father visited, he'd wanted to have Otto changed out for someone more capable, had offered to go to the elder council and see that happen. I'd declined the offer. When my parents tried to actually parent, it went badly.

They'd given up that right when they'd turned me over.

I touched Otto's arm, his fear hitting me hard. All right. These visitors demanding to see me legitimately intimidated him. Who were they? He wasn't even going to be able to get the words out.

Putting up my emotional shields to tune out some of the anxiety, I stepped around him to head to the greeting area.

"Sienna." A whisper caught my attention, and I whirled around to see Joy coming quietly through the hall. We didn't talk in regular voices unless we were in our private rooms. It was just an unspoken rule. She wore all black, the same as me. It was perpetually depressing to never have the option of putting on colors when so many of the people who walked through the temples were always in brighter patterns. I steeled my shoulders. Always whining. That was why they never promoted me to the top position. Somehow, the elders knew my inner thoughts were constantly negative.

"Joy?" She'd said my name but nothing else. "What's going on?"

"The men here to see you?" They were men? I almost never saw men. "I heard they came from space."

Now she had my full attention. "There are off-worlders? Here?"

We didn't get a lot of those, and they certainly didn't come to the women's temple to see us. Distantly located, pretty much as far away from Earth's empires as we could get, we had almost nothing to tempt others to come here. Our psychic abilities were guarded like rare jewels lest someone want to use us, so much so that people didn't even dare mention that they existed. Otherwise, we were a farming planet that didn't even farm that well.

I swallowed. "Why are they here?"

"I don't know, but they've come in with your Uncle Courage." She bit her lip. "Good luck handling them."

Joy scurried away, and I wished for a second that she

was more the kind of person who would have offered to come with me rather than go hide in her room. I ran a hand over my face. Okay. There were off-worlders here. Fine. Whatever service I could provide, I would attempt to do so. My father hated my Uncle Courage. It was a pretty funny name for a man who had tried every which way to scam the world and never do a hard day's work in his life, but it was what it was. He was family, and I had tried to hold onto the idea of mine, even though I lived separate from them.

I made my way to the main room where my Uncle Courage waited. He looked so much like my father, only a slightly more put together version. My father spent his days sewing, hunched over a machine that barely worked. My uncle stood up straight. Maybe it had been wishful thinking when my grandparents named him Courage. He'd never shown any that I could tell.

But then again, I wasn't privy to all of the details of his life. His emotions were rather run of the mill, even if they bordered pretty standardly on jealousy.

A lot of people were like that. It was hard to live in a world where so few ever had even the chance to experience love.

He was with three other men. Two of them were what I would call regular-sized, about the same height as Courage. They wore suits and shoes that looked like they'd never had dirt on them. I stared, fixated at the way the light hit them and bounced off. How did they manage that? We were all pretty dirty all the time in between showers.

The third man was huge. Practically half the size of one of the pillars. I stared up at him, my mouth falling open. How did someone get that big?

"Ah good, gentlemen. As promised, my niece, Sienna."

I forced my attention where it belonged—on my uncle. "Sir?" I stepped forward. "How can I help all of you today?"

There were four men in the temple. That wasn't illegal —who would enforce laws, even if we had any—but it just wasn't done. Men came with their wives and maybe a daughter. Not alone, not to see me. Other than my father.

He smiled at me. "Sienna, these men are from Evander Corporation."

Courage waited as though I was supposed to know what that was. He waited so long, it officially became awkward. I had to say something. "I'm sorry, I'm not familiar with what that is."

The taller of the two men with the unscuffed shoes stepped forward. "That's okay. We wouldn't expect people to know us out here."

I hated the implication that we were ignorant, unaware people. Even when it was true. "How can I help you?"

"Your uncle has been filling us in about some of the amazing things you can do, Sienna, and we are here to offer you the opportunity to take your talents and use them for the benefit of the universe by coming with us."

I managed not to gasp, which I considered a feat because that was pretty much what I wanted to do right then. My uncle had told outsiders about me?

That would be dealt with at another time. For now, I needed to handle what was happening. "Thank you for your kind offer, but I'm not looking to leave." At least not with them. I lowered my shield enough to feel them, and their emotions were dark and hate-filled, except for the big guy, who offered nothing at all.

"Sienna," my uncle scolded me like I was a toddler. It was everything I could do not to cut out his eyes with my fingernails. Yep, I had a temper, and it wasn't pretty. Still, I managed to control myself. Barely. "These men have traveled a long way to see you. I think you should hear them out."

I shook my head. "Not interested."

With that being said, I turned to leave. I was going to send a messenger to my father immediately. He could handle his betraying younger brother and...

"Devil," Evander's man who'd spoken to me said quickly. "Stop her."

Quicker than I could have imagined, the tall, tall man stood in front of me. He sent me nothing. There wasn't a noticeable emotion anywhere in him. Just cold, dead eyes as he stared at me. He shot out his hand, I could hardly follow it, and grabbed my arm. "You don't move until the executives tell you that you can move."

I tried to pull my arm back, mostly on instinct, as I wasn't an idiot and I knew I wasn't wrenching myself out of this man's hold. Not by conventional means in any case.

He wasn't going to manhandle me and keep me here if I wanted to go. They knew about my abilities? Fine...

I zapped the heck out of him. He let go of my arm, falling to his knees as everyone in the room, including my uncle, startled. Yes...they'd feel the residual pain.

"All of you get out. If you come near me again, you'll know my anger." That sounded ridiculous coming out of my mouth, but I hoped they got the gist.

"Sienna," the man in charge shouted. "Make this easier on yourself. We have ways to get you, whether you want to come or not."

Fear threatened to overtake me, but I didn't turn back around and cower. No, they didn't. He was bluffing. He had to be.

———

I jolted awake. The memories of what happened that day flooded my mind. That had just been the beginning. I couldn't catch my breath. I'd been terrified then, and the fear hit me all over again as though I experienced it now, too. Oh, yes. They'd had ways of making me comply, as evidenced by my arm and the virus indicator I now had to live with.

But that hadn't been the first thing they'd done to me.

Strong hands pulled me against Corbin's chest. "You're okay. Just a dream."

I'd never been so glad to have someone to sleep with me as I was right then. It was stupid to depend on others, but he'd said nothing would harm me, and I believed he might actually be able to stand in front of the man who I'd zapped that day and taken to the ground. He'd come back for me. I could sort of remember...

"Not dreams. Memories."

"Ah." He stroked my back with a gentle hand. "I hope how I'm holding you is okay. It was instinct. I can let go."

I would have laughed if I were capable of that at the moment. "It's new for me, too, but please don't let go."

He tightened his hug. "Okay. I won't."

Corbin didn't say another word, which I appreciated more than I'd ever be able to say. Yes, Evander wanted me. I'd played right into their hands by showing them what I could do. My uncle had turned me over like I was something he could barter with.

That thought was what brought on the tears.

CORBIN RAN a strong hand through my hair, which was challenging, considering my hair had grown in the cryogenic sleep until it was past my rear end. I'd always had long blonde hair, but it had never been quite this long. I was going to have to cut it or something. But at this moment, I loved the feel of it. No one had ever done this before.

I'd described my memory, and he hadn't commented much. Maybe there wasn't anything to say.

"They didn't expect much resistance. That's why they only brought one." He continued his stroke. "Am I doing this correctly?"

I lifted my head. "Is there a correct way? I'm afraid, in this case, I'm not any more experienced than you."

He tilted his head. "Do you remember the man's name? The soldier who you zapped and got away from." With his other hand, he squeezed my arm. "They may not have used it. We tended to be numbers or just hand motions. But out of curiosity, did they use a name?"

Actually they had. "Devil. They called him Devil."

His body jerked, and his arms tightened around me, dropping from my hair. "Sienna..."

The door flung open, illuminating the light from the hall for a long second. Enough time for me to see Blaze standing there. "She just said Devil, right?"

He closed the door as he stepped inside. Apparently, he didn't beep to enter. He just walked in. Corbin put his cheek on top of my head. "She did. You were listening."

"Only since she cried out. I'm not interested in your private words. Can't say the same for the others, I have no idea if they're listening. But when someone screams like that on my ship, I pay attention to make sure no one is dying or needs the doctor." He stepped in again. "Although, I was relieved to see you were still here." Blaze paused. "What are you still doing here?"

Corbin went back to stroking my hair. "I'm sleeping in here. She's fine. You listened to her story?"

"I did." Blaze walked toward the bed and sat down. "Is he the one who injected you with the sickness?"

My memory hadn't gone that far. "I don't remember yet."

"We need to know if you do." Blaze's presence had altered the energy in the room. Not necessarily in a negative way, but he'd certainly changed the way the air moved, like he would always take up a lot of the space in any area he entered regardless of how large a room it was. "We should ask Wade if this is a trauma thing, an illness thing, or a cryogenic sleep thing."

Corbin shifted slightly. "We've never had memory loss, and we've been under more times than I can count."

"Yes, but we are as we are, and I can honestly say I have no idea what it does to ordinary people." He rose. "I'm going to go ask Wade."

Exhausted Wade? "It's the middle of the night, right?" It could be mid-afternoon for all I could tell right now.

Blaze sighed. "Yes, it's about three."

"Then I would say let the doctor sleep. He looked pretty tired today." Maybe it was a bad idea to give Blaze orders. I was so used to being listened to as though I knew what I was talking about, even when I didn't. "Sorry, I tend to...tell people what to do."

After a second, he sat back down. "You zapped Devil." I didn't expect his laugh and wasn't sure what to do with it. "Scary motherfucker."

Corbin shoved him in the shoulder. "We're not supposed to curse in front of her. That's what they mean when they say language."

"Sorry." Blaze sat back next to me, kicking off his shoes and stretching until his head was on the board behind us. I was officially in between them, and there was still room for me. I hadn't been wrong about my statement that the bed was huge. "That is going to take some getting used to."

I cleared my throat. "I...I don't really care if you curse. I've only ever seen the words written, and only then because a friend snuck them in and we read them secretly. So...hearing you guys say them is a little bit of a novelty."

Blaze turned, and he must have been looking down at me. I still hadn't made any moves to get off Corbin, and the reality that this was an uncomfortable situation settled on me like I'd just been sprayed with water.

I wiped my eyes and tried to pull off, but he held on. "Sorry, I've been forcing you to hold me."

"No one forces me to do anything." Corbin readjusted me, but didn't let go. "You should try to get some more sleep."

Just me? "Don't you guys need to sleep? I know you said you don't need much, but surely some."

"Tell you what." Blaze patted my back. "Few things, actually. I have no intention of locking you in your room. I should not have said that I did. That was an overreaction. Trenton tells me I have a bad habit of slash and burning when smaller steps would be a more measured, helpful response. He's been...instructive. My instinct is to make sure whatever might harm my men can't go near them. But you're not a harm. You're an enigma."

I was an enigma. That shouldn't have made me smile, except I totally was. "Thank you, Blaze."

"You're welcome. Now go to sleep."

Groaning, I rolled toward him, Corbin's grip loosening a little bit to let me do so. "I can't just do that on command. Can you?"

"Yes," they both replied. It was Corbin who finished their response. "We have to be able to do just about everything on command."

That sounded horrendous. "Well, I can't."

"I could get Wade to give you something." Blaze sounded like he cracked his neck when he stretched it.

"No thanks." Dread filled me. "I think I have enough medicine going on right now."

Corbin slowly rubbed my back, and a second later, Blaze touched the top of my head. After a moment, Corbin readjusted himself so that I lay more on the bed between them and less on him. That had to be more comfortable for him. He scooted down.

"I'm proud of you."

Surprise made me tilt my head. "Why?"

"You got away from Devil. He trained me. Best of the best outside of Blaze."

His leader laughed, a low sound. "I'm not the best. You know that. I'm the leader, but there were better at what I did. That's not modesty. I don't know how to do that. No, that's just factual."

Corbin was long in answering him. I wondered if he'd fallen asleep. But then, he spoke. "There was more to it than that. You kept us alive. Inside. Devil's dead. He could have used you. His men...they died inside, too."

Blaze scooted down until all three of us were lying together. I didn't know Devil outside of what he had done to me, and I wasn't sure I remembered all of that. Still, I was fascinated to hear them talk. They'd been born in labs and raised to be lethal. Yet here they lay with me in the darkness because I'd had a nightmare. How was I to reconcile the two, and why didn't they scare me at all?

I let my guard down a little, which was always a relief. It took constant effort to keep them up. No rush of negative emotion hit me. In fact, both of them seemed calm, relaxed. Corbin was happier than he had been earlier. And Blaze seemed almost drowsy.

"If that's true," he said as he stretched his arm over his head. "Then why did they leave? Canyon? Rohan? Sterling? They faked their deaths and fled to the other side of the universe."

Corbin snorted. "I don't think they faked their deaths. I think Evander told you they died. And there were women to chase. For Sterling anyway. He told me about it during a lull in one of the battles. Diana was here, so this is where he had to go. They didn't even know if she was alive."

Blaze nodded, and the bed moved when he did. "Sure. And Canyon and Rohan chased a possibility. Why not come to me and tell me they had doubts, if I'm so good? Why not tell me they're going to go?"

Corbin shrugged. "I don't know why people do what they do or don't do. I'm not good at people."

Oh I didn't think that was true at all. Just the opposite. He seemed very attuned to everyone. "I don't know them or you, but I never want to disappoint the people in charge of me. I hope they didn't send me off to get rid of me. I hope that I don't make their lives harder. I...I'm thinking maybe they didn't want to let you down."

"Maybe." He sighed. "Or they were afraid I'd kill them. I wouldn't have, but they did have reason to think that could happen. Thanks to people like Devil. Who, like Corbin, I am deeply impressed you survived."

I leaned up on my elbow. This was cozy. I wouldn't have thought I'd like it. Sleeping was a private thing. But I did like them here. I didn't know why Blaze had decided to stay, but it was like I had two guards to protect me from my memories. Right now, I'd embrace the cowardice and take the protection from myself. Maybe tomorrow, I could be stronger.

"How do you guys sleep at all? With your ability to hear everything? How do you manage to sleep?"

Blaze tugged on my arm until I put my head on the pillow. It was gentle. It didn't hurt. "First off, I am sorry I said to you that your people wanted to be rid of you. I don't think that could be the case. I apologize for that, if that hurt you. Like Corbin, I don't know what to say and not. Seems that was mean. I didn't mean it to be, merely speculative. As for sleep? We concentrate on one sound and tune out the rest."

Like a white noise. One of my fellow trainees had to sleep with water running in her bathroom, or she couldn't sleep at all. "I imagine the ship has lots of those. The engines. The...I don't know. Mechanical things."

"Not for me." Corbin put his hand on my hip. "If I start listening to those noises, they'll make me nuts. Artemis... she's a great ship. Great old lady. She just doesn't want to comply with me."

So funny how he talked about her like she was alive. "Maybe you need to say please."

"I have. And lots of other things. I'll get it." He squeezed my hip. "That's not what I've been listening to."

"Funny. Me, too. What have you been focused on?" Blaze put his hand on my back. I loved how they were touching me. Such a natural thing for me, and it meant I wouldn't have to be strained doing it.

Corbin sighed. "Her heartbeat. In the machine."

"Me too."

They'd both been listening to my heartbeat to go to sleep at night? I opened and closed my mouth. What was happening now? "I'm not sure I should apologize for waking up. I mean, that is weird. But it must be odd to lose your steady sound."

"It still worked. Earlier. For me." Corbin snuggled down. "I can hear it. Nice and steady. Little faster right now, but it will slow again. When you close your eyes and try to go back to sleep."

And Blaze listened to it, too? "I'm glad it worked for you guys, I guess."

I had absolutely no idea what I should say right now.

Blaze's voice sounded amused as the same emotion flooded me from him. "People who aren't us don't get it. That's okay. We do."

I supposed that made sense. I didn't know how I'd explain what it felt like to zap someone. It was quiet in the room. I couldn't hear their hearts or anything, but I could feel the way we moved through space. How fast were we going? I actually didn't want to know. It would make this worse. I'd gone from never being around men to having two in the room with me in my bed. Corbin squeezed me again, and Blaze shifted until his hand was on my arm.

They did seem to move together without having conversations, like they were reading each other's signals. One of them rubbed, one of them touched. Were they on some kind of quest to get me to sleep?

"How well can you see in the dark?"

Blaze patted my arm. "Better than you."

I should remember that. And it begged the question—were they coordinating how they soothed me with hand signals I couldn't see in the dark?

Would they tell me if I asked? Did I even want to know, or did I just want to go with the fact that I did feel better having both of them here and it was nice to have them care? How did they know how to do this anyway?

"Is this standard for you two? Taking care of upset women in the dark?"

Corbin snorted. "No. You're the first woman I've spent any real time with. How about you, Blaze?"

"No."

As before, I had no conscious thought that I was going to go to sleep. I just did. It was warm, and they were there to stand between me and any members of Evander who wanted to come and get me. That wasn't right or nice of me to need this from them. They owed me nothing. By contrast, all of the thanks was from me to them and not the other way around. Still, for right then, I'd never felt safer.

I woke up slowly. Like I'd been asleep a very long time. It was hard to know. There was no light coming from the window. The movement of the ship seemed less pronounced, but maybe I'd gotten used to it while I slept.

It was the position that I found myself in that was the strangest for me. At some point, we must have all rearranged ourselves. My head was on Corbin's chest. He lay sprawled on his back, his eyes still closed and his heart beating a steady, easy sound beneath my ear. Blaze had an arm thrown over me, embracing me to his body, which was pressed up against me from behind. The warm feel of his breath caressed the back of my neck in even, gentle movements. Corbin's hand tangled in my hair, his face turned toward my body.

Heat swept through me, and my nipples hardened. I sucked in a breath. Had this ever happened to me before? Not quite like this. We were kept away from men, so it was hard to have fantasies in the temple. But every once in a while, I'd see someone from a distance and think...yep, he's handsome. Sometimes, I'd even wake up with a throbbing in my core like I needed something.

I'd touched myself, but it was always a hollow completion, like I wasn't getting what I needed from my own fingers.

Lying between them and not in a panic, I was definitely as turned on as I'd ever been. Would they know? Could they tell? I winced at the thought. Privacy was obviously not something given in abundance around Super Soldiers. But how far did that extend? They could hear my heartbeat. What else could they tell?

Blaze shifted slightly, letting out the slightest sigh in the back of his throat. He tugged me closer to him, but Corbin didn't let go. It would have woken me if I hadn't already been up. They didn't sleep much, and they were both still out cold. Did that mean that it was still the middle of the night?

I don't know how I realized Blaze was awake. He didn't

make a sound, and I wasn't turned to look at him. But I just knew...like the air in the room had shifted. He didn't move, didn't alter how he held me, but he was awake. As gently as I could to not disturb Corbin, I turned my head to regard him.

His eyes had opened, and he stared at me. His voice was low. "You okay?" He smoothed his hand over my forehead.

I nodded, answering in a whisper. "I don't know what time it is."

"Early." His voice was scratchy. "Thanks for letting me stay here. I haven't slept this well...ever."

"And we could all still be sleeping if you two weren't shouting." Corbin laughed. "Or whisper-talking. Whatever." He rolled over until his back was pressed to my stomach.

I don't know why that made me giggle, but it did. Blaze's mouth twitched into a grin as Corbin groaned. "Seriously. Nothing happening on the ship that needs attention. Anders is fine piloting. He's sort of dozing anyway, because there's nothing happening out there. Trenton and Wade are actually asleep. Kellan is fiddling with the climate control, but hasn't broken anything. We could actually just lie here and do nothing but sleep."

"He's grumpy in the morning when he actually rests," Blaze still whispered. "Always was. Should see him when he comes out of cryo. One time, he actually tore up a med room."

I squeezed Corbin's hand. "Are you going to beat up my bedroom?"

"I don't have any memory of doing that. I maintain it didn't happen."

Just then, my stomach growled. Blaze leaned up on his elbow. "You're hungry."

I rubbed where the sound had come from. "I guess so. I think I remember where there was food. I'll go find something to eat."

Blaze swung his legs over the bed. "Time for me to get moving. I've never spent a day or even a morning in bed. Wouldn't know what to do with that." He turned slightly toward me before he brushed my hair off my face. "Thanks for not throwing me out of the room."

That thought hadn't occurred to me, even if maybe it should have. "Thanks for keeping my bad memories at bay."

"Devil is scary. If I was dreaming of him, I'd be screaming, too." He nodded toward the door. "I'll see you in the kitchen. Do you have anything to wear other than Corbin's clothes?"

I looked over my shoulder at Corbin, who now had the pillow over his head. "No, he gave me a bag of them. Very grateful to him."

I don't know what he said, because it sounded more like a grumble from under the pillow. Whatever it was, Blaze grinned.

"Here," he pulled his shirt off and handed it to me, "wear mine."

Corbin threw his pillow aside. "Are you serious?"

"Smells like you. I want her to smell like me for a minute."

Okay...they had to work this out. I wasn't sure what to do with any of it. I had no clothes, so I was going to have to borrow until that changed. But I was leaving that to them. Deciding that my need to pee trumped whatever argument this was, I hustled myself into the bathroom. Closing the door, I brought Blaze's shirt to my nose. Did it smell like him? I couldn't really discern any scent on it, other than maybe laundry soap and just an overall general masculine scent. I pulled the shirt I had on off me and brought that to my nose. Did it smell different than the one I had on? The soap I'd used before I put it on was certainly evident, but could I detect anything really?

If I ever found myself pressed up against them again, I was going to smell them. The heat inside of me intensified at the thought. I leaned against the door and tried to breathe. I might need a quick, intense, cold shower. Certainly, if they could hear everything, the last thing I wanted to do was to very disappointedly try to satisfy myself. They didn't need to listen while I made an attempt at orgasm and so cruelly didn't get one.

I splashed cold water on my face, put Blaze's shirt on, which I swam in because he hadn't torn it down to fit me the way Corbin had, and managed to roll Corbin's pants up to wear them. Coming out of the bathroom, I found the room empty.

It was bigger without them in it, but also sadder. I'd forgotten to be overwhelmed when I woke up this morning, but now the rush of last night hit me once again. I was on a spaceship named Artemis that Corbin kept calling an old lady. We were going somewhere to drop me off so I could meet even more new people who would be responsible for me.

I took a long deep breath. Okay. This was happening, and there wasn't a thing I could do about it, except try to react in a way that would make this go in any semblance of smoothly. I had to do the next right thing.

Whatever that was.

Why did none of the tried and true things that made so much sense in the temple not work for me now?

Standing here was going to do nothing to improve my hunger, so I forced myself out the door. The hallway was quiet, and fortunately, I did remember the way to where Trenton had fed me. There was a swishing noise always present on the ship, and it was louder out here than in the rooms. Why was that? Had they built her to be quieter in the sleep quarters? How many sleeping quarters were there? I should ask Blaze. It was his ship after all.

Reaching out, I touched the wall. Peeling paint meant someone had to pay attention to the aesthetics here. Depending on how long I was going to be on this ship, maybe I could do that. I'd done it at home.

It would at least give me something to think about. Assuming they had things like paint on board.

My bedmates were in the kitchen, both of them staring at the fridge. They looked up when I came in, and I didn't miss how they gave me a once over. I'd worn both of their clothes. A strange compromise considering how strange an argument it had been to begin with.

"Hi." I nodded toward them. "Do you guys have to stop every so often to get groceries?"

"That would be hard." Blaze pulled out three things from the fridge. "We have some food like that. Trenton made you dinner with some supplies that didn't have to be rehydrated, but mostly what we eat has been freeze dried and could last a long time if we needed it to."

Corbin grabbed plates. "On the few times we've been on a space station, we do buy food."

Anders came through the door. He held a tablet in his hand. "If you guys are making breakfast, count me in." He shot them both a look I couldn't interpret. "Everyone sleep well?"

Blaze pulled out another packet. "Jealousy is such a waste of time."

My cheeks heated up. Yes, of course, Anders knew I'd

slept between the two of them. Kellan probably did, too. My impropriety was absolutely not hidden on this ship.

"I'm not jealous." Anders touched my arm when he went by. "Just surprised. Corbin, yes. You, I wouldn't have thought it."

I held up my hand. "Can we not do this? I...I'm embarrassed all of a sudden, and I'm too hungry to be this uncomfortable."

Anders nodded. "Sorry. I didn't mean to do that. I didn't realize what I said would."

The next few however many days we were all on this ship together was going to be a minefield of me trying to figure out what was going on.

There was a beep, and Corbin pulled out something they were rehydrating. How did that even work?

My stomach didn't care. It chose that moment to grumble again.

BREAKFAST WAS BLAND TASTING, but I was too hungry to complain. Did they eat like this all the time? Trenton came into the room, rubbing his eyes just as I'd finished. He looked around at all of us at the table.

With a yawn, he laughed. "I never see you guys eating in here in the morning. What is the occasion?"

"I think it's my fault." I sipped the water in my glass. "I was really hungry."

"You're entitled to be. These guys don't eat or sleep much, so I was shocked." He poured himself coffee. I'd never had any, but loved the smell. What was really amazing was the machine had turned on without him being in the room and started brewing. He must have pushed a button from his tablet to get it to do that.

Anders shrugged. "I really like food. It was something readily available as more than just a substance plan. We got our required calories and nutrition in one dose and that was that. But I've come to see what you like about it, and I understand why you complain so readily about how we have to eat on this ship."

"Not how." Trenton slid in next to Blaze. "What we *have* to eat. I wouldn't mind so much if we could make more regular stops."

"Sure." Blaze tilted his head. "And let's just let Evander know exactly where we are at all times, too. Maybe we should make them a sign."

Trenton held up his hands. "I know. This is an old argument. We've had it many times. You're the boss, and I acknowledge you understand this battle better than me."

I looked between them. "When was the last time you saw Evander?"

Anders took my hand in his, lacing our fingers together. The same warmth I'd woken up with flooded me again. No one at the table indicated they knew at all. I could almost sigh in relief. Perhaps there were some things they didn't know just by having keener senses.

"We saw Evander three days before you woke up. But we managed to get away from them. Right now, we've been hiding more than engaging with them. However, I would guess that's going to stop. The weapons are sufficiently upgraded now that we think we could have a chance in this game we're playing with them."

Blaze nodded. "The next time we see them, they're ours."

I shivered. "Maybe you won't see them again."

"They have to be destroyed," Kellan said as he entered. "They can't be left to regroup, reform, or bother this side of the galaxy anymore. It's too late to push them through the black hole and shut the door, because Melissa and her motley crew at Mars Station closed that option down. So we have to kill them. Yes, for you, Sienna, but also because we just have to kill them. Period. For the sake of everyone."

"Not necessarily." Wade leaned in the doorway. Some

of the dark circles under his eyes had faded. He must have slept. "Last I heard, and I don't have details, the Chens are rehabbing Evander Super Soldiers on Earth to live pretty good lives. They have that whole Chen Empire-Z Warrior thing they do. I saw it firsthand when I lived there during the war. It's serious stuff. I don't have details, but Amber told me a Super Soldier saved her husband's life by hearing a heart condition."

Anders tilted his head. "Which husband?"

"Shane." Wade poured himself coffee. "You doing okay, Sienna?"

I nodded at him. "I slept really well and," I looked down at my arm, "I'm still at one."

"Good deal." He scooted in next to Trenton. "Any issues with the device bothering your arm?"

Anders shook his head. "I was with Shane a lot. I never heard a heart condition. Who do they have there with better hearing than me?"

"We compete to see which one of us is the most Super of all the Soldiers. It's an ego thing," Kellan leaned forward. "Do it again."

Took me a second to realize of what he was speaking. "I am not going to zap you. If you act like a jerk again, I'll figure out something else, but it won't be the zapping." No, I'd hold that entirely for people like Devil and anyone else who threatened my life. "I shouldn't have done that to begin with. I apologized, and I will again."

He scrunched up his face. "What am I supposed to do with your apology? I want to be zapped so I can learn how to do it."

"You can't learn how to do it. It's just something that women born on our planet are able to do, to certain degrees, sometimes."

Wade leaned forward. "That's fascinating. Why is that?"

"None of us are scientists. We're too busy trying to survive. It's just accepted and, before my uncle sold me out, protected knowledge."

Blaze took a bite of his rehydrated food and pushed it away. "What else can you do? It's not just zapping, right? This is an awful lot of trouble for them to want to know how to do just that. Particularly if others on the planet can..."

The tablet in front of Anders beeped, and he picked it up. "Incoming."

All of them jumped. The ease of the eating changed immediately to a tension I'd not felt from any of them, not even when I'd zapped Kellan the day before. Anders passed the tablet to Trenton, who took it, passing his finger over it several times.

"Two ships. One under attack from another." His eyes flashed with anger. "One of them is a fucking old Sandler ship, and the other one is a transport vessel of some kind with identification from a smaller Dark Planet." He lifted his angry eyes and met Blaze's gaze. "Well?"

A muscle ticked in Blaze's jaw. "I'd say no, if I didn't know what it means to you."

I was missing something here, but that wasn't pressing at the moment. Blaze rose so fast, the chair he'd been in flew backward. "Do it. We're going after them."

Anders was the first out the door, followed by Trenton and Corbin. Then Kellan, with a nod at Blaze, ran after them. Wade grabbed Blaze's arm. "This doesn't fix that for him. Nothing we do to however many renegade Sandler Cartel pieces of shit that are running around fix this for him. I thought your objective wasn't to expose us."

"I told you. No more running. That means Trenton gets his turn. They're his Evander."

Wade shook his head. "I don't know that you should be indulging this."

"People need us. They're under attack, and if we're really the good guys, then I want to act like it. Otherwise, what is the point of any of it?" He spoke through gritted teeth. "And last I checked, you answered to me and not the other fucking way around."

He stormed out of the room. Wade slammed his hand down on the table before he followed them. All of them leaving me there in the room. The ship bayed left, and I grabbed on to the table. Okay. This sucked. What did I understand? Well...we were firing at a Sandler Cartel ship that was attacking people. At least, I assumed we were saving the other ship.

I knew who the Sandler Cartel was. Sandler Space had been terraformed at the same time as the Dark Planets, but had developed more resources. It had to do with the fake suns and the money that had been spent on theirs versus ours. But I didn't need to think about that right now. It was old politics that no one wanted to hear about since nothing could be changed.

I had to know what was going on. Grabbing on to the wall, I ran out to see. I might not know how to do anything on this ship or help in any way, but dang it, I was going to at least know what I was about to get into. Unable to use buttons or knobs was one thing, but I'd always had the best sense of direction of anyone I knew.

I went to the control room, expecting to find it filled with chaos. But instead, the reality was that it was silent. Trenton pressed buttons fast while Anders did the same thing next to him. Blaze stood back and watched, not saying anything.

Where the others were, I didn't have a clue. Blaze put out his hand to me, and I took it because I didn't know what else to do.

"We're fighting with Sandler Cartel." I kept my voice down, not that it would make much of a difference.

He nodded, and then shook his head. "Sandler Cartel is gone. Ended with a gunshot to the head. Garrison Sandler himself got taken out. I've only heard about it because I was technically just coming out of cryo and betraying Evander at the time. But Waverly Sandler, his daughter, killed her father. It was, from what I understand, rather an impressive feat. In any case, that's over. But what is left is a bunch of assholes with ships and the need to harm others. They're basically pirates."

I bit the inside of my cheek to keep from screaming. I knew what those people were. We all suffered because of them. "And you're stopping them."

He nodded. "Yes. But this is personal for Trenton. Sandler Cartel killed his wife before the war. Trenton was on a rampage against them before there was any war. He didn't get to kill Garrison, so he wants to kill what's left of the cartel."

He'd had a wife? And she died? My heart clenched. Oh, that was terrible. Trenton with the long, mismatched hair who had made me French toast was in mourning. My mental walls threatened to collapse, but I held them up. Right now was not the time for that.

Anders hit a button and smiled at Trenton. "All yours."

"Got him." He rocked back on his feet. I expected to see him smile, but he didn't. "They're dead in the sky. Life support is failing. It'll be over in seconds."

Blaze nodded. "Good. Let's go help the other ship."

Trenton didn't turn around. Truth was, I didn't know the man well, had never met his wife. But right then, if I allowed it, I could feel like I did. That wasn't going to help anyone right now. Still, my heart bled for him.

He hung his head before he turned and left the room.

"Come on." Anders motioned at me. "I think it's safe on the other ship. They need some help. If there's a woman on board, it'll go better if you are there."

I swallowed. "If you think that would be of use."

"It would," Blaze answered. "But she's not going near strangers until we're one hundred percent sure this isn't a set up. She can wait and greet them if they come onto our ship. Otherwise, Sienna is on Artemis until we get to the Farm." With that pronouncement, he strode out.

Anders touched my arm. "Come with me."

With no other choice, I followed. "Is Trenton going to be okay?"

"No, I don't think he will. I mean, short of something remarkable happening to him, something he says he never wants, like falling in love with someone else, I can't see that he'll ever be okay. He's lived for revenge. The object of his anger is gone. What's left is not quite the same for him."

That seemed like a lot. "Maybe he needs some time to process. Has he ever done that?"

"Taken time? I don't even know what that is. It's all very foreign to me. I've never been angry at anyone I've killed. I've never felt one way or another about it. Never known anyone personally enough to care about the action I was being sent to do. For that matter, I've never had anyone die that I cared about either."

Now that I didn't believe. "Corbin called you his brother last night. I think you guys care."

"I wasn't listening when he said that. Believe it or not, I try to stay out of private conversations. Easier that way. But I do feel for Corbin and the others here as much as I possibly could for anyone, which is why, I suppose, it's really good that they aren't dead."

We stopped at a window, and he pointed at it. "That's the shuttle leaving Artemis to go to that ship. See the red flames on the inside? That's some kind of fire. I'm not worried about that."

"You're not?" I'd never seen anything like this before. Goosebumps broke out on my arms. There really was a ship flying to another ship. "Wouldn't fire be very bad?"

"Sure, if Kellan wasn't so good at putting them out. It's his specialty. He blows things up and puts out the flames as though he was born to do so." Anders side eyed me. "Which of course, he was."

He was testing me. I turned to stare at him. "Did you say that so you could see how I'd react to it?"

"I don't know, truthfully." He ran a hand through his hair. "Sometimes, I don't know why I do the things I do."

That was troubling for him and quite a bit to handle for me. I let my wall down slightly. He really was confused. It slammed into me. This was part of the unusual aspect of my life that I hated. Why did I have to sometimes feel what others felt? What if I didn't want to know? Didn't want to help them?

Wishing things were different changed nothing. I put my hand out on his arm. It would soothe him, whether he knew it or not. That was why I'd spent years in the temple, to learn how to do just this. "I think you were more thrown by Trenton than you realized."

He nodded. "Large displays of pain are hard for me. I want to run away from them like they're a wound."

"You want to run away, or you want to figure out how to fix what can't be fixed?"

His lips twitched. "Maybe both. How have you all lived with so many emotions all the time? How did you get through childhood? I never had to feel anything. In fact, the need to do so was beaten out of me. All of us. At an early age, and I've found things very difficult since we left Evander."

The ship we watched docked with the ship on fire. It was fascinating to witness, although I doubted I'd see anything else now except the shuttle and the new ship locked together. Did I dare ask Anders the question floating in my head?

"Why did you do it? Decide to leave Evander?"

He was so quiet. Had I crossed a line? He wasn't the only one who didn't always understand social norms. Were there even such things anymore?

"I almost didn't." He leaned against the wall. "I've never said that before. I almost didn't. We woke up to this woman talking in our ears. Telling us things that seemed impossible. It was Waverly Sandler. The one who killed her father."

She sounded like an amazing woman. Waking up Super Soldiers. Taking on and killing her father. I'd never done anything except be made sick and have to be carted around to avoid getting captured. "She's...busy."

"Married to two Super Soldiers and two normal guys. Fearless, I think." Anders spoke with such respect in his voice. I'd never be that—fearless. What was that anyway? How did someone fear nothing? A pang of pain pinched my stomach. I was terribly ordinary. The things I could do? They weren't really mine to own. I'd been born with them. Like my blonde hair and blue eyes. Meaningless when it came down to it.

I had to answer him. What were we talking about? Oh, that woman named Waverly. "Yes. Sounds that way. Fearless."

"Anyway, Blaze jumped right off. He was listening to her. Going to rebel. He was in charge of the whole ship. Hundreds of us. Told us that anyone who stayed with him was leaving Evander and everyone had minutes to get off the ship if they were deserting."

That sounded intense, and it was hard for me to reconcile the two Blazes. There was the one who gave orders, yelled at Wade, started a rebellion, and the one who held me in bed and snuggled. What did it mean that thoughts of both versions of him made me warm inside? That achy feeling he and Corbin gave me. Heck, Anders made me want to whack a woman named Waverly in the arm for being so brave, even though I'd never met her, because he spoke with such fondness about her.

I really was such a flawed individual. When they were teaching people language, they could hold me up in front of children and say here is a physical example of flawed.

"I almost got on the shuttle to leave. A fight broke out. Some of the ones evacuating the ship went at him. I was going. Not to fight Blaze, but because I wasn't exactly ready to leave Evander. I'd just woken up from cryo. I felt like shit. And like it or not, the only home I'd ever had was provided by them." His gaze was distant. "But they attacked Blaze. Whatever else he is and isn't, he's my friend. He leads us. Always has. He was going. I went with him. Make no mistake, I had no great resolve."

Something pinged, and he pulled out his tablet. "They're already on their way back. Wade with the people. Corbin with them. Kellan stayed behind to repair what he can of the ship. They're coming back, and Corbin says they have a mother and daughter among the injured. So my earlier statement stands. It would help to have you."

I nodded. "Whatever I can do. Hey...Anders, at the end of the day, you went with Blaze, you picked the right side, as far as I'm concerned. Who cares if you faltered for a minute when you were tired and grumpy? They were attacking Blaze. You didn't like that."

"I care. I care that I faltered. I'm always steady. Always on. And I killed those guys after Blaze. None of them live anymore." He tilted his head. "I wasn't even angry. Just done. I feel better having talked to you. Clearer. Why is that?"

I could explain it, but I wasn't going to. Not now. They already knew I could zap people and were bringing me to people who would take over my care. The fewer times I had to expose the secrets of the temple the better. My uncle might have had no conscience about giving away secrets, but I did. Wade had told them he could hear me in his head, and I'd confessed to that, too.

"Not going to tell me?" He quirked his lips. "I just spilled to you."

I sighed. "Believe it or not, I'm trying to figure out who to burden with this. Whoever takes me on is going to get a lot. I'm not brave like your Waverly."

He scrunched up his face. "She's absolutely not my Waverly."

I kept going. "It's a secret. Maybe it isn't anymore. I don't know. Maybe everyone knows, but I was raised to keep it secret, and it's going to be hard for me to just start talking about it. I have to keep it for whoever is going to be the one ultimately helping me."

His face fell. "And you don't think that's going to be me?"

"You're dropping me off."

He blinked rapidly. "I hadn't thought about it."

"Well, there it is. I'm not sure I should go ahead and tell this very sacred, at least to me, thing to people who won't be in my life very long." I squeezed his arm. "I'm sorry if you feel like you're sharing and I'm not."

He shook his head. "You have been in my life a long time now. Not awake, but you were here. Keeping Sienna from Evander has been the main goal. I guess that's going to be changing." I pulled my wall all the way back up. His words shouldn't have made me sad, but they had. Or maybe I was just sad to begin with. When I had strong reactions to things, it was better if I wasn't touched by others' feelings as well. Still, as we held each other's gazes for a long moment, I sort of wished I hadn't. What was he thinking? He looked almost sad, but as he'd told me himself, he didn't really do emotions or understand them. Was he? That I wouldn't tell him, or that he'd wasted so much time carting me around? What was he thinking?

I almost asked him, but he took my hand, and then all I could think about was how our hands looked clasped together. Were there people whose lives that were just simple? A man took a woman's hand, and then they were allowed and able to simply like each other? To maybe fall in love? Where they didn't have responsibilities to the whole universe to contend with?

Internally, I sighed. I was so dramatic. There was nothing about me that influenced the whole universe. I was just a girl from a temple on a Dark Planet that no one knew about, who had the bad luck to encounter really mean people who wanted to use her. By contrast, I was lucky these strong, different-minded, unique individuals had decided to take me on as their problem. Even if it was just temporarily.

"They're here." He nodded toward the window where the shuttle approached Artemis. "We should go."

"Okay. Hey, Anders, why did Blaze say he had to watch Artemis? Would she really blow up or something?"

"No..." He tilted his head. "I'm just guessing, but maybe it was more about Trenton. He's probably sitting somewhere making sure that Trenton doesn't decide to steal a shuttle, go find what's left of Sandler, and blow himself up taking them out."

I sucked in a long breath. "Makes you wonder, right? How it would feel to love someone so much that nothing could ever be the same when they were gone? I...I guess we talked about this already."

"Some things bear repeating. It does make me wonder. But then I think about how lucky he was to know that kind of feeling. I don't know if I ever will, because I don't think I'm capable of it."

I pointed to the device in my arm. "Seems my life is too complicated for love. Always was. It was pretty much forbidden, and now, in the aftermath of what happened, even more so."

He winked at me and then grabbed his eye. "That just feels weird. How does Corbin do that?"

I laughed. Despite everything, there could still be these silly moments mixed into the mess.

AN ALARM SOUNDED, and Anders looked over his shoulder. "I installed that. It just tells us when people are coming and going from the ship. Artemis didn't have that. Presumably, you could have come and gone from here with no one knowing. Now, the second a shuttle attaches, it goes off. But then, if the person piloting accepts the attachment, it shuts off."

That begged the question—for as little as I understood what he'd told me—about who exactly had accepted the shuttle. "Who's piloting?"

"Blaze. From a tablet. It's not ideal. There's a half second delay. When we engage, we want to actually be in the control room. But for basic everything-is-probably-fine moments? Yeah...the tablet works, and it keeps us from having to be in there all the time."

That made sense. "Less lonely."

"Less dull." We walked together into a room I'd never been in before. It was huge, the ceiling significantly higher than anywhere else on the ship. How did that work from an engineering perspective? I ran a hand through my hair. I was like a child. A thought occurred to me. Maybe there were books that people gave to children on space travel. I could read one. Start with that.

It would be better than nothing.

With a click, the shuttle holding everyone opened. Noise hit my ears that Anders must have long been aware of. A man cried out in pain. I rubbed my arms. I wasn't a doctor and had no interest in being one. Blood was really not my thing. The fact that I was actually holding out pretty well with the device in my arm was a tribute to the fact that there were a million things happening and I couldn't obsess about that. I'd have thought I'd be puking by now from the grossness of all of it.

Corbin leaned over to speak to the man he rolled out. Wade rushed after all of them. It was, however, the woman and small boy that followed them out that held my attention. She walked, didn't seem hurt, and held the little boy's hand tightly in her hand. My mouth fell open. I knew them. She used to come into the Temple sometimes.

Right at that moment, she saw me and cried out, coming to an abrupt stop. As the man still cried out in pain, Corbin didn't cease his pushing him on the medical table and Wade continued to run after them, but certainly, they both looked between me and the woman.

"Sienna?" She rushed toward me, and as she did, dragging the small boy with her, I remembered her name. It was Brianne, and she hailed from the town right near the temple. I'd seen her maybe half a dozen times. "How are you here? How are you okay?"

She threw her arms around me, and I let her. This was what people did when they knew me, when they understood what it was that I did. Doors opened and closed behind me. I hugged her back. "Are you okay? You were on a spaceship?"

That really wasn't something people who came from our world did all that often. I'd known one family who had left in all my life, and even then, it had been because they'd gotten into some trouble with their neighbors and had to flee.

What was she doing here?

She teared up as she looked at me, which made the little boy with her start to cry. Brianne hauled him up in her arms and then visibly swallowed. "Oh, we all thought you were dead. They made you so sick, and then your father...he rushed through the village to find a shuttle so that they could get you someplace and freeze you? Is that right? We never heard what happened after. Your father never came back and...we thought you were dead."

This was all information I hadn't had. My father rushed me off? How did he even know there was such a thing as cryogenic sleep? And...where was he? What happened? Fear almost took me to my knees. I wasn't close with my parents, but I didn't like the idea of anything being wrong with them.

"Sienna?" Anders said my name as Trenton entered the room. "You know this woman?"

I swallowed. "They're from home."

She hugged me again. People needed to touch me, and I was required to receive their contact, honor *their* need. In fact, what I really needed to do was drop my wall and let her in. Only, I couldn't seem to do it. No. I just didn't want to. Not then.

Brianne dropped her gaze to the ground. That wasn't surprising. On our planet, unless we were related or married to him, we didn't make eye contact with men we didn't know. Except for me...

I apparently had no problem doing so, or even sleeping between two of them.

"These men saved me. I mean, they've been carting my unconscious form around for a very long time." At some point, I needed to pin down exactly how long that was. "And keeping me safe from those people who want to hurt me."

She let out a halting breath. "Things just went so badly after that. The whole planet freaked out. Evander was everywhere with big soldiers." She leaned over and whispered in my ear. "Very similar to some of these men. In size. They ran through all the farms. Took everything, left us with nothing. I swear, it was like the whole planet was decimated. Not that I've seen the whole planet. I...I..." Letting her get it all out was hard. I could just picture what she said. "Then men came with ships. They...they sold us all ships for whatever amount of money we had left. Depending on how much we had was the kind of ship we got. They gave us quick lessons and sent us on our way."

I gasped. "And...and you all just left? On the ships? Now you're attacked...how long have you been running around in space?"

"For a long time." She collapsed against me. "Running out of food. People aren't letting us land. They don't want us. Everything is really hard out there. Lots of people without homes because of the war."

Trenton came over and placed his hand on my arm. "Brianne? That's your name, right? That's what Blaze said anyway." He smiled. "Come on. Let's go see your husband."

She wiped at her eyes. "Yes. We should do that. Thank you for saving Sienna. If she's alive, there is a chance for the universe. She just makes everything better. She's very special. Thank you for being here, Sienna. It's such a gift."

I let her go to Trenton, who held her arm. He looked over his shoulder at me. "We didn't do anything substantial. Her father got her off the planet and others took her in before we did. I'm just glad we got to her when and how we did."

Anders followed Brianne and Trenton from the room as Blaze regarded me. "You can trust me."

"I know that." Or at least, I thought I did. I could trust him in the ways you could people who were new to you. I had the impression of trustworthiness. Last night, I'd had him in my bed. His men certainly thought he was worth uprooting their whole lives for. "It's just..."

What was it, really? It sounded like my whole world was gone. My parents missing. The locals sold some sort of ships and sent on their way.

"You should know that when Dr. Amber Chen was given you on a space station that is now destroyed, she was visited by people who...how shall I put this...made it very clear to her that keeping you safe was pivotal to all of us. That's why it doesn't surprise me that this woman is so attached to you. But I think there is more going on, right?"

I breathed out a long breath. "Blaze, obviously the zapping isn't all I can do. I think you already know that."

"I think that woman held onto you like you might put breath back in her tired body." He nodded toward the door. "I think your home is destroyed. The life you had is over. And I think that if there are things that we should know about you—if every person who encounters you who knew you back there—is going to react like that, then we need to know how to keep you safe. I think you should seriously consider telling us." He stepped back. "Soon."

He nodded toward the door. "Let's go see this woman who knows you but who you don't seem all that enthusiastic to see in the sickbay. She's going to have a fit if Trenton doesn't get you for her."

That extra hearing was a wonderful and sometimes terrible thing.

Was he right? Was I unenthusiastic about seeing Brianne? Shouldn't I be feeling wonderful? I needed information, she had it. And yet, it was as though I suddenly had a burden I needed to haul over a field filled with rocks.

I stared down at my arm. The virus level still read as level one.

That was good. I followed Blaze from the docking room to the sick bay. The closer we got, the more I could hear the poor man screaming.

"Shouldn't he be in the med machine by now?" Or placed in cryogenic sleep. Whatever it is that they were actually doing these days for the sick and injured.

Blaze shook his head. "Not until Wade has him assessed. You can stick someone in the machine with no diagnosis. It doesn't work quite as well or as quickly. But it's better if the doctor can control the thing. And Wade is good. Better than good. The only person who doesn't know how amazingly talented he is turns out to be Wade."

I shook my head. "He's not a Super Soldier, right?" I wanted to make sure I had everyone in the right category. Trenton and Wade were like me, they were regular humans, made in the ways that people generally made babies, and not on the other side of the galaxy in a lab.

"No, we don't make doctors. Or they didn't make us doctors. They had their own, and if we were injured beyond what a med machine turning on could fix, then they put us down anyway. No, there are no doctors in our midst."

We stepped inside, and I forced my stomach to stay steady, my anxiety about anything medical not pushing me over some edge where I puked just from thinking about it.

Anders picked the screaming man up off the table and placed him in a med machine in the corner. "This one?"

Wade nodded. "That'll do. Edward," he spoke to the screaming man. "The pain will stop now. The burns will be gone and the breaks will heal. There is nothing whatsoever that has happened to you that won't get better. You are not going to die."

His words did seem to make the man stop screaming. In truth, I'd never seen a person carry on about an injury before. We had been taught to endure quietly. No one wanted to come to the temple to hear someone carrying on. I'd broken my arm and hardly said a word. Of course, I'd never been burned on a ship I barely knew how to fly.

Brianne sniffed and held his hand. I didn't know him, but if he had gotten a wife, that meant that someone important on our planet thought he was important.

I looked at Corbin as he came to stand next to me. "Is it standard for Evander to give out ships like that? Sell them to people who don't fly?"

He shook his head. "That's not Evander. What Evander does is go into some place and strip it of all of its resources, keeping a portion of the population alive to rework them. They don't sell ships off the planet. Although that's sort of ingenious. Someone figured out how to make money off people's pain. To scare them into going up into space. On ships that are probably badly refurbished." He tilted his head. "There's a word for that, I think."

Trenton leaned against the wall. "Profiteers."

"Aha." Corbin tapped his temple. "Couldn't come up with the word."

Walking away from the wall, Trenton stood to my other side. "That's okay. You guys have only been using vocabulary that wasn't about killing for a short period of time. You probably never said profiteer before."

Corbin nodded. "True."

That was so interesting. Brianne noticed me and opened her arms, her son holding onto her leg. I steeled myself. The woman wanted another hug. Keeping my face passive, I walked toward her and hugged her again.

"Honestly, I don't know what I'd do without you here. It's like the temple came with you."

I wasn't a building. I almost said that, but stopped myself. It was my duty because of what I could do to help her and...

A hand touched my arm. It was Wade. He smiled at me, pulling me away. "Hey, Brianne, your husband is going to be fine. And out of here in two hours. Then he'll be as good as new." He turned to Anders. "Does Kellan have her ship safe enough to fly? Or safe enough for her to return to it?"

Her eyes widened. "Couldn't I stay here?"

"No," Trenton walked toward us. "Sorry, it's not safe here. Right, Blaze?"

Their leader nodded slowly. "Nope. Not safe."

Anders pulled out his tablet and pressed a button. "Kellan says it's safe. He's got all the fires out and the engines reset."

"If we would like Brianne to leave and go back, I could give her husband a lesson on flying and not blowing up the engines before they leave again. And how to best avoid space pirates or Sandler or whatever." Trenton motioned to the doorway. "This way."

He took her by the arm and escorted her out. I watched until they exited. Relief flooded me. I was so glad she wasn't in the room, and that was awful but it was the truth. At least in the temple, I had visiting hours. What would I have done if I'd had to be on all the time? Oh forget, not even all the time. I didn't want to be on at all.

Maybe that was a huge problem.

"Thank you," I nodded toward Wade. "I didn't want to do it right now. I didn't feel like I could."

Wade tilted his head. "Honestly I'm not sure what you were going to do. Hug her? Do you know her that well? Or is there a reason you had to? In any case, she's not my patient. Her husband is, and you're...well, you're sort of my patient, in the sense that you could be again if that number rises. You were uncomfortable. She had to go."

Anders scrunched up his own face. "How did you know? I mean...I didn't get that. Tell me how you saw it."

As an answer, Wade shrugged. "I don't know. I just did."

"Trenton did, too." Corbin shook his head, fast. "I didn't. But he gave Blaze some kind of signal, and you read it, Blaze."

Their leader shrugged. "This time I did. Next time, maybe I won't. Okay. This is almost over. Two hours, then we're on our way back on track. I got a coded response to the one I sent to the Farm. Diana answered me. She wants us to meet her on Mars Station. They're headed there for a meetup with the Chens and the Sandlers. It just makes sense for us to head straight."

Wade groaned and hopped up on the table. "I hate meeting with the whole crew. I know I shouldn't feel that way. They saved me, but I always feel like if I can't find something profound or funny to say, then they all stare at me as though I have two heads or I'm not worthy to sit in the room." He sat up straighter. "Or maybe I don't have to go. I don't need to be in the meeting, right?"

Anders patted him on the back. "They like you just fine, as far as I can tell. Amber does. You're both doctors. She thinks highly of you. You kept things afloat for her when it all went to hell during the war before you took up with us to save Sienna."

I tried to follow their conversation. But it was hard to learn about people I didn't know who were all faceless to me. One fact stuck out. "Is it common for women to be doctors?"

Wade shook his head. "Amber's the only one I know. She really amazed me. Did it during war time."

I rocked back on my feet, filing Amber into the same category as Waverly. Women I hadn't met who were extraordinary, doing things I'd never do. A doctor? I couldn't even stand thinking about blood.

Wade held out his hand. "Come here. Let me look at your arm."

"It's still at one." I held out my arm so he could see. He nodded and let me go. "Holding steady. Looking great."

An alarm sounded, and I jumped. Blaze shook his head on his way out the door. "It's just Trenton bringing Brienne back to her safe ship. And picking up Kellan. Everybody get back to work."

"Um, what should I do?"

He was halfway out the door with my question, but stopped as I said it. "Do?"

"Yes, what should I do? I can't really sit around for the next few days. I'm not used to doing nothing. At home, I did a lot of things." In between visits, but the less said about that the better. "I cleaned. I organized. I didn't cook, someone else did that. I sometimes built things. I've never painted, but if you had some, I could get going on your walls."

Wade examined the read out on the med machine. "We have paint somewhere. I know I saw it."

"We do, and you're lucky because I almost dumped it." Anders smiled. "Seemed pointless. I mean, I've never cared what the ship looked like."

Really? I couldn't fathom not caring about my living space. "Home matters. I mean this won't be my home, obviously, but it's yours for however long it is. There is something to be said for feeling like you care about that place. Then it takes as good care of you as you do of it." That was why I'd spent such an incredible amount of time fixing up my room back at home. It was the only space that was mine, but it mattered. At least to me. "Maybe it sounds dumb."

Blaze threw his hands in the air. "I don't understand human females. Sure, by all means, paint the ship over the next few days. If it makes you happy. Not one of us will notice."

He stormed from the room. Wow. Had I said something to upset him? It was the two Blazes again.

Wade smiled. "I'll notice. Thanks. That would be great."

Corbin nodded. "Sure, now that I know you're doing it. Plus, I'm sure that it'll really smell. We tend to notice that really strongly. The senses things. Let me know if you need help."

With that statement, he left, following Blaze through the door.

Anders squeezed my shoulder. "It'll really brighten the place up. Be good for the eyes to have something new to look at, even if it's just color. Got to go. It's a full-time job keeping up Artemis. Welcome to the fun of it."

I swallowed. They'd hear me anyway if they were listening, and yet I had to ask Wade some questions. "I feel like I'm in a minefield. People come to me, they talk to me. I don't make social mistakes. I made Blaze mad. Why and how?"

"You want me to explain the psyche of a Super Soldier? Not going to happen. I have no idea most of the time. Now? Maybe he's mad because he didn't consider that you'd need a job. Or he's annoyed that we're going to be on the ship another day and a half to get to Mars." He smiled. "Maybe he doesn't want the ship painted."

That didn't help me at all. "I don't have to paint. I could clean and organize or construct shelving or something."

Wade winced. "No shelving. Just another thing to fall when we're attacked. Want to help me?"

I looked around. "As long as there is no blood or vomit."

He threw his head back, laughing, which surprised me. "Good thing you said that to me. I do have a habit of being around blood and vomit. Okay, nothing that will be gross for you." He pointed to a shelving unit. "I think I need to get these medicines labeled. Could really use some help."

That I was pretty sure I could do. "Show me what to do, and I'll get it done."

He was so quiet, I wondered if something was wrong. "I miss it. Strange as that sounds. You talking in my mind."

I forced myself to swallow as I sent him the word. *Wade...*

He sighed. "And there it is. How do you do that? How do you talk in my head? How do you do whatever you do that made that woman want to hug you like that? It was weird. I mean, I'm not a hugger. Not by nature. Even I could tell that was off. That's reserved for people who we know."

"She thinks she knows me." How many times could I put off telling this? "The psychic abilities we're born with on our planet haven't been studied. Who would study them? But I am rather strong at it. I've never been tested. We go, we live at the temple, and someone decided that we would be good at helping people because I can sort of feel what other people feel if I let myself. It's rather painful. Awful, actually. But I do it, and then people feel better after I speak to them about it. That's what she wanted. For me to make her feel better."

Wade stared at me a long time. "Sounds like hell, Sienna."

I covered my mouth, the tears springing to my eyes surprising me. I wiped them away. "Sometimes, it really is."

And he was the first person to ever say that.

I SPENT most of the rest of the day sorting through things for Wade in the sickbay. It was busy work, but organization was something I'd always excelled at, and I was glad for a task that kept me busy. Sometime during the afternoon, the alarm signaling the patient was awake went off, and I exited quickly. It was cowardly of me, but I didn't want to see anyone else from my home planet until I figured some things out.

It would be my job to give and give to him if he needed it—and people who saw me always did. I wasn't sure I had a drop of empathy left inside me. Maybe the cryogenic sleep coupled with my illness bled me dry of what had made me a good person previously. Maybe I was just...temporarily done. I hoped it wasn't permanent. What use would I be to the universe if I wasn't available to help soothe the emotional wounds of those who needed it? That, at least, had been a noble calling.

With nowhere to go except to my room, I headed in that direction, stopping instead in the kitchen on my way. My stomach grumbled, reminding me it was time to eat. I didn't want to have to ask people to feed me. Maybe I could figure this out. At home, I'd at least been able to prepare myself a snack when required, even if I hadn't done the heavy-duty cooking for the temple. We'd had staff for that, and sometimes Joy helped out because she liked it. My heart clenched. What had happened to her and the others?

I chewed on my lip. I had to find out. Who would know? Maybe I had to go back and see the place with my own eyes, get answers. Blaze didn't want to take me, but there had to be others that would. I could figure out how to pay for it. I kept going back to the same issue. Being dependent was a problem, and my only discernible skill was so currently repulsive to me that I was hiding from people who might need my help.

I was just going to have to get over myself and do it.

And charge for it.

How would that even work?

I stared in the freezer and fridge area. None of the food was labeled, but that didn't mean it didn't belong to people. I was their guest, for now, and I didn't want to overdo things by stealing food that might be specified for someone else on this ship.

"Hungry?" Kellan entered quickly.

I looked over my shoulder at him. He didn't look worse for wear, having put out fires and repaired a ship. "Are you okay?"

"Never mind, I was trying the small talk thing. I know you're hungry. I heard your stomach."

I might always find that really, really weird. But then again, I was totally off, so we fit right in with one another in an odd, out there kind of a way. "I didn't hear the alarm signaling you'd returned."

"Really?" He furrowed his brow. "Must be broken

again. Everything breaks on this ship." His smile surprised me. "Just gives me lots of things to fix. Makes the days pass. If you're hungry, why aren't you eating?"

I pointed at the fridge. "Is it just okay to take things? I don't want to steal food."

"Oh yes, all of it belongs to all of us. Communal. Trenton and Wade are both incredibly rich. They pay for everything. After we're done playing cat and mouse with Evander, we'll have to figure out jobs for ourselves. Right now, they seem to just be handling it. I'll pay them back someday. All the food is everyone's."

That was good to know. Looked like I wasn't the only one who didn't know exactly how to function outside of my own little world. Getting a job was so foreign. I'd hated the temple, but at least my path had been set.

I pulled out some dehydrated food that looked from the label like it was going to be meat and veggies. Their dehydrating unit was familiar enough, and I quickly managed the task without blowing anything up. Now, if I'd had to turn on a light, I might have stumbled.

I didn't suppose Corbin could label the whole ship.

When I turned around to sit down, Kellan took the seat across from me. I pointed to my food. "Do you want some?"

"No." He paused. "Thank you."

I nodded. "You're welcome. You guys don't have to eat much?"

"We need large quantities of food but not to eat all that often. We're all trying to adjust to a more human schedule, so that we can fit in for social occasions should those occur."

I chewed and swallowed, trying not to grimace at the taste of my rehydrated meal. This was pretty disgusting. Still, beggars couldn't be choosers. I was glad for the food and determined to let it take care of my hunger.

"Do it again." Kellan spoke after moments of silence.

I supposed I could play dumb and act like I didn't know what he was talking about, but that would just insult us both. "No, I'm not going to zap you again. I can't figure out why you would want me to. From all accounts, it really hurts."

"It did." He leaned forward. "And I want you to do it again. I'm going to work on learning how to do it myself, and I think several repeat performances would allow my brain to figure it out faster."

I reached behind me and pulled out a small can of water. It looked like someone had filled it manually and that this hadn't come prepackaged. Who took the time to do this? "You can't learn to do it."

He narrowed his eyes at me. "You don't know me yet, so you haven't realized that I am actually the smartest person on this ship. Among the smartest ever created in the Super Soldiers. There is nothing that you can do that I can't learn how to do."

I almost scoffed at the ego of that statement, until I realized he hadn't meant it to be that way. For Kellan, that was a statement of fact. In his world, they were all ranked that way. Who was best at what and when?

"How did that translate for what you did for Evander?" I tapped my head. "Your super brain?"

He smirked. "Well, we don't really call it that." Kellan shifted in his seat. This wasn't what he wanted to talk about. I didn't even have to have my empathy open to know that. It was written all over his face, the slope of his mouth, the way he'd made his eyes jump around, looking everywhere but me. Finally, he spoke. "I planned missions. Figured out the best ways to eliminate enemies. Generally, Blaze would send me someplace by myself on solo missions.

I would take out the target, and we wouldn't have to bring in a full-on attack."

I took another bite. "Would you have been like the one they brought to me? Devil? To get me off the planet? And make me sick?"

He didn't answer right away. "Probably not, actually. Devil was higher up the chain of command. He was a planet killer. If they brought him to you, it was only in the midst of thinking they had no use for any of the people he encountered. They didn't care if he ended up destroying the whole place. I was more strategic."

My worry for Joy and the others quadrupled, and my appetite went with it. I pushed aside the meal. He stared down at it. "Pretty gross. I was shocked you were eating it. I think Trenton meant to throw those out."

I smirked at him. Kellan was amusing. He absolutely did not always say the right thing or make any attempt to. Yet, he also said thank you and put out fires on a stranger's ship before fixing it. "You could have mentioned that. Like hey, don't eat that one."

He shook his head. "I didn't want to argue with your choice."

"I wouldn't call that arguing with my choice as much as I might think that was warning me not to make a bad one. I don't mind being instructed in things I don't know." I sipped my water.

Kellan took my hand. "Sienna, please. Let's talk about the zapping. I explained why I can do it. I've asked you to do it. It's not a punishment. It's a request."

I hadn't avoided this conversation with distraction. I squeezed his fingers back. They were tough, like he worked with them and had damaged them enough that he had a lot of calluses on them. "Kellan, I need to explain. The reason no one knows that these abilities exist is that they only come from those born on our planet. There are things people can do there. We like to say we can hear our ancestors in the wind. But it's just the women born with the chance to do what I can do. Even then, it's rare. It's not something that all people can do and just learn how to do it. I... It's like having blue eyes. I just can. It's always women. Men can't do it at all. I'm not being stingy with my knowledge. If I could teach you, I would. But you have two strikes. You weren't born there and you're male."

For a second, he looked like he was going to argue. "What is it genetically that happens on your planet?"

"Beats me. Sorry."

He laughed and squeezed my fingers back. "All right then, don't zap me again. Unless I deserve it. Which I might, because I can be really obnoxious."

"Surely someone with as big a brain as yours can figure out how not to be rude."

He lifted his eyebrows. "You're so pretty, Sienna."

My cheeks heated. Was I? No one ever talked about that with me. I wasn't valued for what I could bring to a husband since I wouldn't have one, and no one ever talked about pretty unless it related to what a woman could give a man in marriage. I didn't think Kellan was thinking along those lines. It was more like he just gave me the compliment.

It seemed so much more important because he had. Was he handsome? He was. And deadly. Yet, he held my hand gently, and I liked him even though he was, admittedly, very rude. But sometimes not.

"Thank you."

He smiled, not the smirk I usually got, but a tantalizing

perusal that made my body flush. My breath caught in my throat.

"You don't have to be afraid of me." His voice was low.

I shook my head. "I don't think I am. As you know, I can take care of myself."

"That is the truth. I'm more beat up than the others. I've been through more fire, more explosions. My body is a scarred mess."

I blinked. He didn't look like a mess to me. I'd seen him and Anders both shirtless. They had been huge, over-whelmingly beautiful in their strength and power. Kellan and I hadn't started off well. But this slightly softer version of him I could probably talk to forever, even with the slight nudges into his being rude in what he said.

"I think you're," I might as well just use the word, "beautiful."

He sucked in a long, audible breath. "I'd like to kiss you."

Wow. This was happening. I hadn't... This was new. "I've never been kissed."

"How is that possible?" He tilted his head when he asked me the question. "Are all the men on your planet blind?"

His words made me giggle. Not something I generally did, ever. "I...I'm kind of a figurehead of sorts. Off limits."

"Well...fuck that. Sorry, language." He shook his head. "So can I not kiss you? I've never kissed anyone either. Not in real life. There used to be these machines they put us in to give us fake experiences that would control our...never mind, I don't want to talk about that right now. Or ever."

I leaned forward to meet him halfway. "You can kiss me."

Was I really doing this? As he rose, he never let go of my

hand. Kellan moved closer, taking the seat right next to me. "I want to be closer."

That was the last thing he said before his mouth met mine. I expected a strong pressure of mouth-on-mouth, considering how Kellan threw himself into conversation. But he was gentle, barely touching me.

I caught my breath and closed my eyes. With my free hand, I touched his cheek, drawing him closer than he already was. His cheeks felt rough against the pads of my fingers, stubble providing a rough contrast to his sweet lips.

He pressed slightly harder, and heat surged through me, finding its way to my face where I was sure my cheeks were bright red. We were both new to this and, I was sure, not quite getting it right. But we stumbled through until kissing him seemed to make more sense. My mouth met his and then his would meet mine.

Kellan pulled back slightly, but only to run his tongue over my bottom lip. My ears rang, and I needed to press my body closer to his. That move, the thing he had done with his tongue, it spurred the thought in my mind. What could I do with my tongue?

I pushed it through his lips. He moaned against me, grabbing me by the back of my neck and yanking me closer. It was rough, but I loved it.

Our tongues danced. That was what it seemed like. I never could have imagined it, and then he abruptly stopped. Panting like we'd both been running, he stared into my eyes. "Trenton is moments away."

"What?" His words didn't want to penetrate the fog surrounding my brain.

He smiled, running a hand down my cheek. "Trenton will be here shortly. I don't mind, but I think kissing is the kind of thing that people do privately." He paused. "Right?"

Was it? "My mind has shut down."

His smile was huge. That I noticed. But a thought dawned on me that pushed all good feelings away. "Kellan..." Utter horror made tears rush to my eyes. "I'm carrying all kinds of sickness. I could have made you very unwell."

He stroked his hand over my wrist. "It says one. You're not contagious, and even if you were above your threshold, I'm not going to get sick. Super Soldier genetics. Better immune systems."

That was all very interesting. "Even for sticking my tongue in your mouth?"

"Even for then. You can't make anyone sick right now in any capacity. Wade went over it with us before he woke you up and..."

Trenton strode in, shooting us both a look as he did. "Yuck. Throw out that food. How did you let her eat that?"

Kellan shrugged. "I'm an asshole." He held up his hand before he winked at me. "Sorry, language."

He was so doing that on purpose. Someone as smart as Kellan could easily adjust to not using curse words. This was amusing to him. "Here's a hint. I don't care if you swear or not. Go ahead and do it. Doesn't offend me."

His smile widened. "And she cuts off the game before it even starts."

Trenton rehydrated something, leaning on the counter. "You two look cozy."

Kellan jumped to his feet. "I have to go figure out what's wrong with the alarm that didn't go off. Thanks for the talk, Sienna. I'll look forward to continuing it later."

He squeezed my shoulder as he passed, the sensation making me want to lean into him and never let go. Wow. One kiss, and I was ready to melt at his feet.

Trenton walked over as Kellan left, setting some new food in front of me. It smelled much better. Some kind of pasta dish. He had one for himself, too, and sat across from me in Kellan's original chair.

"That was the most pleasant I've ever seen him. You're like a miracle worker."

I shook my head. I had to get out of the kissing fog. "He's perfectly nice. A little rough around the edges, I guess."

"To say the least. So you knew those people? The ones who were on the ship. They talked about you like you were a religious figure."

Well...we were going right for that. "I explained it to Wade. Some of the things I can do involve sensing emotion and helping to make people feel better. It makes them want to be with me. On my planet, the role is held with some significance. I suppose religion might be the word."

He stopped chewing. "For real?"

"For real." I let the smell of the pasta relight my appetite and took a long bite. "I'm sorry about your wife, about what happened."

He nodded, not looking up at me. "Thanks. It makes me...very intense when I encounter them." Finally, Trenton lifted his gaze. "But don't do anything about that or whatever with your abilities. I don't want to feel better. I'm not sure how I'd get through the day without feeling really angry and hating what's left of the Sandler Cartel."

I held up my hands. "I'd never do anything anyone didn't want. And right now, I don't want to do it at all. You can keep your hate. It's yours. I promise."

This seemed to satisfy him. "Hey, am I crazy, or was there something going on in here with you and him when I got here?"

Kissing was a private thing. That was what Kellan had said to me. He didn't want to talk about it with others, even if nearly all of the rest of the ship could hear it happen. "I don't know if you're crazy or not. That's the kind of thing you'd have to talk to Wade about."

Trenton's smile shocked me. It was big, huge, and unexpected. "You shock me every so often. I'll decide you're sweet and kind, then you zap Kellan. I ask you a question you don't want to answer, and you coat the words 'fuck off' in kinder rhetoric. I like you, Sienna. The ship is much more alive with you on it. So glad Wade figured out things well enough to wake you up."

I liked him, too. Trenton did speak his mind.

"Kellan said you're rich. I've been speculating on money. What I'm going to do to earn my passage home, how I'm going to support myself. What did you do to earn your credits?"

He finished eating and wiped his mouth with a napkin on the table. It brought my attention to his lips. What would Trenton kiss like? Would it be like Kellan? I needed to stop. One kiss, and I was suddenly a kissing monster.

Or something.

"I didn't do anything. Well, that's not true. I've worked as a pilot for years. I used to fly for Earth. In their military. But my family is old Earth money. They were rich for an incredibly long time. I mean since before the bombs. I don't even know in what anymore. Medicines. Or something to start. Then they sold weaponry after the bombs. We're not as rich as some. Most of the people we're going to see have a lot more money than me. I have enough to fund what these guys need, coupled with Wade, who is richer than me. We take care of things around here."

That was so interesting. "I've never given any thought to money. Feels really foolish now."

"Women don't generally have to. The truth is that most women, even when they're pseudo-religious figures, marry very wealthy men. They take care of it. I know it didn't used to be that way, and I think that things may be changing. If you hadn't had your abilities, I think you'd probably not been thinking about money then either."

I finished my pasta. "Truthfully, where I'm from, it's not about money. It's about resources. Women get married to farmers with big stockpiles or shopkeepers. No one as far out in the Dark Planets as we were had any money."

"Interesting."

His tablet beeped loudly. Corbin's voice came over the speaker. "Trenton, it's Evander."

"Oh shit." He winced. "Sorry. We're in the middle of nowhere space. This is the worst-case scenario to run into them. Strap in, your holiness, we have to go fly like the devil is chasing us."

I didn't have time to hate that nickname. Where did he want me to strap in? I didn't ask him because he ran from the room. Twice now, I'd seen Trenton run, and the last time had been a big problem, too. If Trenton was running, we all should be running.

I didn't belong in the command room. I couldn't even use the light switches. The best thing I could do was stay out of the way. And yet...I wanted to see this Evander ship that chased me. Could I do that somewhere where I wouldn't be a problem?

I ran for sickbay. Wade pulled out all sorts of things, talking to himself. "Corbin is going to burn his arm again."

"Really?" He jumped when I spoke, obviously not

having had any idea I was there. I winced. "Sorry. I'll wear a bell around my neck or something."

He shook his head. "Or I could pay attention. It's me, not you."

"Can I see the ship from here? The one chasing me?"

Wade scratched his head. "Absolutely, you can. Sure. Hold on." He grabbed his tablet. "We should get you one of these when next we can."

He fiddled with his, and I stared down at the picture. Sure enough, a sleek, silver ship rushed past us. Something red seemed to pour out of it, and our shift shot to the side, hard. Wade grabbed me, pulling me to him just in time to hold onto the med machine together.

"What was that?" I was too confused to be as anxious as I was sure I should be.

"Trenton saving our asses. They're firing. He's really good at this. That's why they let him fly. Otherwise, I assure you, one of the others would be doing it. For a Super Soldier to say that someone is better than them at something, they have to be really, really good."

I think he was trying to be reassuring. "Well, I'm hardly in a position to judge. I'm very grateful to all of you and..."

He interrupted me. "Strap in. Over here." He pointed to some chairs he'd pulled down from the wall. I managed to get there without falling over and strapped in as he instructed.

Wade didn't strap himself in, instead, going back to pulling out his equipment. "Why are you safe running around, and I'm locked in?"

He smiled. "Because I'm me and you're you. I'm always going to want to take care of you, Sienna. I can promise you that."

That might have been the sweetest thing anyone had

ever said to me. These men, who had kept me alive and were continuing to do so, came across so rough...until they didn't.

The lights flickered, and Wade sighed. "Something just blew up."

"How do you know?" I looked around. I hadn't heard anything.

He grimaced. "Experience."

STRAPPED to the chair while Wade rushed collecting supplies around the room gave me too much time to think about things. Way too much time. "Wade...that ship is much bigger than ours."

He looked over his shoulder. "It's not about the size of the ship." His smile surprised me. What was he grinning about like he'd just made a joke? "It's really about what you can do with the ship. They don't have Trenton. They've yet to really get us. Don't worry. They push this old lady of ours to the brink, but she never lets us down."

I leaned back. With no control over anything and not really understanding how any of this worked, I had nothing to do but sit with my anxiety. It sucked. I rubbed my eyes. When I was little, I used to worry about everything. Particularly because I was responsible for making people feel better. It felt very dishonest that I was supposed to do that when I couldn't help but feel so completely lost to everything myself. Over the years, I learned to control the anxiousness.

Right at that second, I wasn't doing such a great job.

With nothing else to do, I had to talk. Otherwise, I might implode from thinking about that huge ship that was out there, trying to fire at us in order to board and take me. "I...I guess you got more than you bargained for when you took me on. Couldn't have known that Evander was coming. Now they're your problem."

He stopped what he was doing and walked over to me, sitting down, just in time as it turned out, because the ship jerked in the other direction. He would probably have fallen over. Instead, he leaned back like nothing was happening.

"I got to become your doctor in the middle of a battle on Earth. I took over your patient care. Although I'd been watching you before that, too. So I knew Evander wanted you." He winced. "It wasn't my first time with Evander either."

I looked at his handsome profile. Wade was beautiful, and I wished I could do something about the dark circles under his eyes. Strangely, I wished I had the right to reach out and touch his face, smoothing that wounded looking skin with my fingertips. I didn't, and I wouldn't. But for just a second, I wished I could.

"How were you involved with them?"

He scrunched up his face. "After my parents died, I was left in charge of my much younger brother and sister. I'd just finished Med School early. Things were going crazy in the world. I decided after a few years that we had to pick a side in the upcoming war. And it wasn't going to be Sandler or Evander. I'd seen atrocities. Things I couldn't fathom. I quit my job, and we were heading for this place we call The Farm. I wanted to help. There were kids there. I thought it would be okay. Evander stopped our ship. They were looking for me."

Wow. I leaned forward. "Why?"

"There was a very high up person at Evander who they called Dr. Death. He wanted to find a way into the group. Infiltrate without being caught. They are very careful there with background checks. Anyone can get in and out with ships, but they don't have access to the main areas, they're not privy to conversations with the people in charge. He wanted in, and he knew that wasn't going to happen on his own."

I still didn't understand. "What did he do?"

"He traded places with me. Kidnapped me and put me on a dark planet to mine for a while. Threatened my brother and sister. Then, arrived at the Farm as me. He pulled it off. My little siblings—Madison and Travis—were threatened to say nothing. If they didn't want me to die, they had to stay quiet. Madi was thirteen, Travis was twelve. It was awful. Eventually, he got caught. Stopped. Waverly went through hell because of him."

There was that name again. Would I ever meet her? Would I like her? Would she not like me?

"The group there rescued me. Came and found me, brought me home. I was finally where I'd wanted to be. But not the man I'd been when I left. Wrecked. You've gotten to meet what is left after that."

Since I hadn't seen his brother and sister, they were obviously not here. Unless he kept them locked away. "Where are Madi and Travis?"

"They live at a boarding school on Venus. I sent them there during the war. It's better they're not with me. Madi is almost eighteen. She'll graduate soon, and then...I guess we'll have to talk about what she'll do then."

He sounded so sad that I had to reach out and take his hand. He stared at it for a second, but then squeezed it back.

I found my voice. "Would you be with them if you weren't running around saving a complete stranger?"

"No. I'm not good for them. I think the best thing is for them to be where they are, safe, and away from me."

I hadn't expected that answer. "Why aren't you good for them?"

"They got hurt because of me. Lived with that madman because of me. I decided we had to go and join the fight. Probably if I'd just stayed where we were, it would have sucked, but it wouldn't have been that."

Wade... I couldn't help it. I had to reach out to his mind.

His smile was warm, like a greeting. "I love when you do that."

"Have you asked them what they want? I mean...do they blame you? Are they scared around you?"

He shook his head. "I'm pretty bad with kids."

"Are they still kids?"

His tablet pinged, and he looked down at it. "Blaze is dragging Kellan in. He's hurt. Must be bad if he's coming at all. They all hate the med machine." The ship was relatively steady right now. I unhooked myself. Kellan was hurt? We'd just been together.

I swung around just in time to see Blaze holding up Kellan as he strode fast into the med bay. "The stupid bomb unit blew up again."

Kellan shook his head. "I'm fine."

He was absolutely not fine. His leg...from the knee down. No, I looked away. I wasn't a doctor, not great with blood. The thing to do was to get the heck out of the way. I backed into the wall, knocking a vial over when I did so. I hoped it wasn't important.

Seeing me, Kellan grinned. "Hey, there's Sienna. She's so pretty." His voice slurred, and Wade nodded.

"Into the machine, Blaze."

"I really don't want to go in," Kellan spoke to Blaze. "I bet if Sienna kissed me, I would feel better."

Wade snorted, and Blaze shook his head. "I've never seen him like this."

"Did he take a blow to the head?" Wade examined Kellan, who was now muttering to himself in the machine.

Blaze stared intently at the scene in front of him. "No idea. I wasn't watching."

Wade shined some kind of light into Kellan's eyes, who winced. "Yep. He did."

I had to be brave. I'd been kissing the man maybe half an hour ago, and now he was very injured. I forced myself to walk over. "You're going to be fine."

"Hate this thing," Kellan murmured, barely audible. "But I really liked kissing you earlier."

I had to be so red then, I could light up the night sky. "Me, too. Feel better soon."

How he smiled at me I wasn't sure, but that was what he did just as Wade shut the machine. He shot me a look I couldn't decipher before he placed a strong hand on my back. The machine started to buzz. With his hand still firmly placed, he looked at Blaze. "Are we done? Or are we still being fired on?"

"We lost them. I don't know how he pulls this shit off, but he did." Blaze shook his head, and I couldn't help noticing he stared where Wade's hand rested on my back. Was I doing something wrong?

He dropped his gaze just as everyone else piled into the room. Anders first, followed by Trenton, and then Corbin. They all spoke at once. The general question seemed to be whether or not Kellan was okay.

Blaze held up his hand. "Let's let Wade talk."

"Thanks." Wade sighed. "He isn't currently, but he will be. The machine is going to have to do a lot of work. The bone was compromised. He's clearly hit his head. Rambling on about stuff. And for a Super Soldier to show any symptoms means it's bad. But he got in the machine. He didn't fight it—"

Anders interrupted him. "Another sign that it's bad."

"Correct." Wade nodded. "And he's going to be fine. That machine has handled worse cases than that."

I let my gaze travel from the group, to the med machine, and then finally to the cryogenic chamber in the corner. My illnesses—I hated the plural—were so bad, that machine couldn't even heal me. Thank goodness it could fix Kellan.

Wade still hadn't moved his hand. I liked how steady it felt, how warm. Blaze's gaze was back on it. Was I missing something here?

"Why were you guys messing with the equipment in the middle of a battle? If I'd needed those bombs, we'd have been fucked," Trenton hollered at Anders, then he winced. "Sorry, Sienna."

I waved my hand. "Feel free to curse with impunity."

Corbin laughed, throwing his head back and then stopping abruptly, staring at the rest of us. "What? That was a funny way to put it."

Anders pointed at Trenton. "He was trying to fix it so if you needed it, then it might actually work. I don't know why the bomb systems on Artemis have been messed with so much that they are so weird, but we have to figure it out, or we could find ourselves without them."

Trenton pounded the wall. "Sometimes, things are so broken they can't be fixed, ever. Maybe it is. I don't need those bombs. Not when I'm running and not firing. We can't bomb Evander. They will win every time. They're stronger than we are."

"For now." All of Corbin's joy was gone, and in its place was a serious lethality I hadn't seen before but recognized in an instant, maybe in some leftover anthropological way that meant I could recognize a predator when I encountered it. Not that he was going to threaten me.

He finally finished his thought. "But they have no backup. Evander is mostly on the other side of the galaxy. Whoever is on that ship, whichever soldiers they have piloting, chasing us, still going after Sienna, that's just who's left. Even if they got her, and they won't, they have nowhere to go with her. No way to take her back through that black hole and bring her home to that side of the galaxy. They should just give up. They don't. Fine. We keep doing this. But eventually, they'll need supplies, they'll need repair. They'll need something, and their modern, flawless ship will break. Then they're not stronger than Artemis. Then we have the advantage because this ship survives. I don't know how or what has happened on her. But I know that. What's more, is that so do you. That's why you fly it the way you do. You know she can do it."

Anders patted him on the back. "That's quite a speech there. But yes, I agree with him. We have no choice but to try to fix as we need to. No one told Kellan to do it, he just did. And he's not dead. You won, Trenton. Let's not make a bigger deal of this than it has to be."

A muscle twitched it Trenton's jaw, but he nodded. Whatever he was going to say, he kept to himself.

"Guys, I..." I took a long breath. "This is my fault. My people shouldn't have done this, shouldn't have made me anyone's problem. I won't have anyone killed for me. Or injured." I stared at the med machine. "Please get me as fast as you can to wherever we're going. Mars Station, right? I won't be responsible for this. You all have lives to lead that don't include almost dying for me. Please, Blaze. I have no right to ask, but as fast as you can. Get me where I can't hurt any of you anymore. And thank you, guys, thank you for everything."

I rushed from the room. Kellan had nearly been killed. They were in a constant battle, and for what? Evander wanted my abilities. They'd never get them. Not even all the women on our planet got one. I didn't know why or how they came. It was some genetic fluke that had been created when they terraformed our planet. Too close to the fake sun, too far? How the heck would I know?

I made it to my room before I burst into tears. This crying thing was becoming a habit for me, and not one I loved. Still, I let the tears fall because that is what they had to do, and fighting them was only going to make the whole situation that much worse. There was a time and a place for crying. This one was mine.

All of this was beyond my control. I'd asked for none of it, unless I counted the silent please for a different life I'd made. Surely the universe couldn't have thought I meant this. These men could all be killed because of me.

Eventually, and without even realizing it was going to happen, I drifted off to sleep, tears still traveling down my face as I did.

A knock sounded followed by a beep that was the sound of someone wanting to come in the room. I rubbed my eyes. Trying to talk didn't work right away. I cleared my throat. "Come in."

Anders leaned in the doorway, holding a plate. "You missed dinner. Or at least, you missed when we ate it. Didn't exactly give you a time."

I rubbed my eyes, letting the sheet that covered my clothed body fall away. "Thank you. Sorry to be trouble. I guess I..."

"Fell asleep," he finished. Anders walked toward me. "I think you needed it. You're healing. Or at the very least, you're staving off getting sicker. The meds Wade has in you help your own body fight off the virus and infection. That takes a lot of energy. You need to eat and sleep, a lot. More than you used to. Plus, the whole trauma thing and we got attacked, which is new for you."

He said those things like he was reading off a list. "Anders, did you come up with those responses yourself?"

His smile was huge. "No, Wade gave us a lesson after you left. We're not used to crying. I can only speak for myself, but I wasn't certain what to do with it."

I almost apologized, but changed my mind. I did have reason to cry, and it wasn't the kind of thing I should feel sorry about, I didn't think. "Thank you for the food."

He handed it to me. "Wade is going to come by and check on you, soon. I may have jumped bringing this to you so that I could get some alone time with you."

I caught my breath. "Did I do something wrong?"

"No." Anders sat on the edge of my bed. "I just liked talking to you so far. I feel like the others have gotten more time. Maybe the word is...jealous. I must be jealous."

He might be the calmest, most contained person to ever express that emotion. I took a bite. It was better than what I'd eaten at lunch. What was this? Some kind of poultry? "Why are you jealous?"

His smile was big. "Because Blaze and Corbin slept in your bed. You talk in Wade's head. And Kellan kissed you. I listened to all of it. I'm losing the race."

I blinked. Yes, all of those things had happened. I hadn't

focused on them individually, but yes, when put like that, quite a lot had taken place. In a short period of time.

"Is it a competition?" Were they doing things to get my attention to...what...win something? I stopped eating to look right at him.

"Only in as much as I decided the second I met you that you were mine."

I opened my mouth. I had no idea what I'd say, but something had to be uttered. He'd decided I was his? How did that work? He was incredibly handsome, but I didn't think it worked like that. People had to take time to decide these things. Didn't they?

Anders cut me off before I could speak again. "I know things, fast. That's part of my skill set. Fast decision making. If most people's neurotransmitters take 0.5 ms per synapse, mine take 0.4. That's a significant difference."

I raised an eyebrow. These Super Soldiers and their impressive brainpower. They did like to talk about it quite a lot, didn't they? Still, they clocked brain speed? How did they even do that?

It was like he expected me to understand what he meant based on that alone. "I'm sorry, what does your brain speed have to do with deciding I was, ah, yours?"

He took my hand. "I make correct decisions instantly. I can decide something fast and know it to be correct. I saw you, and I knew. You were mine."

I set aside my plate to get up on my knees. "You may not even like me when you get to know me better. You may regret saying this and feeling this way."

He shook his head slowly. "Let me take care of you, Sienna. I know there may be things started with the others. I get that. This galaxy or world or life, I don't know, we don't do one to one. It makes no sense to. So you like the others, that's fine. I like them, too."

Wow. I reached out and took his hand. "I lived in a temple. I can't have relationships like that, not really. And... I'm sick. Plus, you're leaving me. I'm not staying with you."

He furrowed his brow. "He can't possibly still be thinking that. Is he?"

"I think...I think I can't put you all in any more danger."

He squeezed my hands. "We've lived our whole lives in danger. Keeping you safe at least feels worthwhile. We're built for this. Even Wade and Trenton. We're not made for gentle times. What we're made for is war, pillage, and destruction. This time, I get to do that for a very good reason. I love that idea."

He grabbed his head, and I moved to kneel by him. "You okay?"

"I get headaches. It's a flaw. But not one they wanted to put me down for, because I was still such a good killer that I paid for myself. It'll pass."

Acting on instinct, I reached out and rubbed the back of his head. His hair felt silky. "How long do they usually last?"

"A while." His answer was fast. Was this how he dealt? There were slight lines around his eyes, but otherwise, no other indication that he'd just spoken about being put down.

"Have you talked to Wade?"

He nodded. "Yes, and he's given me a thorough exam. He offered some pain meds, but truth is, I'd rather ride it out most times and then be done with it. Plus, the heavy dose he has to give us to get any pain meds to work have so many side effects, they're basically worse than the pain."

I continued to rub, slowly. "Does this help, hurt, or have no effect whatsoever."

He side-eyed me. "It helps. Thank you. I just want to take care of you, Sienna. I want to continue to do so."

That might have been the sweetest thing anyone had ever said. "How about we take care of each other until I have to leave you guys?"

He closed his eyes. "Come here to tell you I want to take care of you and end up with this headache, and you have to take care of me. Not really great on my part."

"Stop it." I shook my head. "I'm just sorry about your headache."

A ping sounded, and I called out that someone could come in. Anders leaned back a little bit. "It's Wade."

Sure enough, he walked in. "Oh, Anders. I didn't realize you'd come." Like Anders, Wade carried a plate of food. "Looks like we had the same thought. How are you doing, Sienna?" He set down the plate on the dresser. "I've been worried about you, but Anders said he could hear you were asleep, so I left you alone since sometimes that just makes all the difference." I hadn't stopped rubbing Anders' head and Wade noticed. "Headache?"

Next to me, Anders nodded.

"Bad one?" Wade took a step toward us. "Need some help? Want something?"

Anders shrugged. "Just badly made."

"Stop that. All of you talk about yourselves like you're pieces that were strung together for some use, and if you're not perfect, then you're somehow less than deserving. You get headaches. So do a lot of people." Wade sat down next to me. "Not a big deal. I wish I could solve it for you."

Anders smiled. "Wade reminds us that we're humans all the time."

"That's good. I'm going to remind you, too." I smiled at Wade. "I feel less desolate since I took my nap. But that doesn't change the fact that I'm right. All of this time, you could have all been killed and that's entirely on me."

Wade shook his head. "Make no mistake, Sienna, we are doing this for you. However, it was never entirely about you for these guys. We were at war with Evander. The enemy wanted you. It became their job to stop that, in the same way it would have been if Evander wanted a weapon's supply or some hidden plans or..."

Anders held up his hand. "I think that's simplifying it. We were fully aware that we were taking on a human. And we might be cold feeling some of the time, but I can tell the difference between a box of weapons and Sienna."

Wade raised his eyebrows. "When you took Sienna onto the first ship, you were thinking of her as a human or as something to keep from Evander?"

Sighing, Anders smiled. "Maybe it took a day or two, but I got there. We all did."

This was ridiculous. Whatever the reason that they'd done what they had didn't matter anymore. "I don't care about the why of it, just that you all helped me, and it doesn't change the fact that I don't want anyone killed."

Wade nodded. "Well, that's why they keep me along. I keep everyone alive."

"Who keeps you alive?" I smiled at Wade. It was easy with him, comfortable. All of those months we'd spent together when I wasn't conscious must be in there somewhere if I could feel like I knew him already.

Anders raised his hand. "I do. I pulled him out of the way of an explosion once when we stopped for supplies. So I guess I keep Wade alive."

Wade nodded. "Thanks again for that, Anders."

He smiled. "Yep."

"I can't have anyone die for me. Or be hurt for me. I can't. I won't." I shook my head.

Anders leaned his head on my shoulder. "When it comes down to it, Sienna, we can't let Evander get you. What if they can figure out how to recreate what you do? Then a new army of Super Soldiers who can hurt people just with their minds emerges. We won't allow that. Some things are worth dying for." He paused. "Some people, too."

I ENDED up watching a movie on Wade's tablet with Wade and Anders. I lay on my stomach between the two of them watching the funny film. Wade and I laughed at the hijinks the poor farmer had to go through on his planet that wasn't quite a Dark Planet, not quite in the Earth Zone either. As far as I knew, there wasn't a planet like that in existence.

But it was funny just the same.

I wasn't sure if Anders found the whole thing too ridiculous to laugh at or if he was studying it as some sort of commentary on humanity. In any case, he never cracked a smile. Maybe his head still hurt and he just didn't want to tell me.

As I scanned through to find another film—Anders having shown me how to do so—I noticed that Wade was out cold. He slept on his stomach, his breathing low and even. I nodded toward Anders who smiled. He'd probably been aware a lot earlier than I was.

"He never sleeps." Anders whispered. "Or at least, not enough for him. Wade stresses about a lot of things. Doesn't get a good night's sleep because of the worry that comes with it." He reached over me to pull the blanket over all of us. "You slept with Corbin and Blaze last night. Okay if we stay tonight, or want us to leave?"

I almost laughed about the fact that he'd pulled up the blanket before he asked me. If I said no, it was going to be a lot harder to disconnect. "You're welcome to stay, but you might be disappointed. I don't know if sleeping with me is actually all that exciting."

"I guess I'll be the judge of that."

I settled down, rolling onto my side. We were on the opposite side of the bed from the night before, but I didn't want to wake Wade to move him. "How would Wade know if Kellan needed him?"

He pointed to the tablet. "It would sound an alarm. Kellan isn't due to wake up until the morning. Right around the time we get to Mars Station. Blaze listened to you, he sped up the engines."

That was good. Wasn't it? My heart panged. The sleepovers would stop tomorrow. I had more than liked the two nights of this. But I'd been right to tell him we needed to hurry up so that they wouldn't get hurt.

I was sure of that.

We didn't have pillows. I reached over and grabbed three of them from the top of the bed. Handing one to Anders, I kept one for myself and put the third over by Wade so if he rolled over, he'd be on top of it.

Anders hit a button on Wade's tablet before he set it on the floor. The lights shut off in the room. I'd been asleep earlier, and I wasn't at all certain that I was going to now.

Which way should I face? Currently, I looked at Anders, but it might be weird for him to go to sleep with someone staring at him. Or maybe it was odder to watch Wade sleep when I couldn't.

Anders touched the side of my head, stroking a hand through my hair. "Thanks for petting my head earlier. It was really nice."

"Oh." I nodded. He could probably even see me do it, since they were able to view things in the dark. "You're welcome. Headaches suck."

"They do." He sounded amused. "You're wide awake. It's late."

"You should go to sleep. I'll roll that way to let you." I made to turn, but he shot out his hand to stop me.

He leaned up on his arm. "I'd rather talk, in low voices, so we don't wake him."

I wasn't sure we could wake him. He seemed really out cold. "Okay. But if you're tired..."

"I need almost no sleep."

I furrowed my brow. "When was the last time you slept?"

"Couple of days. I've been doing the night flying so Trenton could." He sounded so blasé about the way he simply announced that it had been a couple of days since he slept, as though that was the most normal thing in the world. I might never get used to them and the ways they did or didn't do things.

But he had to be tired. I took his hand in mine. "I never had this, that I can remember, but I'm told that people tell stories when they want to go to sleep. They get read to. So let's tell each other stories." Next to me, Wade shifted, making a small sound in the back of his throat. "In a whisper."

Anders was quiet for a second. "I don't think you'll like my stories. Tell me one of yours. What is the most beautiful thing you've ever seen?"

I had to think about that. I hadn't seen that many things

in my life. I'd lived in a three-square mile radius, occasionally going to a town. And then I'd woken up on this ship. But still, there had to be something I could think of that would qualify as beautiful.

"Oh, there had been this terrible storm. We got them sometimes, but it's okay because we like the wind. On my planet. We harvest it and use it. Anyway, terrible storm. Loud. A real show that night. I watched the night sky, and that was beautiful. Terrifying and beautiful. Somehow, both. It was breathtaking in how frightening it was."

I was afraid I'd put him off with what I said when he didn't initially respond. "I love that. Things can be more than one thing. Beautiful because of the fact that it was also scary." He sighed. "I guess I have to answer my own question. The most beautiful thing I've ever seen was an Evander ship exploding after we blew it up, saving Earth. I know people died. I shouldn't think it was beautiful, but it was us versus them. We weren't on Artemis but a big ship ourselves. It could have been them, could have been us. And when it just burst into nothing...it was beautiful."

I squeezed his hand. "I'm incredibly glad it didn't get you instead." A thought dawned on me. "Why are you all on Artemis if you had a ship the same size as that one?"

He squeezed our linked hands back. "Because they knew our ship. The big modern one Tommy Sandler gave to us, and we needed to be on one they didn't know to run around with you. The idea was to disguise us. Then we sort of took to her."

"Even though she blows up when you try to modernize her?" I yawned. Okay, maybe I was more tired than I realized I was.

"Even then. There's something about being on this ship we've all liked. When she breaks, it just gives us reason to try again. Honestly, I think we might all have lost our minds all of these months if we hadn't had Artemis to look after, and then...it just works when we need her to. Just now, somehow, Trenton got us away. I...I don't really get it, and I feel all right about it. I think it's worked out."

I smiled at him. "You almost sound like you believe in there being some...rhyme and order to the universe that placed us on this ship."

"Don't you?"

I shook my head slowly. "I think that everything is a muddled, chaotic mess that makes no sense whatsoever. No rhyme. No reason. I've never seen any evidence to the contrary. Or if there is some order to it, something driving things forward, then it's a sick entity who just wants to cause people harm."

He stroked his finger down my nose. "This from the woman who lived in the temple?"

"Maybe because I did." I shook my head. I was very dour right then. I didn't even know why. Disgruntled. It wasn't like I didn't ask the universe for things. I did. I complained in my head all the time, but it wasn't like the things I asked for or thought about came true. Not in a way that made sense.

He leaned over and kissed me gently on the lips. I caught my breath. I hadn't seen that coming. It wasn't like Kellan, who had asked me. Anders had just done it. His lips were soft against mine. He didn't push, didn't look for more. I kissed him back, but he quickly pulled away.

"Goodnight, Sienna. Maybe in the morning, the universe won't seem too bleak to you. Maybe tomorrow, we'll both see something beautiful. I know I'm looking at something now that takes my breath away."

I caught my breath. "Goodnight, Anders." I didn't have

his pretty words to draw on. I was still too stunned from the kiss to think at all. "I...I hope you sleep well."

He put his arm over my waist. "Close your eyes. You're actually tired. I can hear it. If you try to rest, you will."

I'd never really know if I did because he told me I could, or if I really was tired.

I woke up with Wade thrashing next to me. I rolled over, staring at him. He was having a nightmare, saying something I couldn't understand, but it was clear it was terrible. His head moved back and forth on the pillow.

Anders lifted his head. "It's a bad one. Has them a lot."

I rolled toward Wade, putting my hand on his arm. "It's okay, Wade. Just a dream. Or a bad memory, but it can't hurt you now."

He didn't stop. Wade didn't sleep much, but apparently when he did, he slept deeply.

I took a deep breath. Waking up from sleep made this hard, but he needed me right then, and I didn't mind being there for him, not even a little bit. *Wade.* I sent the thought to his mind. *Just a bad dream.*

"Sienna." He tugged me close without opening his eyes, but his thrashing stopped, his breathing steadied.

I took a long breath. He was okay. I'd also managed to keep my internal shields up. Half-asleep, I could have lost them and felt his whole nightmare with him. Maybe I was stronger than I used to be. Or just lucky.

"Did you talk in his head?" Anders rolled closer to me, adjusting his body so he was pressed up on the side Wade wasn't. "How can you do that with him and not with me?"

I sighed. "I did. We've spent more time together. It's some sort of connection I can form based on time alone. It's not as though I like one person more than another. My brain forms connections. Can't explain it."

He kissed the back of my neck. "Then we'll just have to spend more time together. I want you in my head, Sienna."

That was funny. I didn't even want to be in my own. They so didn't want me running around in theirs. I was pretty much the definition of a mess right now.

━━━

Wade woke up before I did. I had no idea if Anders had gotten up before him, but when I opened my eyes, they were talking to each other. The dark circles under Wade's eyes weren't visible. He'd actually slept well.

His smile at me could have warmed the room if it were cold. "I understand I have you to thank for my not waking up in a panic last night." He brought my hand to his mouth and kissed it. Butterflies traveled through my stomach. "Thank you."

"Does that happen to you every night?"

He rubbed his eyes. "Only on the ones that I sleep. I didn't mean to conk out here. Sorry."

I shook my head. "I liked having you guys. Think I might be getting used to having company in my bed."

I blinked. That sounded quite different than I'd meant it. Wade winked at me. "We might have to make a schedule. Kellan's going to want in." Wade grabbed his tablet and looked down on it. We hadn't heard it, so everything must be okay with Kellan. "Maybe Trenton will."

Anders shook his head. "Not yet."

"Guys." I swung my legs over the bed. "I'm leaving today. Or at least leaving you guys." I looked down at my wrist. Still at one. Such a relief. I lifted my eyes and met Wade's gaze. "It's at one."

He nodded before he took my hand in his. "I know. I

looked while you were still sleeping." Wade kissed my wrist near where the device was hooked up. "Does it hurt? Irritate?"

I shook my head. Sweet of him to ask. "No."

"Sienna," Anders caught my attention. "This won't have been the last night. Some people might take longer to... catch on to what is supposed to be...but it'll happen."

I could pretend I didn't understand him, but that would be insulting to both of us. "Anders, there is no supposed to."

He shook his head. "We can keep having this argument until I change your mind."

Wade let go of me to walk toward the door. I immediately missed his warm presence. "I'm with Sienna on this. There is no supposed to be. That doesn't mean we can't have what we want. We just have to make that happen. Maybe. Things tend to explode and suck around me." Wade stopped and turned around. "Hey, look out the window, Sienna. That's Mars Station we're approaching. Trenton made incredible time."

That was just what I'd asked Blaze to do, and he'd listened. Trenton had gotten us here. I wanted to spare these guys the risk of being with me. So why did it feel like I was about to turn around to look at a nightmare?

Anders still hadn't moved out of my bed. "It's not the prettiest sight you'll ever see. Not beautiful. I don't think Mars Station is much to look at. Not like Earth or Venus. Or The Farm. Someday, that place will have a new name. What do you think? Would you put Mars Station on your list of beautiful?"

I forced myself to look. In the distance, seemingly floating in space, and getting slightly bigger every second that I stared at it as we approached, was a dark, spinning circular object that must be the station. It was huge. To see the whole thing, I would have needed a larger window scope. This was Mars Station. Did that mean that the planet was somewhere nearby?

"I'm not sure what I'm looking at. It just looks cold from here. Like a piece of machinery spinning in space. I don't know what to make of it."

Anders got out of bed. "It won't seem cold on the inside, but that's a great description from here."

"Are we near Mars? This is Mars Station, right?"

He made a sound in the back of his throat a second before he put his arms around me. I steeled myself not to like it. This was all going to go away. This kindhearted soul would be a memory for me. Was it better to let myself feel how wonderful this was and remember it forever, or to not let myself feel it all? This morning had been wonderful. Yesterday had been, too, and we'd been attacked. I couldn't have held back the warmth if I'd wanted to. Anders was watching with me, even though he must have seen this a million times. Or something like it.

Finally, he answered me. "We've passed Mars. I'm sorry I didn't think to wake you."

"What happens now?"

He leaned his chin on my shoulder. "We eat breakfast."

That wasn't what I meant, and I suspected he knew it. Still, his point was made. One thing at a time.

━━━

I worried the entire time we disembarked that I was going to feel sick upon stepping foot on the station. It spun the entire time I watched it, but I didn't feel a thing differently. Just another thing I didn't understand about my surroundings.

I sucked in a breath as I looked around. The landing bay

had been quiet. There had been one person waiting who took a tablet from us. He hadn't spared me a glance, but now that we were in what Blaze called the promenade, there were people everywhere. I'd never seen so many in one space.

Shops were open, and people called to each other, called to us to come buy things, and in an eating establishment, they were actually singing inside.

"It's like they think the war is over," Corbin spoke to Trenton next to him.

"Denial." Trenton nodded. "Let them pretend. They know what happened here. This place was dead in the sky, and if Evander gets to rebuild, gets the chance to take Sienna and remake their one ship to ten, they'll be running for their lives again."

My mouth fell open. "Is that a possibility?"

"Kellan thinks it is." Trenton winced. "Sorry to scare you."

No one would have known Kellan had woken up in the med machine this morning. He looked entirely put together, as though nothing happened to him at all. His leg was fully healed. "I think the capability is there for them to build a ship within a ship. We need to get into that ship and break it up from the inside."

"If only that wasn't a suicide mission." Wade shook his head. "We go do that, and we're not getting off."

Blaze silently observed the scene in front of him. Finally, he spoke. "We'll figure out what we're doing next now. First, we should—" He cut off speaking. "And here comes Nolan. Are we getting arrested or welcomed?"

Trenton laughed. "Hard to tell with his body language. I can't read him. Wade?"

Wade lifted his eyebrows. "It's bad if you want me to

tell. Um...I think we're being welcomed. Has anyone done anything to piss him off lately?"

A bald man wearing earrings who looked like he could lift three of me and not break a sweat stopped in front of us. He wasn't as big as the Super Soldiers, but boy, was he close. "Gentlemen. Welcome. You didn't blow up Artemis. I appreciate that. More than you'll know."

A smile twitched on Anders' face before it disappeared fast. I might have imagined it.

Blaze answered him. "Nolan. I'm surprised to see you. I was going to seek you out."

"Heroes get personally greeted." He eyed me and then went back to looking at Blaze. "So you guys get me."

Trenton shook his head fast. "Heroism would mean we got them. We haven't."

"You saved the girl. I assume this is she?" Nolan smiled at me. "You must be Sienna. Everyone has been anxious to see you awake."

My cheeks got hot. Was there anything more unnerving than knowing all of these people had seen me when I'd been unconscious? "I hope I don't disappoint." I looked down at my shoes. They didn't fit, but Corbin had cobbled them from one of his, and they had to do for now. A strong hand touched the small of my back, and I forced myself to look back at Nolan. It was Kellan touching me. I appreciated the confidence boost. Where had all of my steel resolve from so many years gone? Had it vanished with the illnesses Evander gave me? Eaten my self-consciousness as it wreaked havoc to my immune system?

"Well, come on guys. Follow me. You have a guest wing. Seven rooms. Everyone will be at the meeting later. The whole leadership crew. Sandlers and Chens arrived a few hours ago. Diana's been here for a week, and Waverly arrived yesterday. It's like the old days." He stepped forward. "You're feeling okay?"

Wade glared at him. "I wouldn't have her up if she wasn't safe."

I blinked. What had I just missed that Wade understood? Nolan nodded. "Just had to check."

"If you want to know, just ask. Let's not play games. That's C.J.'s bullshit." Wade strode ahead following Nolan, who laughed before he answered him.

"No, my brother C.J. has turned over a new leaf these days. It's truth all the time."

Wade grumbled his response. "Bullshit."

A thought occurred to me. These men knew each other. All of them. They'd been to war together, had done things that meant they understood each other's questions without actually having to have the question. I knew this well. I could have done that with Joy. She would have said 'want some' and I would have known she meant was I thirsty. This was hard. I was a stranger on this station, surrounded by people who all knew each other well.

Homesickness struck me. It hadn't been perfect, but it had been mine. That was something, and more than others probably had in this cold, metallic universe that spun, even if I couldn't feel it beneath my feet.

I tried to pay attention to my surroundings in case I needed to find my way back, but Nolan pressed so many buttons to open so many doors and eventually placed us in a lift that soared us to the sky before it let us out that I was sure I'd never find my way in any situation ever again.

"Hey," Corbin whispered in my ear. "It's okay. I can hear your heartbeat. I know I'm not supposed to mention it, but I can. You're nervous. This place is okay. As safe as anywhere. It got blown up before the onslaught of the war, but they rebuilt it even stronger."

I hadn't been worried about the soundness of the station. Well, at least not before he'd said something. "Thanks."

Nolan motioned toward a door. "Sienna, you're in there."

"Thanks."

Everyone waited like I was supposed to do something. I forced my back straight. "Do I just walk in? Does it just open?"

"Oh." Nolan shook his head. "I didn't realize. Sorry. Yes, it'll open for you when you walk in. No one gets on this floor except the seven of you. And you can lock it from the inside if you want to keep them out."

Corbin gestured toward it. "I'll show it to you. Save me a room. Not next to Trenton. He snores."

"Fuck off." Trenton laughed. "I don't snore."

Corbin stepped toward my door, and it opened. I followed him in.

"Give me a second, and I'll label stuff for you." He smiled. "Pretty similar to Artemis."

It was. The light switch was where it had been on the ship. A lot was the same. I walked around, looking at things.

"You'll get used to this. I don't know how long we'll be here."

I nodded. "I'm staying until someone else takes responsibility for me, I suppose. I need to find a way to earn enough to get back home. But that might be later. I can't get anyone killed. Why had I thought this would be better? There were six of you on the ship. Thousands of people here. All of them at risk because I stepped onto their station."

"Sienna." Corbin strode over to me fast, pulling me against him. "No one blames you for this. Evander wants you. Not your fault. It's something that happened to you."

"That's true." I forced myself to breathe. "But now it's mine to deal with. I'm a walking incubator of illness, and Evander could show up with their scary stuff and kill everyone. Somehow, even though I don't even know how to use the switches to turn on the elevator, I have to work this out. Only I can do it. And I don't have the slightest idea how."

Corbin shook his head. "You're not alone."

He didn't understand. Even in his arms, I totally was.

I SHOWERED and went about my business of getting ready, which included putting myself back into Corbin's too-big-for-me clothes. It took less time than I hoped to perform the task, and I didn't have a clue what I was supposed to do now. I sat down on the bed. I didn't need another nap. If anything, I wondered if I might never sleep again. My nerves were shot. I rubbed at my eyes. What were the guys doing? Should I go and find out?

A ding sounded on my door, and I smiled. Company would be delightful, something to distract me from the fact that I really didn't know what was going to happen next and I had no control over any of it. Did anyone have the ability to dictate what happened in their lives?

I pressed the button—thank you, Corbin—and opened the door. Four women stood there staring at me, and behind them, Kellan leaned against the wall, watching. He nodded at me.

"Ah, hello." I spoke to the new faces staring at me. "Can I help you?"

They must not be too much of a risk, or Kellan wouldn't have let them near my door. I didn't think.

"Hi." The one all the way to the left spoke first. She was small and beautiful with dark hair and violet eyes. "You're Sienna. Sorry, it's different to see you awake. I've been so excited to meet you. I took care of you for a while. Before Wade. I'm Amber." She put out her hand. "Amber Chen."

I reached out, instinctually to shake. "Yes, right. Wade has told me your name. I'm Sienna. But then you know that. Um..."

She grabbed my arm, gently but firmly. "Look at this. He did it, made some changes, but it worked. Different than what you have, Diana." Amber stared at my device. I snapped out of my shock and ripped my arm back, rubbing the spot that she held. Was this how it was going to be now? Was I going to be some...exhibit for everyone to look at?

I stepped back, and the woman—Amber—her mouth fell open. She spoke before I could. "I'm so sorry. That was completely rude. I'm a doctor. I came up with the initial design that Wade used, but that is no excuse. Totally and completely rude. I apologize. So sorry."

Somehow, the apology made it worse. "That's okay. I..."

"You don't want to be grabbed out of the blue just because she had a moment of suddenly feeling giddy that her system worked," the tallest of the group spoke. She had red hair and kind eyes. "I'm Waverly, and I'd have done the same thing you just did. We're not making a great impression. Let's start again. Welcome to Mars Station. I mean...I don't live here, but I'm welcoming you just the same."

This was Waverly. My mouth fell open. "You're the reason the Super Soldiers revolted against Evander."

Her cheeks turned red. "It was a chance...I'm glad it

worked. Yes, that was me. I didn't really do anything but leave them a message. It was nothing."

It certainly wasn't nothing. She'd changed their lives so much that they were barely recognizable. "I think that you may be underestimating what you did."

She shook her head. "I can't really think about it. Feels like it's not me. Like it's not something I really did. But that's not why we're here. I swear, we didn't come for Amber to paw at you or for me to talk about myself."

Amber winced. "I am sorry. Truly."

Waverly laughed, a low sound. "These other two are Diana Mallory and Paloma Sandler. Paloma is Amber's sister and my sister-in-law. Melissa Alexander, who runs this place, is Diana's mother."

That was a ton of information. I rubbed the back of my neck. "It's nice to meet all of you. How can I help you?"

At home, I'd know what they wanted. They'd have come to my temple to get my help, whether I wanted to or not. As far as I knew, they didn't know about those things. Unless the guys had checked in and told everyone everything. I supposed that would happen since I was leaving them. Had it already?

"We think we can help you," Diana spoke at last. "Well, Paloma can. She's good at this. The three of us tagged along for fun. To get a little break from other things. I'm sorry. I'm rambling." She hadn't said very much. Did that count as rambling for her? She continued. "My uncle Nolan told me that you were wearing clothes that looked like they belonged to one of the Super Soldiers. We thought we'd take you shopping. You just woke up. You have nothing. Let's get you fixed up."

I looked down at my clothes. Yes, I was a bit of a mess. But there wasn't a thing I could do about that right now. "I don't have any money, so these clothes I borrowed will have to do for now. Even though I'll have to figure out how to do that while I'm looking like this."

Paloma met my gaze. She was stunning. So was Diana. In fact, all four of the women in front of me would be considered physically gorgeous. Waverly with her sweet gaze and sunset hair. Paloma with her sharp brown eyes and high cheekbones. Amber looked like she'd stepped out of the definition of the word stunning, and Diana, she was tiny and curvy, an incredible combination.

I hadn't been raised to concern myself very much with what I looked like. Still, I'd never felt more like a fish out of water. Although, I'd experienced the uncomfortable sensation frequently of late. At least two of these women had done extraordinary things that I knew about. If I had anything to bet with, I'd say the other two had as well. They were probably a force to be reckoned with.

Motioning toward my room, I invited them in. "I don't have anything to offer you, but I'd love it if you wanted to come sit down."

"Sienna," Paloma finally spoke. "I know how it feels to have nothing. My story is long, but all I can say is that there were people who helped me when I was lost in the universe, utterly alone with no credits, no hope, and no future."

That made no sense. "Isn't this your sister and your sister-in-law? How could you have been alone?"

"Long story I will tell you sometime when I cook you a meal. Just as I'd like to hear your story. In fact, we'd all like to hear it, because who you are and why they want you is turning out to be really important. But beyond that, it would make me really happy to get to do for someone what was done for me. I know that you've been on Artemis with a bunch of people you don't know, and maybe you're sick of strangers. I get that. Only, strangers are only strangers until we know them, right? We can afford to buy you clothes."

Kellan walked away from the wall. "She can afford clothes." He held out a tablet. "Here."

I stared at his tablet, my stomach clenching at what I knew he was offering. "I can't take any more from you guys. I've already used up your time and placed you guys in so much danger, I can't imagine it. You've done enough for me."

He held the tablet up even higher as though I couldn't see it. "Sienna, Trenton is asleep. I can wake him up and get him to tell you that the credits are worthless to him and he'd really like you to buy what you need, or you can just believe me."

I sighed, taking the tablet. "Thank you. I'll thank Trenton when he gets up."

Waverly put her arm around Paloma. "So you don't get to pay. Looks like Sienna has...help, already. Do you think you'd let us come with you, Sienna? We know the best places to go on the station, where they won't take advantage of you. A shopping day. I hate buying clothes, but I don't mind doing it with them. We can be fun. Get a coffee. Some fun before this evening's meeting that is sure to be doom and gloom, because all meetings are doom and gloom."

I smiled, despite my dour mood. Waverly must have one of those personalities that just made people want to be happier. "I'd love to get a few things that fit. And some company sounds nice."

Diana nodded, pointing down the hall. "This way. Back to the elevator. I'm not shopping, and I won't be a help, but I like the company. And the coffee. That'll be good. The baby had me up all night." She pointed at her jaw. "Teething."

That sounded...awful.

I had two bags of clothes by my feet and wore a whole new set by the time I sat at a table on the promenade with the ladies I'd spent the day with. They were nice. My initial impressions had been correct, but I hadn't counted on liking them as much as I did. They'd done extraordinary things, but seemed to have no ego about it.

Waverly nodded toward the other side of the shopping center. "Have you noticed your security?"

"My security?" I looked around. What did she mean?

She pointed. "Kellan. And Corbin. They've followed us most of the day."

"Really?" I finally saw where she indicated. "I didn't know they were going to do that. Should I ask them to go? I mean...why are they following? Is it not safe here?"

Diana laughed. She didn't do that much, but when she did, it was really fun to see. "It's safe. And we're all being followed. Who's on you, Waverly?"

She rolled her eyes. "Canyon is around. I caught sight of him, which means he wanted me to about an hour ago. You, Diana?"

"Damian never lets me out of his sight, and I guarantee Sterling is listening." She shrugged. "I like it. I'd rather have their eyes and hearts with me all the time than ever be alone without them again. I've had enough of that to last a lifetime. If forever means all the time, that's fine with me."

Paloma took a sip of her coffee. "I have Quinn. I can't see him, but he's here somewhere. I guarantee it. And Amber..."

She shook her head. "There is some member of the Z Warriors around. Probably one of the Super Soldiers that Amari recently inducted." She turned to me. "The Z have always been very intense. Add to that the Super Soldier aspect, and my husbands feel like they finally have the perfect bodyguards for me."

All of these women had multiple husbands. That wasn't unheard of on my planet, but not as common as here. I wasn't even sure I understood everything they were talking about, although I wouldn't mind time like this, years to get to know them. As long as I could figure out some way I could contribute, some way I wouldn't forever be on the outside.

But none of them lived here. Mars Station belonged to Diana's mother, and these women had their own lives. If I did manage, someday, to know them, it wouldn't be here. In this noisy, metal, spinning place.

I could see the beauty in the design, the colors, the way it was laid out so everything had a place. It was like a remote piece of art—sterile on the outside, but vibrant if I looked more deeply. Could people really live here their whole lives? Could they spend massive amounts of times on ships or stations? Could they live off planets forever? Never see a real sunset or experience actual sunlight?

Diana, Paloma, and Amber had spent their childhoods here.

They were all living on planets now.

Diana caught my gaze. She leaned forward. "I know it's overwhelming. Almost too much. Too many people. Too much stuff, like you're existing inside a machine designed for war and commerce. Space stations are just places people go to buy things they need and leave. It's weird to spend time here, knowing you're basically in a transport area. Coming and going. Coming and going. My mother thrives in it. She likes the impermanence. No one matters, really, except the few who stay. I'd rather have consistency."

I blinked. "How did you know what I was thinking?"

"Most of the time, I have no idea what people are musing about. And then sometimes, I know entirely. I can't really explain it." She smiled at me.

I shook my head. "I specialized in knowing what people needed, what they were thinking. But now? I have no idea what's going on. Everything is a big giant mess in my head all the time. If you could sort me out, you're rather remarkable."

I'd gotten all of their total attention by speaking those words. As fun as this had been, the shopping and chatting, they wanted some answers from me. The meeting was coming up, and it was about me. Blaze had brought me back so that the people here could figure out what to do with me now. They had to know me. They had to understand. The trouble was, I didn't know myself.

That troubling thought made me lift my head to stare at the fake world around me once again. It really did seem like it wasn't real here.

And then like something out of my nightmare, I saw him.

My mouth went dry. There, across the promenade, looking at us—no, *me*—was the man that I'd remembered from the day Evander tried to take me. The Super Soldier they'd brought to scare me. I'd had to zap him to get away.

It was Devil.

Where had he come from?

I wasn't the only one to see him. I'd no sooner caught my breath on a cry I didn't mean to make than Corbin rushed at him, his long hair strung over his shoulder as he got in Devil's face. He hollered at him. I couldn't hear what he said over the noise in the promenade, but Devil shook his head, fast. Kellan appeared on his other side.

Devil lifted his hands up in the universal sign of surrender.

I started to shake. No, I couldn't let him take me, wouldn't let him put all these people in danger.

Amber jumped to her feet, grabbing my arm. "Sienna? You okay?"

I shook my head. "No, that man. He's here to hurt me. I know him. He...he tried to kidnap me."

She looked where I pointed. "Oh, that's Devil. No. Sienna. He's not here to hurt you. I'm sure he's here to guard me. Shift change. Remember I told you about the Super Soldiers who work for my husbands now? He's one of them. Amari, my oldest husband, he rehabbed him. Well, rehabbing."

"Are you listening?" Paloma was on her feet fast. "Sienna says that he helped to harm her. I don't think she gives a shit right now that he's suddenly part of the Chen Empire."

"Paloma, for goodness' sake, I'm trying to explain," Amber yelled at her sister.

I didn't care. Let them work this out among themselves. Who worked for who. Who was doing what. All I knew was that man was dangerous.

"Hey." Anders strode over to me. "He's not getting anywhere near you."

No, he really wasn't, because Blaze was in Devil's face now, too. But they were surrounded by others who were equally as big, all of them dressed in black with purple sashes, the same uniform that Devil wore.

Devil shrugged off Corbin and pushed at Blaze, who held steady, almost unresponsive before he spoke through gritted teeth. I wished I could hear what they were saying. It was just far enough it all sounded like noise and not actual words.

Wade ran over to me. "You okay? What's going on here?"

I swallowed. "That's Devil."

He swung around. "What the fuck?"

"Wade." Amber grabbed his arm. "He's not a threat. Okay? He's with us. He's guarding me."

"Oh, I assure you, Dr. Chen," it was Anders who answered, "he's still a threat. However you dress him up."

Someone grabbed onto Paloma's hand, and she shook her head. "Quinn, I'm fine. I'm not in any danger here."

"Better to leave it. Come on, P." He put his arm around her shoulder, bringing her with him. "We'll see all of them at the meeting when they've had time to cool down their tempers."

"Wade." Amber really wanted his attention, but he wasn't giving it to her at the moment as he searched my face for something.

"Are you okay, Sienna?" He took my hand in his. "We can get out of here. That man isn't going to get anywhere near you."

Mars Station security swarmed the scene. I could have laughed. They were half the size of the Super Soldiers. Others were around us. Everyone was talking, but not to me. It looked like the people watching my new friends wanted their ladies out.

Trenton joined the crowd. He was fearless in the face of all of those Super Soldiers.

Devil broke free of everyone, Blaze grabbing him and shoving him back. They were in each other's faces with only Trenton trying to separate them.

I didn't want Devil closer. I could practically feel that

day back home when he'd been brought to grab me, my utter terror, the idea that my uncle had sold me out...

All of it hit me as though I was living it again. I didn't think about where I was, didn't consider what could happen, I just opened myself up and zapped him. Hard.

He grabbed his head, falling to the ground as Blaze whirled around to stare at me. I hadn't broken any rules. He told me not to zap his men, I hadn't. We weren't on his ship anymore either, and he was turning me over. I didn't have to feel bad about this. I didn't...

My walls were down, the shielding I'd learned to do fled, and all of a sudden, a promenade's worth of emotions struck me at once. Devil raised his gaze to glare at me. That was the last thing I could coherently think as my knees went out.

Never in all of my years had I had so much...everything assault me all at once.

Wade grabbed me, not letting me hit the floor. "It's okay. I've got you."

That was the last thing I heard before my world whited out.

━━

"You're okay." Trenton's soft voice reached me, bringing me back to wherever I was. It was quiet, just the sound of a beeping machine. A cool hand pressed to my forehead. "Think she just got a little overwhelmed."

Wade answered him. "Her vitals are good."

I opened my eyes. "Sorry... I didn't mean it."

Trenton stared down at me. He raised one eyebrow. "Are you apologizing for fainting after you took down Devil with your brain?" His smile was huge. "We didn't know he was here, or he'd have been handled without you seeing him."

Wade's face appeared in my view. "Not so simple, actually. He's under the protection of the Chen Empire. He's not an enemy combatant. He was captured and rehabilitated by Amari Chen himself. But we can keep him away from you, and that is happening already."

I sat up, slowly, still feeling sort of dizzy. "I had to open my natural shields up to do that. It's hard to explain. It's like deciding to release an emotion. I let it go, and then I can zap. But then I have to take in everyone else's emotions to do so. There were so many people on the promenade. It was too much."

Trenton pulled me against him, and I placed my head on his shoulder. He hadn't touched me like this before, but I did need the hug. He smelled like cinnamon. What had he been eating or drinking? I smiled against the scent.

"What would happen if you weren't overwhelmed? If it had just been a few people. Or one."

I sighed. "If it had just been one, I'd have sort of taken on their emotion, helped them to handle it by lessening it. Taking it away."

He squeezed me tighter. "Then it becomes your problem to deal with whatever emotion they're feeling?"

I nodded. "Pretty much the idea. That's why those of us that can do it are shut away. We're kept to minimal contact so this kind of thing can't happen."

"Like a professional empath. Seems like a huge amount of bullshit to me. Do people in your profession lose it early? Like if all you're ever feeling is sadness and pain or pent up...I don't know...anger. Or whatever. It has to be hell."

Wade put his hand on my back. "I told you before. I think it's awful."

Trenton rocked me slightly. "Don't ever take my pain, Sienna. I need it to stay upright."

I laughed, throwing back my head, and he grinned at me. "I'll keep that in mind. I'm selfish, actually."

"How do you figure that?" Wade turned off the beeping machine.

"I don't want to do it, don't want to help others. I have this gift, and I don't want to do it. That's pretty selfish."

Trenton shook his head. "That's called self-preservation. I wouldn't want to do it either. Hard enough dealing with my own emotions."

The door opened, and someone I didn't know strode in like she owned the place. It occurred to me a second later that she did. This must be Melissa Alexander, Diana's mother. They were both dark haired, but I didn't think Diana looked that much like her, more like the man who stood behind Melissa. Her eyes were the same as his. That must be Diana's father.

I hadn't yet heard his name.

Melissa spoke, looking at me, not Wade. "How's the patient?"

"I'm better. Thanks." I put out my hand. "I'm Sienna McKinnon."

She took my offering and shook. "Melissa Alexander. This is Geoff, one of my husbands. You're feeling okay?"

I nodded, and that seemed to satisfy her.

"What happened on that promenade? How did you do that to Devil?"

I opened my mouth to answer her when Wade interrupted. "I don't know that Sienna has to answer that. It's a skill she has. She uses it to protect herself, not for other reasons, and she's not a threat to you or to anyone unless they come after her in some way."

Trenton rocked back on his heels. "She's gentle."

I didn't know that I was gentle, per se. I looked between them. Trenton and Wade were worried. They'd really not liked her question.

"On my planet we have things called honeybees. I'm told they were put on all the terraformed planets. Are you familiar with them?" I asked Melissa.

She nodded fast. "Very. We have them here for the arboretum and had them on Artemis when Cooper used to grow plants there."

I hadn't known there was a greenery on Artemis. At my unasked question, Trenton shook his head. "Long gone."

"Oh yes, you guys just came off Artemis." Melissa nodded to herself. "How is she? Holding up? And as for your bee statement, Sienna, I suppose what you're telling me is that you only sting when attacked. I understand you. But you need to understand that I have to protect this station. You're carrying an unlicensed weapon, essentially, in your brain. I don't know what to do about that."

I sighed. Neither did I. It certainly looked like I wouldn't be staying here.

ALMOST EVERYONE in the room was a stranger to me, and yet, they were here to help make a decision about what happened with my future. The women I had met. Melissa, Diana, Paloma, and Waverly were all now people I'd started to get to know. The guys—I had to somehow not think of them as my guys because they weren't that, not in the way that the rest of the men in the room belonged to the women here—were people I knew. And then there was Devil.

Otherwise, I recognized Nolan from when he greeted us and several of the others from the scene in the promenade. Everyone else was entirely new to me.

And all of them stared.

"So let me get this straight," one of the dark-haired men sitting with his hand on Amber's shoulder addressed the room. I didn't know his name, but he certainly seemed like he was used to having the full attention of everyone speaking. "She buzzed Devil, who is here under my protection, because she recognized him from when he worked for Evander."

Amber visibly swallowed. "Amari, you have to understand, the last time she saw him was when he caused her harm. She's defending herself."

"I understand that. And I actually don't find it that odd that she can do that. We move energy in the Chen Empire. It's a logical step to use it that way. I'm fascinated. But I want my man protected and guarantees she's not coming after him again."

Blaze shook his head. "Then maybe you should get him off the station."

I looked between them. Guarantees? How was I supposed to do that? If he came after me—

They kept speaking. "He's here with me. As one of my guards. Devil has my confidence. We've all come to trust him immensely." Amari—I now knew his name—nodded toward Devil. "He saved my brother's life."

"Then you're being foolish." Blaze was so calm when he uttered that phrase, I could almost not believe he'd said it. "And I've never known you to be. Not at any time when you and I worked together were you ever anything but savvy and smart. Yet here you are, in possession of Devil, the deadliest of the deadly, the perfect Evander soldier, and you're trusting him?"

From where he stood, leaning on the wall, Devil shifted. It was a small move, but I noticed it. Not that I had any idea what it meant. He might just not like being talked about. I certainly detested the feeling. Like bugs crawling around on my arms.

"It's been a year since the majority of the fighting ended. People change. Particularly in the Chen Empire. You changed, why can't he?"

Blaze shook his head. "I was never the perfect Evander soldier. Trust me, I never lived up to him."

Devil lifted his eyebrows. "Still jealous?"

Amari's hand shot up so fast, I could hardly follow the movement. "Not helpful right now."

"Okay," Melissa interrupted all of them. "Listen, I get it. You want him protected. I don't think that Sienna is looking to hurt him. I can certainly understand how it happened, and that's that. Enough. What I want to know is what to do from here?"

I had to speak up. "I'd like to go home."

"Well, that's obviously not happening." I didn't know who the man sitting next to Diana was, but he was tall, like a Super Soldier, and had that kind of feel about him, as though he was just a bigger presence than anyone else who wasn't like him.

Next to Waverly, a man with odd-looking eyes shook his head fast. "Out of the question. You can't go home." He turned his head to address Melissa. "No, this is the most easily defendable position. We all stack up here and wait. I mean, it could be years. We'll send ships in and out, keep a rotation, and eventually when they come for her, we're ready."

The blond man next to Paloma drummed his fingers on the table. "Let's be honest, Earth is the most easily defendable position. But we aren't doing that, because it's not rebuilt and it is here."

"We're working on it, Sandler." One of the other two who looked like Amari shook his head. "If you want to stop building your fancy ships and help more, we'd go faster."

The so-called Sandler rolled his eyes. "Not criticizing, just stating fact. So we'll take some of my fancy ships, and we'll surround Mars with them. See if we can draw out Evander. Give you Super Soldiers a break."

I stopped listening. No one had paid attention to what I said. Not a soul. I wanted to go home, and they didn't care.

But really, why should they? I was a problem for them to solve, not a person.

Wade patted my leg. "It won't be forever," he spoke in a low voice. "This will work better than what we were doing, and then you'll be able to go from there. Just until we get rid of the Evander ship so they don't build more from this one and overwhelm us again."

I supposed I didn't have a choice. But that was the story of my life.

Everyone started talking at once again, but I zoned out. It was like I didn't need to be in the room at all.

Wade grabbed my arm as we exited. "Hey, listen, I uploaded the formulas I've been using on you into the main computer that should be sent to all the major ships, in case you ever need to exit on one fast and you don't have me with you. Just tell the medical personnel to look for it."

I sighed. "Do you think that's likely?"

He shrugged. "I'm not going anywhere. They can dart around in space without me trying to draw in Evander. I'll stay on the station, but I like to imagine the worst-case scenarios. And so I thought—"

His eyes widened a second before a large hand shot out and took him by the neck. I cried out but another hand covered my mouth. Struggling, I didn't know who held me as I watched Wade crumple to the ground, passed out.

"Don't panic. He's fine. Or will be in a few moments." It was Devil's voice in my ear. "I have a device in my pocket that gives me a few minutes that your group can't hear you or me talking. If they try to find your heartbeat, they won't right now. That's going to scare them, and they're going to try looking for you."

We were in a long hallway that should have led to the lift, but right now, we were all alone. What was he going to do to me? I geared up to zap him, and then he spoke again, stopping me in my tracks.

"I have to make this right with you. The Chens are big on that. Making things right. I did you a great disservice, stealing you from your home and giving you to the executives. They've made you sick. I didn't know they were going to do that, but truth is, I would have taken you anyway because back then, I did everything I was told to do. I heard you in there when no one else did. If you want to go home, I'll take you now. Is that what you want?"

He let go of my mouth. I could have screamed, only I didn't. Instead, I dropped down to check Wade's pulse. Sure thing, he was out cold but breathing, and his pulse was strong. Okay. I could think. He was offering to take me home?

This was Devil, who had hurt me, who had kidnapped me, who had...he wanted to make things right?

"You're very smart. I can always tell. We're running out of time. They'll come looking any second. In fact, I think Blaze and Anders have both cued in. Corbin now. What is it? Are you coming with me? Am I taking you home?"

This was what I wanted, but I had no time to think. "How do I know I can trust you? Blaze doesn't. They think you're just about the most dangerous, untrustworthy person out there. How do I know you're not going to bring me to Evander?"

He shook his head. "You don't."

I took a deep breath. I wanted to go home, and if he wanted to take me, he could do it easier than this. I'd be out cold just like Wade. No, he'd asked. That wasn't the move of a person who wanted to deliver me to the enemy. The people here didn't care that I needed to see my home with my own two eyes, or that I couldn't stand not knowing what happened to Joy or my parents.

Nodding, I put out my hand. "Take me home."

His smile was small but present. "Let's go."

———

I stared at the man I'd just run off with and wondered if I'd lost my mind. We were in a small vessel. It had one room beside the main control area where Devil piloted the ship. A tiny bathroom was attached to a living-slash-sleeping space that also had a bathroom attached. Two chairs up front were for the pilot, Devil, and the co-pilot, who I guessed was me on this one. Not that I had any idea what I was doing. There was a med machine next to the small couch that converted into a bed in the back.

Pulling my knees to my chest, I regarded Devil. He was handsome. I wouldn't have thought so before, but now I could see it. His face was long and oval shaped. He had a well-trimmed beard, and his brown hair was long and up in a bun at the top of his head. I didn't think it would be as long as Corbin's if he let it down. It was also slicker looking. He was neat and well put together in his uniform. The last time I'd seen him, he had been in a uniform, too. But this one was different. There were dark circles under his eyes that led me to believe he wasn't sleeping well.

Of course, I hadn't seen a person yet who slept well.

"Wade will be okay?" It was the third time I'd asked. He'd taken care of me, and I'd left while he was knocked out.

Devil tapped furiously on the control panel. "I'm sending Master Chen a note explaining things, that I need to make this right with you. That way, they can call off whatever hunt they've started on the station. I'm sure Wade will be fine, but I'm asking after him."

He leaned back on his seat, and when I didn't comment, because there really was nothing to say, he spoke again. "They should have had you on a ship like this. I mean, Artemis is old, right? How did they expect to beat Evander like that? Blaze should have known that. I trained him. Or a little bit, anyway. Fast and sleek. He'd have gotten you away quicker."

I raised an eyebrow. "In a two-room shuttle? I was in cryogenic sleep. He needed a doctor and a crew. Artemis did just fine for them. I'm grateful. It might have been better for them if they'd left me asleep." Tiredness wrapped itself around me. "I just want to go home, and I've caused nothing but trouble. They must be relieved to be rid of me."

Anders' words from the night before wrapped around me. He'd wanted to take care of me. If only such things could actually be. "I don't want anyone to be hurt because of me. I don't want Evander hurting anyone else. That includes you. If I'd had any more time to think about it, I probably wouldn't have done this because I wouldn't want you hurt."

He side-eyed me for a long moment. "Evander can't hurt me any more than they already have."

I tilted my head. "They could kill you."

"That would be a cessation of the pain. Not the opposite." He shook his head. "Don't get me wrong, I'm not looking to die. I'll make this up to you by bringing you home. I'll keep you safe from Evander while you figure out what's next. That'll be one less thing on my conscience keeping me up at night." He smirked. "Words I never thought to speak. Fucking Chens." He said the last two words with amusement in his voice, not hostility. Clearly, the man liked the Chens.

"What other things have you tried to make up for?" It might have been a bad idea to ask the question. Maybe I really didn't want to know.

He shook his head. "You're the first. They haven't let me out a lot yet, and I'm not sure they'll let me out much after this. But it is the right thing to do, even if it comes with restrictions to personal freedom. Again."

I didn't know what the Chens did or didn't do, but it sounded like there was a story there. I just wasn't sure I should get to know Devil more than I already did, which was not at all. "I don't remember what happened to me."

"You wouldn't. Your friend was threatened into drugging you. I made her afraid, and she did it, and I took you when you were asleep. You weren't made sick in front of me. But as I was locked away to be frozen asleep again, I did hear them say we were under attack. Presumably, that was whoever rescued you from them."

It was hard for me to imagine my father leading some kind of fight to get me back, but that must have been what happened. This was the problem. I had to go home to get answers. I couldn't live with this big gaping hole in my life. What had happened, who had done what... I had to know. Maybe that made me selfish that I hadn't done just what those people wanted from me. I could have stayed on Mars Station.

And waited. And maybe gotten them all killed.

Conflicting emotions rushed through me. I couldn't remember ever feeling this unsettled before. Had I ever been so torn up?

I rubbed my face. "I think I made a mistake. I'm being so unkind. The least I could have done was wait on Mars Station. A million things were done for me while I slept. It's not okay that I broke the rules."

"Do you always just obey?"

"Yes. What else is there to do? We don't get to determine our lives. From the moment we're born, they're sorted out for us. One thing to another, but the path is there. Mine has gone off kilter, but that doesn't change that—"

"Do you hear yourself?" He quickly interrupted me. "You might as well be working for Evander. We do get to decide our lives. You wanted to go home. If that isn't the case, I'll take you back to Mars. Or Earth. Or wherever you want. But don't do it because someone told you to do it. You're a person. We all get to say what to do with our time. Yours is already cut short. I mean...fuck...they shot you up with incurable diseases, and I can't imagine that thing in your arm is going to keep you healthy permanently. Don't waste time being good when you could be happy."

I sat back in my chair and leaned my head against it. There was a time and place to be, as he put it, good. I knew this to be true the same way that I did anything. But he wasn't entirely wrong either. I was sick. It was hard to get my mind around that, as though the fact that I knew it hadn't made it sink into my mind enough that I understood it. That didn't even make any sense. Why was I so confusing, even to myself?

The deed was done. I wasn't going to question it. "Take me home. Thank you, Devil."

He nodded. "No need for thanks. This is a quest to self-improvement for me." He winced. "Sometimes I feel like Shane these days. Never mind. I'm doing what I'm doing because I'm doing it."

"You could have just said I'm sorry. I probably would have forgiven you, and you could have moved on from whatever this is without having to run into the Dark Planets." I might be stating the obvious, but there it was.

When he smiled, half of his mouth lifted up in amusement that almost looked sardonic. "I'm not sorry." He held up his hand. "And the thing about saying that is you have to mean it, as far as I can tell. I know this goes directly against what I said to you about my conscience. So I will try to explain what can't be explained. That time...my whole life up until the point that I got dumped on the Chen's doorstep, it feels like someone else lived it. And also doesn't. It's like I've had two lives. I feel terrible for the things that I did in the sense that I should, but I can't seem to feel anything about them at all. But I can't sleep because of all the things that other person, who also happens to be me but not, did. So I'd better figure out how to make amends for what he—I—did, so that I can sleep again."

"You're right. It makes no sense. Sounds like you're just as screwed up as me. Two people with no idea what we're doing traveling through space together on a ridiculous mission that maybe we shouldn't be doing at all."

It surprised me so much when he laughed that a grin hit my face before I could overthink it. Maybe the experience startled him as much as it did me, because his eyes widened. Whoever this new Devil was, he must not laugh very much.

"Well, life isn't dull. I'll give it that. I was born on the other side of a black hole, and I spent a huge amount of time training people to do awful things on behalf of a corporation that created me. Now, here I am. Yep, not dull."

I nodded. "I was born so powerful with an ability human beings don't have unless they're born on my planet. I was so good at it, they decided I should probably be a spiritual leader so that I could help people feel better about the shitty things in their lives."

Yep. I'd said shitty.

I giggled, which made him grin again.

"You're right. Life is strange. I didn't think I'd be sitting in a shuttle with you, ever." I shook my head. "Considering that just a few days ago, I was certain that you were the stuff of nightmares."

His smile faded as he nodded. "I am. I still am. Make no mistake. There will always be part of me that will be him. That other me. The one who makes me feel sick, but who I can't really feel. He's always in there."

That should have made me run, but instead, I put out my hand and squeezed his. He stared at where I touched him as though he'd never seen two people holding hands before. He gently squeezed me back. "You're surprising, Sienna. I can see why they're all in love with you."

I shook my head. "No one is in love with me."

"Trust me that I can hear things you can't. I can...tell heartbeats, as you know. The way that they breathe. The shortness of it. The way it sounds, they...never mind. It doesn't matter. You just need to trust me that I know."

"They took care of me for a long time. They've done enough."

"You're right. Although, I doubt they'd see it that way." He motioned toward the controls. "Want to fly for a bit?"

That was funny, but I didn't feel like laughing. "I can't even use light switches. I lived a pretty powerless life in terms of electronics, machines, whatever. Corbin had to put up signs in places so that I'd figure out how to use them."

"He was always incredibly nice. Out of the whole group. I have no idea how he made it without being put down. Yes, he would do that. Not surprised. I'll teach you.

Most things are built to be what we'd call user-friendly. If you were working for me, I'd tell you to say that you should put your hands out and ask yourself if you wanted to do something, where would be the closest, easiest thing for you to do that with?"

I rubbed my face. "How do I know what I want to do in this particular case?"

"Well, you want to fly it forward. Tommy Sandler makes these ships so morons can fly them. You are not that. It's very point and click. I kind of hate it, except that it really is the best. So I did the pointing. All we have to do now is click. So to speak. The ship is pointed in the right direction. You want to make it go faster. What do you want to do?"

I put my hands on two pointy stick-like things that were poking out farther than anything else. "These."

I really hoped that didn't put me suddenly in the moron category.

He nodded fast. "That's it. What do you want to do with them to make it go faster?"

I thought about it for a long second. "Push them forward."

Devil let go of the controls. "Have at it."

I did. It took me a second to feel the engines speed up beneath my feet, but they were there. The ship went even faster. It was stupid. I'd really done nothing, but I was flying. "Can you show me the rest?"

"By the time we get you home, you won't worry about light switches. Everywhere you go, you'll have a general idea of what to do. As much as anyone."

I loved that idea. "Thank you."

"Don't thank me."

I was seeing a pattern here with that. He didn't want to

be thanked. "I wish there was something I could teach you. This is going to be one sided."

"Tell you what? If you promise not to zap me again, because I really hate that, we'll call it even. I don't think my brain can take a third Sienna zapping."

I held up my hand. "Unless you give me some sort of reason to zap you, I won't again. We can call it a truce. I won't think that you are a nightmare, and you won't worry that I'll hurt you."

He nodded. This Devil wasn't who I had expected. Not even a little bit. He was taking me home, and for that, I would be grateful. Something beeped, and he pointed at it. "That's the communicator." Devil stared at it for a second. "Wade's fine."

Devil grabbed the sticks in front of him that were the same as the ones I'd gripped earlier. He pushed them even harder, speeding up again.

"Everything okay?"

His nod was fast. "Yep."

For just a second, I wondered if he was lying.

I MUST HAVE FALLEN asleep in the chair, because I woke up suddenly, not having realized I'd conked out at all. I rubbed my eyes, and Devil looked over at me.

"Hey." He smiled. "Did you sleep well?"

I nodded. "Sorry, I didn't used to be the person to just fall asleep. I almost needed none at all. It's either the medicines keeping me alive or the illnesses themselves. I'm always sleeping now."

"It's nothing to worry about." There was a blanket on my lap that hadn't been there before. Devil must have put it on me. That was so...sweet.

I wouldn't have thought it of him. "Hope I wasn't snoring."

He snorted, which made me smile. That was why I'd said it. "I wouldn't care if you were, Sienna. Things like that really don't bother me. But no, you weren't."

"When they didn't have you out cold on the ships in cryo sleep, where did you live? Sleep?" The question occurred to me just as I spoke the words. I didn't know that about any of the guys. I knew what they did now, but nothing about before.

He ran a hand through his hair, letting it out of the ponytail holder as he did. It fell to his shoulders. I'd been right. It was neatly trimmed and sleek.

"They had beds for us. I was a commander, like Blaze, but I was more advanced than he was. Older by a few years. So we only had to share with one or two people, instead of the ten the others did. It's not like we ever went home. Once they released us from the juvenile encampments, we worked all the time. It was cryo or the dorms on the ship. That was it. I didn't really have a concept of home until I saw how the Chen Empire works. They gave me my own place to sleep. A kitchen. Bathroom. It was totally bizarre at first."

I smiled at him. "Kind of like how I feel on this ship."

"Right. But eventually, I got the hang of most of it. And so will you. It's not like you were pulled out of the past. You lived on a terraformed planet with a fake sun that was created by colonists fleeing genocide. Right there, you know a tremendous amount of shit." He winced. "Sorry."

I shook my head. "Go ahead and curse. I'm going to make us some food."

"I can. In a little bit. I just don't want to leave the controls just yet."

A thought dawned on me. "Are you nervous about something? Is Evander after us?"

"No. Evander is nowhere to be seen. They won't catch me. Don't worry about a thing."

He was lying, but I didn't think it was about Evander. "When you want to tell me the truth, I'll listen."

Devil turned to look at me. "You could tell?"

"Yep." I left the small control room and walked toward

the tiny kitchen. Okay. I knew how to use the equipment on Artemis, and Devil had told me that most things were set up so that we could use them instinctually. If I didn't know what to do, I'd try to wing it and hope I didn't burn anything down.

In the end, I managed to rehydrate and heat up two meals that looked pretty decent. I just had to hope I hadn't stumbled onto another disgusting meal. I'd never thought about the food we'd eaten at the temple as special, but it turned out we were practically gourmets.

"Hey, Dev." I came in holding the plate. I'd decided on the nickname somewhere between the rehydrating and heating. I didn't like calling him Devil, so I wasn't going to do that anymore. Unless he objected. I set the plate down in front of him on the console, but it didn't touch the buttons and levers. "Here you go. Hope the nickname is okay."

He took a bite and smiled. "This is great. Thanks. Never had a nickname before. I like it. You eating?"

I sat down. "I probably should before my next round of passing out." I took a look at the device on my arm. It read two. I stuttered. It had been at one the whole time I'd been awake. Now it was at two? My chest felt tight, and I had to remind myself to breathe. "I..."

A strong hand stroked my arm. "What's wrong?"

The contact helped. "My number went from one to two."

"What does that mean? Are you okay?" He scooted closer to me. "Explain so I can help. This is what I do. I fix things for people."

I believed him. But he couldn't help in this. "I'm okay. Wade gave me an indicator. I can see what the level of virus is in my body. Anything under ten is okay. He said it might jump around a bit. I'm okay. It's at two. It's just never been above a one."

He nodded. "Then two is okay. And it could be that you were hungry or that you just woke up. Or any number of things. You were in cryo before now. Maybe you're going to level out, say at a five, and that'll be where you hold. Don't worry."

We didn't have a doctor with us. "Don't let me make you sick. Put me in that med machine if I get too high, okay?"

"I'm a Super Soldier. I'm not going to get sick."

I rolled my eyes at him. "You guys don't like each other, but you've all got that same ego going on. I'm loaded with Evander sickness. I bet some of it could make you sick, considering that Evander is where you guys came from. They probably have something in their collection to wipe you guys out if they had to."

"Now that's a disturbing thought." He hadn't let go of me yet, and his strong hold on my arm helped more than he could ever imagine. "What we need is to get on that Evander ship and find your cures. I'm surprised the guys didn't try that."

I never wanted to see that ship again, ever. "Not such an easy thing to do."

"Evander is not unbreakable. Sterling and Damian, two of Diana's husbands, managed to take us down, and Nolan boarded us with a crew that took us down. They can be beaten. That just wasn't what those guys were trying to do with you. The question is why."

I didn't know the answer to that. "The impression I got was that they felt it their duty to keep me safe beyond anything else. It was all about hide and deflect. Not getting caught. They all found it frustrating."

Dev winced. "That's why Blaze and I never got along. We wouldn't have done that if I'd been in charge. I would have seen it as protecting you to take down that ship."

"So Blaze is more cautious than you are." I could see that. Also, the utter frustration at having to remain cautious, even if he wanted to do something else. It was probably why he got so moody. "Maybe there's a middle ground."

"Probably, but I've never found it myself."

Did anyone? "Do you think that's possible?"

He shook his head. "I know less than anything about anything. Trust me on that."

I didn't believe him. It seemed like he knew quite a bit about quite a lot of things. Not that I was going to say that. I stood up and stretched. Did people stay long periods of time on this shuttle? They must never get claustrophobic. I'd not thought about it on Artemis, but she was pretty big. I was going to notice I was in a small, walk-across-in-thirty-seconds sized ship before long.

On this ship, I would notice I never saw the sky.

Why hadn't I known all the years at home how much I would crave real sunlight if I didn't see it for a while, or how much I needed a blue sky?

I rubbed my eyes. Okay, these thoughts weren't helpful.

"You all right?" He didn't look at me as he asked, but he'd noticed I wasn't.

"Could you tell because of my heartbeat?"

Dev smirked at me. It was sort of adorable. Wow. Who would have thought I'd ever think this man was cute?

He shook his head. "I knew because you made a small noise that I think meant you weren't okay. I could tell if you were scared or sick or exhausted from your heartbeat."

I wanted to run my hands through his hair and see if it was as soft as it looked. I wanted him to keep his eyes this warm and happy, to not retreat to the glacier glare he'd had that day when he'd come after me or in the hallway on Mars Station.

Maybe it was the small quarters we were in, or maybe it was that he was the only one to listen to what I wanted...or maybe he was just really, really handsome. I bit my lip. All of that was probably true. And yet I still couldn't not think about the six men I'd left behind, even though they were probably glad to be rid of me. Even Anders, who had told me he wanted to take care of me.

I'd been a huge burden.

Whatever happened now, I had to stop being that.

A thought dawned on me, and I sat down. Maybe it was none of my business. He might very well tell me to mind my own business and I'd do just that. "How did they ever get you? You're...you're something of a legend. How did they capture you?"

His smile was fast. "Thanks for that. A legend, huh? Probably more like infamous. Your Blaze doesn't like me, and I can't imagine those guys who worship him do either. Anyway, that doesn't matter. How did they get me? I'd been up for eight straight days, and despite the fact that we don't need as much sleep, I had to get a few hours. I closed my eyes. They picked right then to attack. I woke up in the middle of the attack. And..."

Dev's voice trailed off. I didn't push. He'd finish if he wanted to.

Finally, he did. "Maybe I was sick of it. I'd had a chance to see how people lived around here before we pillaged them. How there were these huge family groups that were fighting together. It seemed nice. I never imagined they'd take me in. I just didn't want to hurt them anymore."

I threw my arms around him from the back of his chair.

His body stiffened for a second before he stroked my arm that I held over his chest.

"I guess even I had a limit."

"Thank you for taking me, Dev."

He squeezed me back. "You're welcome, Sienna. I'm really glad for the chance to do this. Thank you for letting me."

I'd gone in such a short period of time from being completely afraid of this man, from zapping his brain, to embracing him like we were old friends. Life had been totally unpredictable to me lately. I almost couldn't recognize my existence anymore.

I let go of Dev before I did something ridiculous, like run my hands through his hair or stroke his cheek to feel his whiskers. I couldn't lose track of reality. We really were just strangers.

I had to remember that. Everyone in my life right now was a stranger. But I was going home. That was key. There would be people there who knew me, even if others had left. Home, I would get some answers.

━━━

"Sienna," a gentle hand shook my shoulder, "we're here."

I blinked, rubbing my eyes. I was on the couch. I'd come into the small secondary room to clean up the food and sat down on the couch to rest. "Guess I conked out again."

Dev nodded. "That's right. Question for you. One of the drugs that Wade is using to treat you, does it have a drowsy property?"

"He didn't say that to me. I suppose it's possible. It may just be that I'm constantly using so much energy to stay healthy." The thought made me look at my wrist. It was still at two. That was good. No further surge. Of course, one would be better. This was life now. Watching the numbers.

Making a noise I didn't understand in the back of his throat, Dev offered me his hand. I took it and let him help me up, even though I could have done it. His hand was solid, strong, and hard against my own. He wasn't soft, except maybe inside, and I wasn't even sure about that.

Dev grabbed a water and passed it to me. "Are you hungry?"

I really wasn't. "No, thank you. Did we land? Did I miss it?"

"No, I'm going to set down the ship now. If you're not hungry, then we'll get right to it. I want to get on the planet sooner than later."

That seemed an odd thing to say. "What's going on?"

"We're being chased, and I don't want anyone telling me that I can't bring you down there." He waved his hand. "Not that anyone can do that. No one outside of the Chen brothers tells me to do anything. But I'm trying to avoid having a fight, for your sake. So let's do this thing."

I grabbed his arm. "Who is chasing us?"

"Artemis. Those guys were not okay with me taking you off Mars Station. They've been trying to catch us ever since, rather impressively. I've got them on long-range sensors, which I think they must know, because they keep falling off the sensors. That's remarkable." He shook his head. "People don't fall off the sensors when I'm running them."

A lot of that was completely foreign, like he spoke another language. "I think Trenton is supposed to be extraordinarily good at flying. They must be really upset that you knocked out Wade." To chase us across the galaxy really showed their level of pissed.

He shook his head as he made his way back to the

control room. I followed behind him. "Then why are they following me?"

"Because I took you." He didn't turn around. "And I get it. They want you back. But I'm not going to let them just have you. I need you to know that. I can't. Buckle in. You could get hurt."

As I did what he instructed, his words banged around in my head. He couldn't? Why not? "Dev—"

He shook his head, effectively cutting me off. "We'll talk about it later. Let me get you home for now. The rest can wait. For a little while. There are a couple of options I need to mull over. Things I won't like, things they won't like. Everyone is going to have to deal, and we aren't people who do that. I..." The ship jolted, but he didn't seem concerned. "Never mind. This isn't your problem. It's ours. You're pale. Are you scared about the idea of me talking to them? Or fighting with them?"

I instinctually touched my hand to my throat. "No, crash landing."

He smirked at me. "So little faith in my skills? Here." Dev pushed a button on the console, and suddenly, I could see outside. Sure enough, there was my planet. I'd seen pictures of it from the sky before, but never witnessed it myself. Tears rushed my eyes. Yes, it was blue, green, purple...that was what it looked like.

"Thank you," I whispered, slightly too overwhelmed to talk.

"You're welcome. But make that the last time you thank me. As the Chens would say, you humble me. And I don't like to be humbled."

We didn't speak again until he set us on the ground. Dev must have remembered where we'd been the last time, because I could see the temple in the distance. Well, what was left of it. I caught my breath in my throat. I'd thought I'd been prepared for this, but I absolutely was not.

He shut off the view screen, and without a word, I followed him outside.

The sun hit my skin like a welcoming beacon, but that was the only thing wonderful about getting off the ship. Otherwise, the place was destroyed.

I rubbed at my arms. "Dev, I really don't know how long I've been gone."

He came up behind me, the heat of his body warming the chill that the sight caused inside of me. For a second, I wondered if he could block out the sun and if that was something I wanted. Maybe it would just be better to have nothing here at all.

"Three years. Almost exactly. Tomorrow is three years."

I closed my eyes. "I've been putting off knowing that for sure. I couldn't... I didn't want..."

He put his hands on my shoulders. "I get it. You didn't want to know, because that was too big a number. But now you know."

I forced myself to swallow. "Dev, if that was three years ago, why is it still such a mess? Shouldn't this be rebuilt?"

He audibly sighed. "Let's go look. We don't know what they've done. Maybe it's not all as bad as here."

Dev took my hand, and I walked with him. This small amount of the world had been my whole existence. I'd never seen more of the planet. There were no people around, and that was different, too. Unless they'd all gotten on various ships and taken off to the sky. It was hard for me to imagine. These people were farmers and merchants. They didn't fly ships.

And yet, I knew from firsthand experience that some were. We walked in silence. I actually appreciated that about Dev. He wasn't trying to make conversation. That was hugely helpful right now, since my mind was a bunch of gobbledygook and I might not be able to coherently speak.

Eventually, we reached the town that was the last stop before we reached the temple. Everything was closed except a market up ahead. I'd never purchased anything there. Others did that for us. But I knew the owner, because his wife came to the temple and I'd helped her through three miscarriages. They'd eventually gone on to have four boys, but that did nothing to eliminate the pain of the first three.

Sometimes, we could pretend that this far out in the Dark Planets, we were immune to problems of the Earth variety. Sure, we had fewer things and were constantly inundated by pirates. But we also didn't have to play politics like they had to. And yet, the same problems that Earth had with conception and birth happened here.

It was hard to have any children, and the ones that were born were almost always boys.

I pointed to the shop next to the market. "That's my parents'. They're tailors."

Dev nodded slowly. "It's hard to imagine having parents. I know people do. The Chens are parents, but just the very idea that people are raised in a home with the people who had them blows my mind." He shrugged. "Let alone parents who own a shop."

I rubbed the back of my neck. "I wasn't raised by them. They gave me over when I was quite young. The temple raised me. But yes, I had parents."

I walked over to the outside door and peeked through the window. It was empty. The clothes that hung everywhere, the radio that always played music, were all gone. It was just an empty shell of a building.

"Someone's coming out of the market." Dev placed himself between me and the street. He was so big, it was actually hard to see around him, but I recognized the squeal and the voice when she shouted.

It was Kristy Webster, the woman whose husband owned the market, and who I had helped over the years.

"Sienna," she shouted again. "You're back. We didn't believe it. They said you were probably going to die."

The thought made me look at my arm. It was still at the number two.

"She's not going to die." Dev spoke through clenched teeth. "Sienna, is she safe for you?"

I nodded, but he couldn't see that, which occurred to me after a second. "She is." I stepped out from behind him, and he didn't try to stop me. "Hello, Mrs. Webster."

She rushed me. As people always did. And threw her arms around me. "Oh, we have all felt so awful with you gone. So completely terrible. I...I never thought I'd get to feel good again, but here you are."

I swallowed as my arms went around her like a sense memory. People hugged, and I hugged back. I'd been trained to do so a million times.

She shook and waited. All it would take to make her feel better would be to open my wall and let her in. Kristy would pass her feelings onto me, and I'd take them. She'd go on for days relieved, just because she encountered me.

The problem was...just like the people we'd met on Artemis, who we saved, I didn't want to do that for her right now. I'd done it for years. Trained since birth, practically. People asked, and they received.

But I had a device on my arm that told me how sick I

was, and I wasn't in the mood. I might never be again. I didn't really feel like I had a duty to do so. When I lived in the temple, the people paid to keep me alive. I had to help them, as I existed based on their goodwill. It was circular, although that had never occurred to me before now.

Only I was tired of owing, tired of being indebted. No. I wasn't going to do that right now. I had enough to carry on my own without adding her burdens to my shoulders right now.

"I'm sorry, Mrs. Webster." I let go of her and stepped back. "Not today."

She blinked rapidly. "Oh...I see. I..." Her cheeks turned pink. I'd never wanted to embarrass her. That wasn't my intention. "I didn't realize..."

"That's okay." I smiled at her. "No harm done. Just not today. Now, maybe you can help me with some information. This is Devil," I introduced him with his full name. That nickname was just for me. He'd probably think that was dumb, but there it was. "And he brought me home so I could get some answers. What happened here? I got pieces of it, but I wasn't ready to hear them. Could you tell me now?"

She nodded fast. "They took you off planet. One of the Evander people told my husband that they were going to force you to obey, to make you sick so you'd comply. He told us so we'd never fight. Alan didn't listen. He told your father. They made plans. Your dad and several others led an assault. I'm not sure why it worked."

Dev snorted. "They didn't think there was even the possibility that it could work. Or that it even would be attempted."

"Well, they got you, but they couldn't just bring you all the way here again. They'd just come back. So they took off running. Honestly, I have no idea. Alan came back, but your father and mother never did. They said they were going to protect you. I have no idea. I just don't. Then Evander came back here and punished us." She looked down. "They destroyed everything." She waved her hand. "As you can see. Then these people came and sold ships. It's been a whole mess." Kristy visibly swallowed. "Are you...are you okay? Did they save you? Make you not sick?"

Dev put his arm around me. "She's okay. Come on, I'm going to take her to the temple."

"There's no one left there." She sighed.

He scooted me on. "We'll be there. So then there will be two people there. That's something."

THE TEMPLE WAS GONE. Well, that wasn't technically true. The building was still mostly there. Someone had blown out the windows. But the whole feeling of it—the way it had seemed sort of otherworldly while I remained hopelessly flawed—was gone. It was just a place now, like any other empty building. I'd lived here, and yet, it was gone.

I wandered from room to room, looking at things. Any traces that I'd existed in these walls were gone. Joy was nowhere to be found, as though she also vanished from space and time. The elders, the ones who had come before me, their rooms had been raided. This place had been formed when the unusual abilities that I and others had started to appear, and now it was nothing.

"You okay?" Dev watched me from a doorway. He leaned against the side, taking up most of the space between the rooms.

I had a headache, but my wrist number remained at two, so I supposed that I was actually fine. "Not any sicker."

He furrowed his brow. "That's not what I meant. This

is a big deal. What they did here, to the planet, to the people, that's what I used to do. I've just never seen it from this end before. The aftermath. I was the cause of this kind of thing. Me, and the others you know. This is what we did to planet after planet, place after place. This, and then some."

I nodded. I knew that. I wasn't unaware of who it was that I'd been spending my time with lately. "You didn't do this. You don't have to take responsibility for it. Own your own sins, and leave the ones that aren't yours to other people."

Dev opened and closed his mouth. "I did take you. That, I did."

"I don't remember it. The last thing I remember is zapping you." I walked toward him. There was nothing for me here. Not the temple, not Joy, not my parents. This had been a mistake. But still, it was mine to make, and I'd needed to come here more than anything else. I had no idea what to do next, but there it was. My past was here, desolated and gone.

I didn't consciously know I was going to hug him, but that was what I did. People hugged me all the time when they needed things. I'd been expected to do it. Maybe that was why I wrapped my arms around Devil and didn't let go, even though he'd given me no indication that he was a hugger.

As soon as I realized what I'd done I tried to let go. This was an invasion—I knew that better than anyone—but he held on, not letting me release him.

"I can apologize for doing this."

Dev laid his head on top of mine. "No, don't. I've never had a hug before. I like this one."

"I really should have asked." Even as I said the words, I

closed my eyes. He smelled really clean, really fresh, so completely different than the rest of this place. "I'm overwhelmed, but it's no excuse and..."

"Sienna," his voice was low, "I like the hug."

Okay. I wasn't going to overthink it. In the future, I'd give it more thought, but for right now, he was all right and so was I. "What do I do now? It's all gone. I have nothing left here. What do I do?"

He didn't let go as he pressed his nose to the top of my head. "Fuck."

That wasn't the response I'd been expecting, not even close to it. "That bad? My future is that dire? I mean...we could go back to Mars Station and..."

"No." He tightened his hold before he gently let me go. I swayed for a second before I found my feet. "That's not why I cursed. They're here. I thought we'd have a little more time. That guy can really fly that old ship. I'll give him credit. He'd have made a great Super Soldier."

It took me a minute to follow what he'd just said. "Artemis is here?"

"Yep. They landed. And they're not wasting time. I've got all of their heartbeats." He ran a hand through his hair. "Do me a favor, and don't get in the middle of what is about to happen. They're going to have to work this out with me. Yep, they can hear me. I'm saying it, and they can hear me. Well, almost all of them can. My point remains. Don't get in the middle of it." He winked at me, which was a surprise move. "Don't zap me either, please."

I swallowed. The guys couldn't be very happy with me right now. I'd run off after everything they'd done. If they wanted to yell at me, then I supposed they had every right.

A light in the distance caught my attention, and I turned toward it. Everything on the planet was so damned dark now, that even the smallest amount caught my attention. This wasn't a small glare, it was a big one.

I held up my hand to shield my face. "What is that?"

"A light that we sometimes used to illuminate the night sky temporarily like it was day. Turn around. It'll only get brighter as they come closer. They're just letting me know they're fully-armed." He shook his head. "I'm not impressed, Blaze. I don't give a shit how many toys you have. Come and talk to me."

There was a pause, and then Blaze's voice pushed out into the night. "Talk to you? You're lucky I'm not fucking pulverizing you, you piece of shit."

Wow. I caught my breath. Devil merely tilted his head. "Kindly remember that there is a lady present."

"Remember it?" Blaze moved so fast, one second, I couldn't see him, and the next, he was in Dev's face. "Did you remember it when you stole her off a station and took her out into the universe only in your small, nothing shuttle with only you to protect her? Did you think about the fact that she's a lady when you pulled this stunt? I don't give a shit what you told Amari Chen. She's ours. Not yours. And you had no right to fucking do this."

I swallowed. "Blaze..."

"No." Dev shook his head. "Sienna, don't get in the middle. Trust me on this."

"Trust you?" Blaze outright shouted now. "You're the one who gave her to Evander to begin with. You did this to her."

"That's right," Dev shouted back. They were so close, their foreheads were practically touching. "I did. And this was my chance to even start to make it right. What wouldn't you do for the chance to fix anything you've done? Anything you did for Evander that keeps you up at night?

Think about it. The shit we did didn't go away because we had the chance to change. We're not forgiven. So I took the chance to listen to someone I hurt, and I am trying to figure out how I can even begin to fix it. You wouldn't have done the same thing?"

Blaze grabbed Devil's shirt. "I won't let you destroy her. She's ours. Mine. I keep her safe."

"You didn't listen to a word she said in that room."

I couldn't stand this. Dev had said to leave it, but they were talking about me, about to come to blows over me. How was I supposed to just stand here and...

"Don't," Kellan pulled me back until I was against his side. When had he gotten there? I looked around, not seeing anyone else. He turned me to look at him. Against me, I could feel how hard he breathed. He must have been running. How had Blaze gotten here so fast?

I shook my head. "He only did what I wanted. I needed to come here, and he made that happen. That's all."

"Oh." Kellan laughed, but it was joyless. "There is so much more than that going on here. I'm so glad you're okay. If you wanted this, needed it, you could have told me. I'd have done this for you. We all would have."

"Kellan." I squeezed his hand. "You said no. You all said no. Not to mention, you were leaving me. Blaze told me that. I wasn't your responsibility anymore. You were giving me to Melissa or something."

He took my cheeks in his hands, smoothing his thumbs over them. It would be a restful, sweet gesture, if Blaze and Dev weren't about to kill each other. "I was never going anywhere. I'm sorry you thought that was a possibility."

"Got her?" Anders was there, followed by Corbin. Then Wade and Trenton. Everyone was talking. It would be easy to get lost in Kellan's words, in the kindness in his usually hot, angry gaze. But then Blaze shoved Devil, who grabbed onto him, and they both went down to the ground.

I gasped, and Kellan turned me around, all but handing me to Wade. There was a crowd of very big men between me and the battle between Blaze and Devil.

"Are you okay?" Wade tugged at me, getting my attention.

"Am I okay?" I shouted over the noise. "No, they're going to kill each other."

He winced. "I don't think they're going to do that. But there are things to work out. I'm so sorry he got the jump on me like that."

Got the jump on him? "I'm sorry I left you on the ground. You've saved my life, and I left you there."

"Sienna. This is Devil we're talking about. From what the guys have said, he's a master manipulator and a really scary guy. If you think you ever really had a choice, you're mistaken."

Okay. I couldn't take any more of this. That wasn't the Devil I'd gotten to know over the last day or however long it had been. I couldn't even keep track of the time anymore. Not without any sun coming and going. All I knew was that I didn't want this. Not a fight about who did what and when. I was in the remnants of my home, a place that had been special and was now dead. And each and every fucking—yes, I cursed now in my own head—one of them was acting like little fucking boys.

"Stop," I shouted, placing every bit of power I had into it. Even though I didn't zap anyone, the same power that moved through me when I did traveled then. I wanted them to hear me. They just had to *stop*.

Standing in front of Kellan, with their hands over their ears, Trenton, Corbin and, Anders winced while Wade stumbled backward. They spread out enough in their action that I could see Blaze and Devil on the ground doing the same.

I panted. I'd never done that before, hadn't known I could. It was as much instinctual as anything else. My heart raced, and I had to put my hands on my knees just to try to breathe. "Don't do that. All of you. Please. Stop. I need you not to do this. Not over me. Not ever. Just no." I wasn't making a lot of sense, rambling. A strong hand came to my back. Wade.

He knelt down, meeting my gaze. "Sienna, deep breaths. Okay? I don't know what you just did, but you're panting."

Devil and Blaze both stumbled to their feet, coming to the crowd around me.

The world tilted left and then right. I knew this feeling. It happened sometimes with the zapping. I stared at Wade for a long second. "I'm going to faint."

━━━

"I can't believe he let him on the ship." Anders spoke somewhere nearby in a low voice.

"I can," Trenton answered, as he stroked a hand over my head. It had to be him who'd done that, because his voice was so close. "I think they really bonded in the day she was away with him. I can see it. The same way that we feel, he does. It was let him on the ship, or potentially lose her to him. He's not going anywhere. If Blaze isn't going to kill him —and that stop she blasted at us certainly told us she doesn't want that—then he's with us now."

Anders sighed. "You don't understand. He taught us all at various points. He's scary."

"Yeah? So are you," Trenton answered.

I moaned, unable to stop the sound as I officially stirred from my stupor. Everything sort of hurt. Trenton's hand stopped moving. "Hey there." His voice was soft. "You're okay. Wade has checked you out and declared that you aren't hurt or sick. Just used a ton of energy. Passed out. You needed a few minutes. He's gone to try to get either Blaze or Devil to take a little medical care. I doubt that will happen, but he left you here with us."

I tried to sit up and then gave up on that. Not yet. "I do sometimes pass out from the exertion of zapping. I've never done what I did earlier. How long was I unconscious?"

Anders walked over, sitting down next to us. "About an hour. No big deal. You're on Artemis. And that thing you did? That's why Evander wants you. It's not about the zapping. It's about the potential."

Groaning, I forced myself to sit up, but the room spun. Fuck. Yep, cursing again. I hated this. Trenton gently put my head on his shoulder. "Just rest. There's no rush."

We were back on Artemis. And if I'd heard correctly, then Devil was with us, which I liked, but was going to be challenging. Trenton smelled like cherries. I hadn't scented them in years. I closed my eyes, not to sleep, just to be. "Where are we headed?"

"At the moment?" He sighed. "Nowhere. We're just in space, drifting while we regain our composure."

The truth of my life returned to me. I had no one and nowhere to go. Tears I wished I wasn't going to shed came to my eyes. I didn't try to stop them when they streamed down my face. Why bother? I had no wherewithal at the moment to do anything about them.

"Hey now." Trenton kissed the top of my head. It was a lot of affection from him, but right then, it didn't feel wrong or too much. I liked it, wanted more. He was very soothing. "What are these tears?"

"I have nothing. I thought... I don't know what I thought. Maybe if I went home, there would be something. Someone. But there wasn't. An old woman I know a little who wants me to fix her and nothing else. I have no people, no home." I repeated myself, but some things bore repeating. "I'm sick. And...I don't know what to do. I guess I have to go back to Mars Station and just wait to be caught."

Trenton kissed me again. "You have people. All of us, even Devil, who we don't like, are your people. You're not alone. And as for Mars Station, let's talk about it. Tomorrow. We'll head in that direction, but maybe it makes sense to go somewhere else."

Anders took my hands in his. "None of us have people. Well...Wade has people, but he's scared of them because he's already let them down. How about we be each other's people?"

"You were getting rid of me."

The door to the med bay opened, and Kellan strode in, heading straight for me. "No, I'm sorry you thought that. I'm sure Blaze didn't mean that either after the first second he said it. You're one of us. Trust me, when we realized we lost you...it was bad."

"Understatement," Trenton whispered.

The door opened again, and this time it was Corbin coming in. He took the seat on the other side of Trenton while Kellan sat on the floor next to Anders.

I had to say something. I just had no idea what. "I wanted to go home. I didn't mean to be trouble."

Kellan rolled his eyes, which surprised me. But then he spoke fast. "Devil, who has been told to stay in his room, would like you to know that you're not trouble."

Trenton snorted. "You know he's only in there because he's choosing to be. We can't really restrain him."

The door opened, and it was Wade who came in. "Blaze is taking a shower, and then I think he's coming here." He stopped talking. "Sienna, are you crying?"

I wiped at my eyes. "Apparently."

That was when I caught sight of the number. It had jumped to three. My heart stuttered. "I think in addition to everything else, I'm getting sicker."

"Wade?" Trenton shifted but held me on his shoulder. "Do something."

The doctor approached fast, looking down at the number. "Still a low number. Let's see what happens after you get some real rest."

"She'll come with me." Blaze spoke as he answered, his hair wet. His eye was swollen, but he obviously didn't care or Wade could have fixed that. He put out his hand. "You're going to get a good rest. We'll figure out tomorrow, tomorrow."

"I'm coming," Kellan announced, rising. "Two is reasonable."

Blaze nodded, once. "Fine, but, Corbin, make a schedule. Everyone, even Devil, is on it. I'm not going to have a pissing match and upset Sienna anymore. He'll show himself for his true colors soon enough. Give me a minute, Kellan. I want to speak to her in my room. Alone. And I mean it. I want you all to behave yourselves and stop listening. Sterling insists they all make efforts to behave. We need to start doing that. Five minutes." He put out his hand. "Come with me?"

I put my hand in his. It was warm, and he squeezed my fingers. That had to mean he wasn't going to yell at me, didn't it? I wasn't sure I could take any more today. I needed time to get strong again. It wasn't a natural occurrence for me. Or at least, it didn't feel that way lately.

We walked in silence until we got to his room. I'd never been in it before, but it looked just like mine. The door closed behind us when he stopped me and pressed me against the wall.

"Two things. I've never been so scared in my life as when I realized he had you and had taken you from the station. That's first. Second, I'm not good at listening. I think he's better at it now. The Chens did that for him. I've had no...reprograming, no Chen Empire and how they teach people to do things. I didn't hear you. That's what he told me. I didn't listen. Next time, I will, but you have to make yourself explicit if I'm not getting it. There will never be a time that you have to run off with anyone else to get what you need. We'll always—all of us—be there for you."

My tears flowed again. "Blaze, you were leaving me. That's what you said—"

"I changed my mind fast. Should have told you that, too. I apologize." And then he kissed me. With tears running down my face, making me a snotty mess, Blaze kissed me like he couldn't exist another second without having done so.

I had no idea how much I needed it until he did it, but then my knees gave out. I'd have fallen if he wasn't already holding me against the wall. He sighed and deepened the embrace. He cupped the back of my head, the other holding me up by the waist. A second later, he adjusted how he held me, tilting my head up so he could kiss me even deeper. I didn't know what to think, had no idea what he would do next, if anything. I was as novice at this as he was. He pulled back, just long enough to swipe his tongue over my bottom lip.

My whole body decided to wake up and heat up at the same time. His body was hard against my curves, and if I wasn't mistaken, getting harder by the second. Finally, he pulled back. "You will know to trust me soon. I'm even going to put up with him because I can see that you have bonded with him. But I'm never stepping aside for him. You were mine from the second I rescued you from Earth. I'll share you, but I won't lose you."

"I...I didn't know you all wanted me this way. I'm sick. I'm lost in space. I'm...not a great catch right now."

He smoothed his thumb over my lower lip. "Starting tomorrow night, we're all getting alone time with you. They'll be no doubt in your mind what we want then. You have people. And you'll never, ever be alone." He nodded with his chin. "Go climb in the bed. You can wear my shirt." He went to a drawer just as a knock sounded. "It's safe, Kellan."

The other man walked in. He nodded to both of us. "Work some things out?"

"Did you actually not listen?" Blaze didn't look up as he grabbed his shirt and handed it to me.

"Nope. I'm working on manners."

Blaze snorted. "We'll see how long that lasts."

I expected them to leave the room so I could get changed, but they didn't. Blaze threw his shirt aside and leaned against the wall. "If it would work for you, Sienna, the guys can figure out some suggestions of places we can go with you and let you pick in the morning."

With his shirt in my hand, I rocked back on my feet. "Sure. That'll be fine. I'm going to change in the bathroom."

Was I talking really fast, or was that just in my mind? I rushed toward the bathroom. That kiss had been...wow. But then again, the one with Kellan had been pretty mind blowing, too.

I quickly changed into Blaze's shirt and came out into the room. Both the guys were shirtless—and beautiful. I sucked in a long breath. They were stunning.

Kellan patted the bed next to him in the center from where he sat. I walked toward him, their gazes tracking my every movement. I wasn't their prey, but I could have been by the way they watched my movements. Shivers traveled up my spine. I climbed into the bed, covering myself up quickly with the blanket. The room looked just the same as mine, only these sheets smelled like Blaze. Clean, but with the distinct scent that made him Blaze. Minty almost, but with a dash of something inherently male. He climbed in the other side.

With a wink, Kellan turned off the light on the tablet next to the bed, bathing the three of us in darkness.

"I have a question, if that's okay?" I cleared my throat. "What made you decide to let him stay?"

Blaze tugged me toward him while Kellan rolled closer to be pressed up against me on the other side. It was the former who answered me. "I think he would die for you. It's hard to explain. I don't like him or trust him with myself, but it was very clear to me as soon as you fainted that he would die for you. I want anyone around who would be loyal to you like that. As far as I'm concerned, we can't have enough people who want to protect you in our corner right now. He's fine. Not any more injured than I am, and we'll all be better after a good night's sleep."

Kellan kissed the back of my neck gently. I froze, the pleasure of it rendering me temporarily without the ability to think.

"Do you snore, Sienna?" His voice held amusement in it.

"I...I don't know, actually." I'd never been told one way or the other.

Blaze readjusted until he faced me completely. "No, she doesn't. I think you'll find what we've all found, that it's very easy to sleep with her. We all missed the sound of your heartbeat last night, Sienna. Wade and Trenton can't hear it, but it was like they felt the absence, too. No one on this ship slept last night."

Kellan put his arm around my waist. "You do have a home. It's with us. Close your eyes. You need to rest."

I didn't think I'd get any sleep, but then my eyes closed.

I RAN TOWARD THE TEMPLE, being chased. I looked over my shoulder, but couldn't see who chased me. It was a faceless, nameless person. All I knew was that they wanted to kill me. I cried out for help, but the people lined up in front of the temple were turned away, and no one even turned to look at me as I yelled. My father was up ahead, but then I blinked and he was gone.

Tripping, I hit the ground, unable to catch myself. Blood gushed out of my chin, and it was almost impossible to roll myself over. Somehow, I managed, and as I stared up at the person who wanted to kill me, I...

"Sienna," a voice reached me in the darkness, calling me from that moment, and I jerked awake. Two sets of strong arms embraced me, but it was Kellan's voice who had brought me from the darkness.

He kissed the back of my neck. "Just a dream."

Blaze smoothed the hair off my forehead. "Bad dreams are such a pain in the ass. They take what is supposed to be revitalizing and turn it to scary, disturbing."

I laughed, some of the fog moving from my mind. "Well put."

"Thanks." He kissed the end of my nose. "You're okay."

"I woke you guys up. I'm sorry. I can go calm down in the bathroom."

Kellan kissed the back of my neck again. "Or you can stay right where you are and let us try to comfort you. Although, it's fair to say you're lying in bed with two people so far from being able to do that, we might as well be speaking a different language."

I turned slightly until they let me lie on my back. "That's not true. You're all very comforting."

He stroked a finger down the side of my face. "Well, we want to be. We're all completely here for you. Could probably get five other people in here to help you, too. We could make a whole thing about it."

His words made me almost as warm as lying between Blaze and Kellan did.

Blaze cuddled down, his nose in my hair. He sighed before he spoke. "What were you dreaming of?"

"Is it a good idea to talk about it or a bad idea?" Kellan yawned. "I can't remember. I've never gotten to talk about my dreams at all."

"I was going to the temple, being chased, couldn't see who was doing it, and there was no one to help me." I thought that summarized it pretty well.

Blaze continued to stroke my hair off my forehead. "We chased you across the galaxy in record time because we care what happens to you. I'm sorry you're still feeling alone. I get it. I think most of us feel alone most of the time, even when we have people. Or maybe that's just true for anyone who has ever really felt lost. I was born that way. Alone. Lost. Kellan, too. I don't know if Trenton or Wade would feel that way about their beginnings, but they certainly get it now. The good news? You have choice. You can go where you want, and you don't have to go anywhere you don't. The only stipulation is you have to let us keep you safe from Evander."

I'd never heard Blaze talk like this before. Maybe it was the darkness and the way that made everything always feel sacred. Maybe this would feel different in the light, less like he was saying something monumental. But I liked it like this.

"Tell me what you want, Sienna."

That was such a big question. "I don't even know what I can have. I just can't…I mean, I'm sure I'd get used to Mars Station. I'm sure I could get used to anything and anywhere. I'm not saying I'm not adaptable."

Kellan kissed my neck again. "It's okay. Tell us what you don't like about it. You don't have to make excuses or justifications before you say what you want. There's no right or wrong answers."

What did I want? I'd never had a choice until Dev had taken me back home. Other than that, since the moment I was born and my abilities started showing, I'd had a destiny. Not a choice.

"I need sunlight. I don't think I can live on a station with fake light and no real movement of time again. Not for any length of it. I think that might make me nuts."

Blaze nodded slowly, but Kellan let go of me. "I'm going to go work with the guys and make a list of places that work like that. Get some more sleep. I'm up now, and my mind is spinning. When it's morning, we'll have some examples of things you can have."

I turned toward Kellan. "Are you sure? You don't have to run off in the middle of the night."

"I need almost no sleep. Blaze is still tired. Besides, I think this is technically going to be his night on that list he has Anders making. I'll get my own, eventually."

As Kellan threw on his shirt, remaining shoeless, he rushed from the room. Next to me, Blaze laughed, a low sound. "He loves a project. Always did. I used to..."

His voice drifted off. "You used to?"

"When we weren't in cryogenic sleep—where most of us had our worst nightmares—I used to give him busy work on the ship. The thing was, it never was busy work for him. I'd ask him to get something working better, even if I didn't need it to, and he would get it done. Inevitably, I'd be grateful I'd asked. We'd have a reason everything went better, because Kellan fixed it. This will be that. In the morning, there will be the best choices there could be for you."

I ran my finger down his nose. "I don't remember my dreams from cryo."

"You should feel grateful for that."

I supposed that I did. "Thanks for talking me through this."

He was quiet for a long moment. "Be one of mine. Belong to me. Different than the rest of them do. And I don't mean solo. I think they'd all kill me if I suggested it. I mean...just be mine. Let me take care of you like I do them."

I pressed my mouth to his. "Does that mean you won't leave me? Won't dump me off and make me someone else's problem?"

His mouth moved under mine into a grimace. "I won't ever leave you. And if you leave me, I'll chase you. We both know that now. If I don't hear you...when you need something...bang me over the head until I do. I'll get there. I haven't had training in the Chen Empire on how to be human. I don't know that Wade or Trenton have been the best examples. They might need some training, too. Maybe you can teach all of us."

I shook my head. "I think I might need some training. I don't really fit in doing normal things. I had no idea what to do with the nice women who took me out on Mars Station. Waverly. Amber. Diana. Paloma. I didn't fit in."

He kissed my nose. "Well, you fit in with me. With us. We can be a ship of misfits. How's that? Say yes. Let me keep you safe from Evander and tucked against my heart."

I wanted to be Blaze's. I wanted to be part of this group. They hated Dev, and yet they'd let him on for me. They were going to fit him in somehow. They wanted me. This was the most judgment-free zone I'd ever been in.

"Yes, keep me, Blaze. Let me be one of yours. Part of this family you made."

His smile was broad against my lips. "I'd never thought of it like that. But yes, we're family. I think you might very well be our center, Sienna. I love that idea."

I kissed him, harder this time. I wanted the connection, needed it, in a way I couldn't remember feeling before. Was it possible to make sentiment mean even more if the physical connected it? I only felt people's pain, never these moments.

He breathed hard against me. "If we do this... I'm as new to it as you are. I've only ever experienced it in a machine that they'd put us in to restrain our sexual urges. I'd see images, feel things, but they weren't real. I don't want to disappoint you."

I shook my head. "I think I might be more apt to disappoint you. I've never had any experience. Not even a machine. What kinds of things...did you like?"

His smile was fast. "I can't even remember right now. I

guess we'll both stumble through, and, sweetheart, I can guarantee you won't be disappointing in any possible way."

Giggling at the idea of stumbling through, all laughter escaped me when he kissed me again. Instead, heat moved through my body, stealing all mirth from the moment and replacing it with seriousness I'd never felt the likes of before. I wrapped my arms around his neck, drawing him closer until I could caress the hair on the back of his head. He kept it so short, there wasn't much for me to run my fingers through, but I had the need and so I did it anyway.

Blaze caught his breath for a second, his body hardening. Still, he didn't rush the moment, just kissing me as I did him, lying in the darkness like we had every right to be doing this. Which somehow, we did.

He placed his hand on the side of my face, stroking his thumb heavily against my cheekbone. Suddenly, I needed this more than I ever did anything else. Blaze was air. I had to breathe him in. He continued to kiss me, but in the moments that passed, it became more intense. He ran his tongue over my bottom lip before he pushed it between them, dancing with my own. He tasted like mint, and I might very well get addicted to it. The man was beautiful. Lethal. And right then, all mine.

His total focus on me, it overwhelmed my senses, keeping me in the moment with him. What did it matter what happened anywhere else, as long as I could be wrapped up in Blaze?

Blaze might not know what he was doing, but his kisses indicated that he did. I sighed, but that quickly turned into a moan. The back of his short hair wasn't enough anymore. I had to pull him closer, practically digging my fingernails into his neck when I did. He jerked against me, getting harder, the bulging in his pants growing ever more present as the minutes ticked by.

He traced his hands over all of my curves.

I clenched my thighs together, not sure why I did that. I truly had no idea what I was doing. I just needed this need that was forming inside of me to do something.

"Blaze. I don't know..." I wasn't sure what I was even going to say to him right then.

"I do. I think."

I was glad he knew what I didn't. Blaze pulled my shirt over my head, discarding it to the side of the bed. Without his shirt, he was a daunting figure, and now that we were both that way, the only thing I wanted to do was press my nipples against his skin. Acting on instinct, which was all I could manage in the moment, I gave into the primal urge.

He reached between us, taking my nipple in his hand and squeezing it. A jolt of pain rocked through me, but it was beautiful, easy. I loved it. How could pain be pleasure? I didn't know, but I wasn't complaining. As he moved toward me, the covers we had shared scrunched up and fell over, draping over the side of the bed like a waterfall. For a second, I was stunned by the feelings, as though small things could have large significance in moments like this one, enough to knock me from thinking altogether.

I laid my palms against his chest, scraping my fingers gently over the muscles, the distinct lines of them. Blaze wasn't the biggest man on this ship, and yet he exuded power as though he were made to lead, made to be in charge, and all of that came from the cells beneath his skin. They coated his body in command.

Reaching forward, I planted a kiss over his heart, mostly so that I could feel his heartbeat. He had an advantage over me, he could hear mine drumming away. I needed a sensory touch to do the same. And I was so glad to have it.

He kissed my neck, the place on my shoulder that led to my collarbone, and I had no idea what to do in return. I kissed him wherever I could reach him, his chest, his arm. His chin. He smiled at me, warmth in his gaze, and what I now recognized as ownership. That was okay. Right then, I wanted to be owned by him.

I wanted to belong here, and I wanted more of what Blaze was doing with his hand. He stroked down my spine, stopping right over my butt. My whole body tingled. Oh hell, I needed...something. I bit down on his chest, and he moaned, a loud, filling sound that moved through my body.

Blaze stared down at me. "Do that again."

He liked it? That was great, because if he hadn't, I really wouldn't have wanted to have made him mad. That would have defeated the purpose of these moments.

I bit down again, tasting the salt on his skin. He moaned, this time his body jerking. "Fuck. I just remembered what I used to do in that machine."

He had? I opened my mouth to ask him what that was, but he'd scooted down, throwing the remainder of the blanket off the bed entirely. Blaze wasn't gentle when he spread my legs apart. Cold air hit me on the hot, aching spot of my core that wanted him in a way I'd never wanted anyone before. His mouth came down on me. I gasped. I hadn't thought that was going to happen. I mean, I guess I knew it could, but not to me, and oh...yes.

First, he started with the bundle of nerves that sometimes throbbed when I thought too much about this stuff. He tongued it, and I gasped. His mouth was warm, his tongue soft and gentle.

"Blaze." I grabbed onto his hair. "I...I..."

"Just relax. I promise you're going to love it. Let me."

I was certainly not going to say no. Then he tongued me inside. I couldn't believe how his hot breath added to the sensation, how I wanted more and more. What was this build up inside of me? I'd never felt anything quite like it before. Soon, I was crying out, digging my hands into the back of his hair. He didn't stop, didn't try to pull away. Blaze jerked his hips against the bed. That was sexy. Funny. I could hardly think, but I could focus on that.

As the pleasure faded, I panted, unable to catch my breath. My heart raced. That was...that was...

Blaze looked up at me, a smile on his face I'd never seen before on him. He scooted closer until he could kiss me. "That was wonderful. Thank you."

He was thanking me? I'd been the one to have the orgasm. That didn't make much sense to me. No, I pulled him down, and he let me. "We're not done."

With an intense gaze, he kissed the end of my nose. "We don't have to."

"I want to."

"Okay." He slipped down just a little to position his cock by my entrance.

I stared up at him for a second. Pleasure still raced through my veins, and I was sure I could handle anything and everything. Were those nerves on his face? No, I had to imagine the stress I saw there, because Blaze, leader of Super Soldiers, couldn't possibly be worried about having sex with me. Could he?

I didn't get to dwell on those questions. He pressed inside of me, gently, but he was huge. My muscles clenched around him, and it seemed like it took forever for him to be able to push inside. I winced. There was pain involved in this, and I hadn't realized it would be this much discomfort. But then he finally made it all the way in.

Blaze sighed, staring down at me. "I'm hurting you."

"Yes, but it's lessening." I didn't want him to pull out. Would that undo everything we'd just done? Why did people like this?

He shifted slightly and pressed his finger on top of my clit. Oh, that I liked. Much better. He did it again and started to move slightly. My body almost sighed, all of it relaxing. Yes, I liked this. I more than liked it. The more he did it, the better it became. Eventually, it didn't hurt at all to have him inside of me. In fact, there was a rightness to it. I giggled. He was *inside* of me. That should have been bizarre, but it wasn't. I spread my legs wider, lifting my hips to meet his thrusts, and oh yes, it was so much better.

I held onto Blaze, not caring how this went anymore. I just wanted more, wanted him...no, needed him. Blaze moaned against my ear. Once, then again. He was quiet, but not for long. Soon, he was meeting my moans. We filled the room with the sounds of our pleasure as our bodies pushed against each other, wanting more and more.

And then finally, and somehow all of a sudden, it was over. I came against his cock, but he wasn't done. I held on while his body shuddered in mine, finally coming on a sigh that was the most beautiful sound I'd ever heard.

For the longest time, we stayed like that. I held onto him, hearing his breaths and trying to find my own. This was...wow.

He rolled me over and slowly pulled out of me, his mouth on mine when he did. Blaze jumped from the bed, grabbing his covers and throwing them onto the bed while he walked to the bathroom. He came out holding a wet rag that he used to wipe me.

We hadn't said a word to each other, and I didn't know what to say. What was traditional now? He scooted next to me, pulling me against him. "I get it now."

Lifting my head, I studied the hard angles of his profile. "What's that?"

"I get what it is to be human. I didn't, I don't think, until this. To be human is to fight tooth and nail to protect this, to protect you. Sienna, you were already mine, but now, I'm not ever letting you go. Wherever you want to go, whatever you want to do, I'll take you there. Forever. Do you understand? I'm yours."

I kissed his chin. "I wouldn't want to do anything without you."

He smiled over at me. "Good. Although I've done so much... Never mind, not right now. Scoot down. You need to sleep, and I'm going to try to for solidarity."

That made me laugh. Maybe it shouldn't have, but it was funny. Blaze shook his head. "I wasn't even trying to be funny."

I knew that, which made it even funnier. That was how I fell asleep, still giggling on and off, in his arms.

If he slept, I really had no idea. All I knew was that when my dreams went dark, they quickly scurried away, sent somewhere else by a strong hand on my back and the feeling of being held in the arms of the strongest man I'd ever known, who just shared something with me I'd never imagined having in my life.

Maybe I really wasn't alone. Not even in sleep.

━━━

I woke when Blaze got out of bed. He turned toward me, kissing my cheek. "You don't have to get up. I just need to speak to Devil. Go over the rules if he's staying on this ship with us."

Was that his intention? Didn't he need to get back to the Chen Empire? My head was still too fogged from sleep to think that clearly. "Is it morning?"

"Yep. But early. Sleep some more. I'll send someone to bring you breakfast."

No, they weren't here to wait on me. I forced myself to sit up. Had my body ever been this sluggish before? I admired Blaze as he dressed. He really was so muscular. After I sat up, I put my hand on his arm just to feel his skin beneath the pads of my fingers. He stopped dressing to smile at me. I might never get used to him doing that so readily, so easily.

Blaze was so serious most of the time.

"Evander will never get you, Sienna, but neither do you have to spend your life hiding some place you hate. Today, we decide where you want to go. Okay?"

I cleared my throat. "Most of all, I don't want anyone getting hurt. I needed to go home, to see it, but now that seems foolish. Everyone here could be hurt because I did that. Or even maybe more than just here. If they want me that badly, it's sort of my duty to hide and see to it that no one else is injured."

"That can be your choice." He pulled his shirt over his head. "But I sort of hope it's not. I looked around that room when I wasn't focusing on the right things with you, and all I could see was people who somehow manage to have very great lives despite how awful things have been. They've been through hell, and I'm not making light of that, but shouldn't we get to try to have that chance? Don't we get to say that we're planting ourselves somewhere and making it work, even if it means fighting Evander right there, too?"

I swallowed. "I don't know, Blaze. I've never had much of a life when it comes down to it. I've always lived mine for other people."

He leaned down to kiss me. "Well, get ready to feel what it is to have all of us live for you."

That was so sweet, it made me want to cry. It couldn't be that easy. Nothing ever really was. Not for me, anyway. In seconds, Blaze was done dressing. I chewed on my bottom lip. Pick a life, Sienna. Really?

I SHOWERED, ate, and drank coffee before I found my way into the command center. As he'd promised, Blaze had sent someone—namely Anders—to bring me some food. He'd told me where everyone would be waiting for me. And sure enough, they were.

Walking in, my cheeks reddened as every gaze in the room turned toward me. They all had to know what had happened with Blaze and me. Their ability to hear everything would make this sort of thing awkward for sure. Well, except for Trenton and Wade. They couldn't hear, but I was quite certain by now they'd know from the others.

Only no one looked at me with any unusual emotions on their faces.

"Morning." Wade sat at the end of the long table. "How are you feeling today?"

Ever the doctor. I looked down at the readout on my arm. It held steady at three. No movement up or down on me. "Looks like I'm feeling well."

His smile was fast. "Don't assume you have to go by the

numbers on your wrist. You can decide if you feel well based on just how you...you know, feel."

Trenton threw his head back. "Wade is not particularly articulate this morning."

"And you are?" Wade threw his cup at Trenton. Fortunately, it looked to be empty, since nothing spilled.

Corbin shook his head. "Keep them up one night going over things, and they both end up acting like little boys who need naps." He turned to wink at me. "You doing okay this morning? Blaze take good care of you last night?"

Trenton spit out his coffee, and my cheeks heated up so badly that I wasn't sure they'd ever cool down. "Um..."

Trenton shook his head. "Nope. Corbin, that's one of those things we don't do. In this scenario, that's a no-no."

For his part, Corbin looked around the room, confusion showing in the way he rocked back on his feet. "I wasn't talking about the sex. I know we're all supposed to act like we don't know about that. I was asking how she slept."

Was it possible to curl up in a ball and roll out of the room and just keep rolling until this conversation stopped? Was it...

Blaze walked into the room, followed by Dev. They both looked at me for a long second before Blaze shot Corbin a look. "Stop embarrassing her. We talked about this. Well, Trenton did. There are topics that are just better unsaid."

He threw his hands in the air. "I didn't say them."

What were the other topics? I almost asked, but Kellan walked fast to the front of the room. "Should we go over what we all discussed while you were, ah, sleeping?"

Devil laughed as I sank deeper into my chair. "Sure. I mean, yes, please. I'd like to hear what you worked on."

He nodded. "We came up with a list of five places. All

of them have pluses and minuses. As far as I'm concerned, there are really only two that would completely work."

"Kellan." Anders shook his head. "Show her the whole thing. We don't all agree with you on there only being two."

Devil leaned against the wall, his concentration on what they were doing up there. Whatever issue they had with him, no one was acting like he didn't belong right now. Had Blaze sorted the whole thing out? Or were they all just pretending to be fine because I was there?

He nodded like he thought what Kellan had on the board was correct, while in the meantime, I couldn't figure out what I was looking at. I was like a child again with how little I knew about anything. I hadn't cared for ignorance then, and I liked it less now.

He pointed at a map. "First up is Sandler Space. There is a moon in the center that is habitable for life. It gets sunlight about twenty hours of the day. And a nighttime rotation of eight hours. You don't seem to sleep more than that, Sienna. Not that we can tell. I mean, we've had no time to work on a schedule or figure out your routine, but for the most part, it doesn't seem to any of us that you sleep that long."

"She sleeps in spurts," Dev spoke up. "Like she needs it all of a sudden. But no, I don't think eight straight hours at a time, so that it is not too little of a night for her."

I held up my hand. "Eight would be plenty, and even if it's not, it's not like there aren't shades, right? We can darken rooms, can't we?"

Kellan looked at Anders. "She makes a very good point."

"So this one is complicated because Sandler Space is very unstable right now." Corbin spoke from the corner. "No one is really in charge there, which is fine. Let the people work out their own governments. We don't need companies like Evander to step in and create stability or whatever."

I didn't follow his thinking. "Why is that a downside?"

"Because of the potential for uprising," Devil answered for Corbin. "And he's right to think about that. I wouldn't have. I would have seen it as a positive. Easy to hide in chaos. But we're not hiding anymore, according to Blaze. We're going to settle and face an attack head on. So the chaos doesn't add benefit, it decreases it. If we're waiting for Evander. We don't need to also worry that some idiot who wants to control the moon shows up with a machete. That screws up the planning."

Trenton rose. "Or even worse, the guy with the machete is not an idiot. He has legitimate claim for the place, and we have to kill him when he actually deserves to be there. My fight has always been against the Sandler Cartel. The people who supported him are still there. If I have a vote, I'd rather not go there."

That made complete sense to me. "You have a vote. Everyone has a vote. Listen, I'm not even sure I should have one. I just don't want to live without the sun. As for the rest of it, I think it should probably be all of you who decide. I'm sort of beyond my depth here."

Anders was by my side so fast, it made my head spin. One second, he wasn't there, the next, he was. "You're not beyond your depth. The concept of home is foreign for me. For Corbin. For Kellan and Blaze. Devil may have more of a sense of it, having been on Earth, and Trenton and Wade both once had one. But most of us didn't. We want to make you happy. After we beat Evander, we can stay wherever we've picked. We can make a go at it."

Wade ran a hand through his hair. "Been a long time for

me. But yes, I remember, and honestly, I'm not sure that one place isn't as good as another. What will we find? People. Some of them will be great, others awful. Some of them might even betray us. That's what happens with homes. They let you down. I don't care where we go, as long as we stay together."

I lifted my head to regard him. "That's not true though, is it? You picked a home, sort of, for your brother and sister. How did you go about doing that?"

"Venus wasn't thought to be on anyone's hit list during the war. The school was good. It seemed like a good fit. Honestly, I just wanted them safer, which meant getting them away from me."

Corbin pointed at the board. "Venus is on our list."

Now, that caught my attention. "Really? We could go to where Wade's family is?"

"We could." Corbin smiled. "As he said, Venus isn't on any important targets list. Give us time to buckle in, to get ourselves set up to handle the assault. They might not look for us there. Although, if it were me, that's right where I'd look for us. I'd have someone sitting there waiting to see if we showed up."

I rose, sitting still didn't seem to go with how jittery my hands were. I just needed to move. "So we can't go to Venus. There are kids there we can't put at risk."

"There are kids everywhere." Devil walked up behind me, placing his hand on the small of my back. It was a comforting presence. "Kids live everywhere we would go. Unless we found an abandoned planet. They do exist. But it would have nothing we needed set up to survive. We'd have to start from scratch."

Corbin ran a hand through his hair. "I think that could be kind of awesome. If we weren't at risk of being attacked by Evander. Like if it were just the eight of us, I can't think of anything I'd like more. Just make some world for us. Start over. Who cares about social norms or trying to figure how to fit in with other people? We have our own little spot of the universe where we can just be ourselves."

Dev shrugged. "You're smart enough to figure out how to fit in socially, if you want to. That became very clear with the Chens. When I went through their indoctrination time. Anyway, you are certainly intelligent enough to work that out, if I remember from your training."

They all turned to stare at him. Devil had just brought up a time when they'd really all hated each other. Blaze cleared his throat. "Let's keep going."

"I can't mention that I trained them? Before you did? I can't even bring up that I actually know them?"

Blaze smirked. "I thought you were really good with social norms."

"Okay." Trenton swung around in his chair. "Enough with that. I don't personally hate you, Devil, if that helps. I mean, I could kill you because you took our girl, placed her in danger, and were ultimately responsible for her being sick. But I don't hate you. I don't equate hate with death. Anyway, next up. What's the next planet?"

They never got to answer, as Kellan jumped to his feet, his eyes on his tablet. I guessed he was flying Artemis. I never could tell which one of them was doing that. "Incoming."

Everyone dashed from the room except Wade, who grabbed on to my arm. I stared at him for a long second. "Evander?"

"Yep. Come. You're with me."

I got to my feet just as we jarred left, an explosion rocking the ship. Wade and I both went flying. I hit the table next to me, and Wade went into the wall. My ears rang from the explosion, and a second later, Wade was next to me.

"You okay?" he shouted at me.

My head spun, but I forced myself to sit up. "I think so. What the heck happened?"

"We got hit." He pulled me against him, and we walked together, or maybe a better description was limped, from the room. "It happens sometimes. Depending on the damage, they'll do a few things. I know they don't want to evade anymore. They want to conquer. I have no idea what role this will play, if any."

Alarms sounded, and he had to shout for me to hear him. Wade wasn't moving much better than I was. Maybe he was just more used to it. They had been at war a long time before I woke up from cryo. This was likely not his first time.

We made it to the med bay, and he patted the table. "Jump up. I'll look at your ankle."

That was when I spotted the blood on him. I gasped. "Forget me. I twisted my ankle. You're bleeding. Badly."

Blood dripped down his leg, I could see it pooling around his ankle where his pants were up a little bit from his shoes. He shook his head. "I'm sure it's nothing."

Wade? I spoke in his head to make my point.

"Maybe I shouldn't say this, particularly now, but when you do that, it makes me instantly hard." He rubbed his eyes. "Fuck. I shouldn't have said that."

I liked it. I'd have liked it more if he wasn't bleeding, there wasn't an alarm blaring, Evander wasn't attacking, and we weren't being thrown around in the sky.

"Are you okay? I mean, I know you're bleeding, but you don't seem exactly yourself."

He rubbed at his eyes. "I don't know. I think I may have hit my head. But we'll deal with that in a few moments. Doctors don't go into the med machine in the middle of a battle."

We jerked left again, and I held onto the table to not fall over. Wade did the same. He shook his head. "Let me look at your ankle."

"Let's not worry about my ankle. I can put weight on it. It'll wait until after we deal with whatever this is." I swallowed. "Let's look at your ankle and talk about your head. You get on the table."

He stared at me for a second before he stumbled onto the shaking table. There had to be a better system for handling this than shaking, dangerous ships. Did people really just live like this?

And it was my fault.

Wade ripped his pants, that were torn anyway, and dropped the bottom end. "Yep. I'm a little dizzy."

Whether that was from his head injury or the fact that blood gushed down his leg was questionable. I stared at his knee. Okay. I hated blood, but I was going to be brave about this and take a look. He had a huge gash, and blood rushed out of it, but there was nothing visibly in the knee. That was something. I hoped.

"Um, that doesn't look good. Right?"

He winced. "No, it doesn't. And truthfully, I have no idea what did it. I'm a little bit out of it. We are going to treat these things until I can get in the machine. First things first, we need to clean it and flush it out."

His voice was getting more and more slurred the more he spoke. That was a very bad sign. "Wade," I touched his shoulder. "Listen to me. You're not okay. You need to go in that machine right now."

He held onto my arms. "You're right. I think it's my head." He squinted at me. "Don't know how I didn't notice."

We could figure that out later. "Into the machine. Sooner in, sooner out. Okay? But I don't know how to run the thing."

"In this case, just press power and go. Not perfect, but it works, mostly. Fuck." He put a hand on his eye, and I tried to help him down and into the machine, which was made twice as hard since Artemis was officially dancing in space. It was loud. Alarms were sounding and I had no time to be scared, because the doctor needed me to take care of him, even though I had next to no idea how to do this.

Well, I had some idea. Press power. Press go. Yes, I could do those things. I hoped. Or I'd scream for help, and one of the guys would hear me and come. Even though that would mean they were stopping what they were doing, which I was sure was more important than helping me press power.

Despite my obsessing, I got Wade into the machine. He helped more than he hindered. "Power. And Go."

He sort of nodded. "I'll fix your ankle when I get up."

"Sure." I bent over and kissed him. Surprise showed in his eyes before he closed them. I quickly shut the lid on the machine and hit power. Lights flickered. That was a good sign that I'd done something correctly. Then I hit go. A whooshing sound started.

Oh thank the universe, it worked. I let out a breath I held. But now what?

I didn't have a job in this situation, except to hold onto something and manage not to fall on my face. I'd no sooner thought that than another explosion, similar to the one earlier, happened again. It didn't matter how hard I held on,

I flew backward into the wall. My head rang, and I sank down to the floor, darkness pulling me under.

I woke to pain and strong hands lifting me off the ground. It was Anders.

"Sienna? You with me?" His voice was low, rough. There was black soot on his face, and his shirt was torn. That was the first thing I thought through the pounding in my head, before a second thought dawned on me in utter horror.

All my shields were down.

Every bit of the mental imagery I used to close down the use of my power was gone. Why? I had no idea. This had never happened, not since I'd learned how to do this as a child.

I was wide open, and whether I wanted to or not, I was going to take on everything that Anders was feeling right then. It rushed at me, and he gasped.

"I can't control it." I managed to tell him as his pain hit me hard. Not of the physical variety, but every terrible thing he'd been carrying around inside of him for...well, forever. I laughed. It wasn't funny, but these guys thought they weren't dealing with real human interaction? Oh, they certainly were. And then some.

Loneliness. Pain. Terror. Those were just some of the few. Anger. That was a big one.

"Sienna, you don't have to do this. You don't have to take it."

So he was feeling the transfer by now. How could he not? "I...I don't mind, Anders. I can't stop right now. I can't control it. And it's you."

As I spoke the words, I meant them. This was Anders. He was one of mine. Why would I have this ability, if not to help him? "Give it to me."

He shook his head, but didn't drop his arms. It would be hard now, even for a Super Soldier. Oh, his pain went deep. I closed my eyes against it as my raging headache warred with the pain from Anders. His was worse. Tears leaked from my eyes. This poor man. How was he getting through the days feeling this all the time? I opened my eyes to gaze at him.

"No," Anders spoke through gritted teeth. "I'm not forcing this on you. That's my pain. Not yours. But...damn. I can see why they want you. Fuck. It's like a drug. It's taken control of me, and it's like euphoria."

I touched his cheek. "Nothing to do if I can't stop it."

I wasn't even sure if I wanted to. I could do this. It was something I could do. He needed this.

"Yes you can." He flared his nostrils. "You're hurt, so you need to dig deep for the strength. I know you can do it." He called over his shoulder. "I need someone. Now."

The ship wasn't shaking. Did that mean it was over? I drifted, just the pain moving me to tears, nothing to do but endure it, nothing but endless nothing. Nothing to look forward to. They weren't my thoughts. They'd been Anders' at some point. Not currently. He wasn't in that much emotional strain at the moment, which was great.

"Look at me." He shook me gently. "Breathe with me. Count to four and search for it. You can find the will power to shut it down. You're in control of your abilities. Not the other way around. Breathe with me."

The door opened and closed. Devil was there. He was equally as beat up as Anders. If he came over, I'd get his pain, too. The dual experience might be too much for me. I'd never tried doing this for more than one person at a time. Not to mention, I'd never done it with my shields down either.

"Don't come too close," Anders spoke over his shoulder. "Go get a sedative. We might need it. And your ship had a med machine. Get that moved in here just as fast as you can."

Dev didn't argue. Instead, he turned and ran.

"Look at me," Anders ordered again. His shoulders started to slump. He'd need to sleep after this. Maybe for a good long while. Letting go of the stuff we lugged around inside of us was hard. Maybe the hardest thing in the world. "Come on. You can do it, Sienna. Find the ability to block me out. I know you can."

He believed I could do that? How funny. I wasn't sure I could even lift my arms again after this. Still, he looked incredibly sure of himself. So I did what he asked. I looked. There they were. My walls. Not that they were physical walls. They were more like mental blocks I'd put in place to keep this ability where it belonged, locked away, unless I said otherwise.

They were mental pictures I used that looked like literal walls. Yes, I could see them. As a rush of loneliness threatened to drag me under, I pushed at the images until they moved in my mind like a picture book. Quickly, they took place, moving where they were supposed to be, where they should have been the whole time.

Drip by drip, my openness to his emotions shut off like a leaky faucet being fixed. We stared at each other, both of us breathing hard. He touched the side of my cheek. "How long does it last?"

"What?" My thoughts were clouding over again. It was hard to think. "Are we safe?"

"No. But we are momentarily okay. How long until my pain comes back to me and leaves you?"

That was a hard, loaded question. "Some of it will never

return to you. It'll stay with me until it dissipates. Some of it will return soon. There are some types of grief that I can't keep away from you. They're yours; they're not mine to keep. They're too much."

He nodded. "I don't want you carrying my burdens. They're not yours. You've done nothing to earn them, you don't need their punishment."

"It's what I was made to do." Why didn't he understand? If that illustrated anything, it was how out of control I was to any of this. I'd been born with these abilities. Who was I fooling, thinking I could decide when and where I used it?

He kissed me lightly on the lips. "You're concussed. You're scared and not at your best. But let me assure you, that was not what you were made to do. I can see why they want to weaponize you. I won't let them. You're mine." He paused. "Ours. Wade has more time in that machine. So we're going to put you in Devil's."

The aforementioned man ran in, pulling a machine behind him that was being pushed on the other side by Corbin. Dev swung around. "I've got the sedative from my ship."

Anders nodded. "We're going to give her a dose and put her in the machine. The dose because I know what you're feeling right now, and I don't want it messing with your healing."

What was I feeling? Too much. I closed my eyes. I could ignore this. I'd gotten good at it over the years. This had been a daily punishment for existing that my life forced me to endure. Take other people's pain, and live with it. If they just left me alone, I could lie there and ignore it.

"I don't know that I need meds."

Anders shook his head. "I won't do it if you say no, but

I'm asking you not to. The machine works better if you're not feeling like hell when you get in. Emotionally. It's the brain waves."

Corbin and Devil both squatted down next to me. Dev touched my cheek gently. "I'm sorry you got hurt, Sienna. This will be okay."

I nodded. "Okay. Give me the dose."

Why the heck not?

A HAND BRUSHING hair off my face woke me from the haze where I floated.

"Hey there, beautiful. Time to wake up. They gave you quite a dose of that sedative." Wade's voice drifted toward me, and I forced my lids open to look at him.

Everything was sort of foggy. "What's going on?"

"You and I had matching concussions." He kissed the end of my nose. "We're both okay, now. I heard you in my head when I woke up."

Had I been calling out to him? "I don't remember doing that."

"I love that you reach for me in your sleep."

I reached up close enough so that he could kiss me, and he did. We weren't in the med bay. That was all I knew. Other than that, my sole focus was on getting Wade to kiss me. I wouldn't have known before that moment that it was possible for my nipples to ache. Were we alone? I didn't know, but I suspected we were. Wade was quiet in his desire for me. I doubted he'd be speaking such sweet words if we were in the presence of others.

Of course, we always kind of were.

I smiled at the thought. It was amazing how well I'd adjusted to that.

His own grin met mine as our lips pressed together. "I'm not sure what's making you smile like that, but I like it."

I brushed the hair off his forehead. "Feeling a little bit goofy."

"They completely gave you too much sedative, but I applaud their effort to do something for you so you'd heal better. When did you get concussed? I have very little memory of the time between the explosion and the med machine."

That made sense. He'd been pretty dang out of it. I looked around. Okay. I was in my room. But something felt off. Different. I rubbed at my eyes. "Something is wrong."

He nodded. "We're not in space."

I sat up. "Where are we then? Mars Station?" That hadn't felt like this. It was the lack of the rumble of the engines I was feeling. When we'd docked on Mars Station, it had still been there. Just this deep, ever-present rumble that I'd managed to tune out over time, but now, couldn't help but notice the lack of.

"No. We're somewhere in the Dark Planets zone." He lay down next to me, staring at the ceiling. "You and I slept right through a really big crash landing."

We crashed? I'd never heard of that happening. "What? Is everyone okay?"

"Yes. Which is good, since I was too out of it to help. Everyone is utterly fine. Even Anders, who conked out for a couple of hours after his encounter with your abilities."

I bet he had. His pain was deep inside me now. I'd shed it eventually. Until then, I had to live with it. Not that I would tell him about it. My melancholy would be my own.

Learning to fake being happy was one of the things I'd been trained to do. I was good at it.

"So we're somewhere in the Dark Planets. Where is Evander? Did we get them?"

He sighed. "That's the problem. We don't know. Our sensors are damaged, the coms down. We got a distress call out to Mars Station, we think, before it all went to hell. Then Trenton managed to get the ship down safely before it all blew. Poor Artemis. She's had better days."

And here I had been asleep through the whole thing? "I...I can't believe I slept through it."

"Well technically, the machines kept us that way. As long as they were working, we weren't waking up before they wanted us to. I took you out about an hour ago. Brought you in here."

The sound of a buzzing, saw-like sound reached my ears. I forced myself to sit up all the way. "How are you feeling? And what is that noise?"

"That is, I think, Corbin cutting us out of the ship. Right now, we can't get off. He's sawing through the doors to get them open so we can exit. Then they will assess the damage and figure out if we can fix her or abandon her."

Abandon her? I hadn't been on this ship very long, but it felt like we should do better than that. Just because she was older, and maybe not at her finest, didn't mean we should simply leave her here to be looted or whatever. She'd kept me safe when I'd been in cryogenics. This was once Melissa Alexander's ship. I imagined she had lots of stories. No, whatever we did, it couldn't be abandonment. Even if someone didn't quite fit in the world, that didn't mean we just up and threw them away.

I rubbed at my eyes. I was really getting personal about

Artemis. The guys wouldn't just rid themselves of Artemis unless they had no other choice. I didn't think.

"Should we go help?"

Wade grinned at me. "We should. But you're in no condition right now. You're still doped up."

I looked around. Was I? "How can you tell?"

He pointed at my eyes. "That way. Your pupils. They're not quite right yet. Come lie down. They've kept the temperature nice on this part of the ship for you. It is a million degrees out where they all are."

"That many, huh?"

He winked at me. "That's a totally accurate description. Scientific and everything."

I liked this version of Wade. He was so easy going right now. It was almost as if I'd taken his pain away, too. "You're very relaxed."

He drew me to him, and I put my head on his chest. "Well, you kissed me before you put me in the machine. I've been in an excellent mood ever since. And then there was the kissing just now. Puts me in a pretty good mood."

His heart beat steadily. "I keep thinking dark thoughts, Wade. You might want to run away, not get closer."

He was quiet for a moment before he placed a gentle kiss on my temple. "What kinds of dark thoughts?"

"The kinds that are wrapped up in the fact that everyone is potentially getting hurt because of me. The kind that wonders if I shouldn't have just let Evander have me, because then my father would be okay and not missing, and you all wouldn't be wrapped up in this shit. The kind that feels pretty worthless, since the only thing I can do is something I don't want to do. The kind that realizes I have no value on this ship to help anyone."

The screeching of the saw got louder. Was that a good sign or bad? I didn't even know.

Wade placed another kiss on my temple. I loved that he did that. It was so gentle, such a caring thing to do. "I don't like the idea that you'd give yourself to a corporation that makes babies in labs in order to send them to battle. That kills the babies that maybe don't measure up in infancy." He rolled over, bringing me with him so that we faced each other, side to side. "I often feel useless on this ship. And overwhelmed by the fact that I can't do what the Super Soldiers do. Trenton never feels that way, and I wish I had his abundance of self-worth."

I swallowed. "Do you ever wish you hadn't been saddled with me?"

"I don't think of it that way." He brought my hand to his heart. "I followed you. They came to get you, to keep you from Evander, and I ran after you. Before I'd ever met you. Sienna, I'm devoted. Even in that chamber, you did something to me. Forgive me if that is weird or too much. But it's real. And that's the best I can do."

"It's not too much. I'm just wondering how I can be worth all of this mess. I'm one woman with a moderate amount of power. Why all this fuss from Evander? Why chase me around the galaxy? Why crash ships? Why put lives at risk?" It felt good to say these things aloud.

He tilted his head. "Sienna, you brought Anders to his knees. By the time I woke up, he was out cold. But I heard all about it. That is a man who, if the stories are real, once took out an entire brigade by himself on some planet Evander wanted to take over. You brought him to his knees. Think about the implications of that. You could undo Super Soldiers. Not to mention, if they steadily used you to clear them of whatever weighs them down emotionally, they don't have to put down quite so many people in their crews from emotional bombardment."

I hadn't thought about any of that. Truthfully, I'd presumed it was my zapping skills they'd wanted. "I'm one person. Even me with my abilities, I couldn't do all that."

"So they figure out how you do it, and they weaponize it, basically. Take a bunch of young girls and force the abilities onto them." He groaned. "This is not stuff I want to dwell on too much. Makes me really, really angry. Like I'm going to go steal a shuttle and figure out how to open the black hole and just blow them mad."

I stared down at the number on my wrist. It was up to five. I held it out so he could see. "It's up."

"You were concussed and you overused your abilities. Let's see what twenty-four hours brings."

I nodded. I supposed that made sense. "Okay. I get really nervous about the numbers. It weighs on me."

Wade nodded. "I've got you, Sienna. And you're not a burden for me. You're...redemption."

I kissed him then. Yes, we were crash landed somewhere in the middle of who knew where. Evander could be coming for us any second. We were literally stuck inside of the ship. Right then, I needed Wade. I wasn't going to overthink it. If someone needed us, they'd come get us.

I climbed on top of him. I was no expert on this, having done this exactly once. However, some things were more natural this time. I at least had an idea of what I was going to be doing.

Except, three kisses in, it was clear that I didn't.

Wade pulled back, breathing heavily. "You want to be on top? That's how you like it?"

I opened and closed my mouth once before I could

finally speak. "I don't have that much experience to know. It was just something I was trying."

He winked at me, letting go of me to put his hands on the headboard. "I shouldn't do this with you right now. You're half-zonked. But the thing is, you kissed me when you were perfectly sober. I think you do want me."

I stared down at him. I wasn't feeling particularly loopy. But maybe I just didn't know. "I do want you. I've wanted you from moment one."

Okay...yes, I would probably not usually say that.

His smile was slow. "We're going to try this again when you're not still on sedatives." He kissed my chin. "But for right now we're going to cuddle."

He was hard. I could feel it, and I wanted to grind myself against him. I'd never had the urge before. It was everything I could do to restrain myself. I slowly climbed off him. I was sure he was right.

Only it really, really sucked.

———

I must have dozed off again, because when I woke up, Wade was reading on his tablet. He scanned through fast, swiping the page, and then the next page. How did he do that so fast? Wincing, he kept turning. Something he was reading he didn't like.

"Hey," I said, sitting up and rubbing my eyes. "You okay?"

He set down the tablet. Did he not want me to see what he was looking at? "Yep." His smile was fast. "Morning. Again. I told you that you were out of it before."

I smiled at him. Yep, even I could feel my head was clearer, and thanks to that, Anders pain was much closer to the front of my consciousness right then. I pulled my knees up to my chest and put my forehead on my knees. Loneliness. I shouldn't be feeling them, the emotions weren't my own. But they were Anders' and he lived like this. If having no choice but to drop my shields had done anything to relieve this for him, then I was grateful to it.

Still, I shouldn't be feeling alone when I was pressed up next to Wade on the bed.

He rubbed my back slowly. "Any physical pain I could help with?"

I shook my head. "No. This is...the aftermath."

"What is that you feel?" He kissed the back of my neck. "I'm not a great emotions guy. When we get our comms back up, I can have you talk to Ari. He's a psychiatrist. I am more like a let's-fix-the-bone-and-cure-the-disease kind of a person."

I leaned on him instead of my knees. "I'm feeling lonely. But I don't want to get into too much about this, because they're not my feelings and Anders doesn't talk about these things, I don't think. And they're his private emotions. I just have to kind of deal with them now."

Wade chewed on his lip. "Hate to give this up. Only I know what has to happen. Stay here. Don't move, okay?"

I stared at him as he gently set me against the headboard. "You're leaving?"

"Yep. But you won't be alone. Just wait a second."

Wade threw his blanket off of him and walked quickly from the room, putting his shoes on as he did it. I told him I was lonely, so he left? I groaned. Seriously, I might never understand men. Had I gone too dark? I probably had.

What did he mean I wouldn't be alone? I threw my feet over the side of the bed. I rose to chase after him when I spotted his tablet. What had he been reading when I woke up? I touched it, and the screen cleared from the save power mode to show the page he'd been reading.

It was some kind of medical reading. Why had he been making that face about it?

The door opened, but it wasn't Wade coming back. No, Anders stood there. He was shirtless and sweaty. I set down the tablet. "Are you okay?"

He visibly swallowed. "Are you?"

We stared at each other across the room. There was always a certain amount of awkwardness that went on when running into someone I had cleared at some point. That was why I preferred not to see them. But it was different this time with Anders. He belonged to me. Or at least, he wanted to, and I loved the idea as well.

I didn't feel uncomfortable, more like relieved that I'd been able to help.

He crossed to me fast, drawing me to him. I put my head on his sweaty chest. I never thought I'd like this sort of thing, but I did. A lot. Who cared that he was a little messy right now? He was here.

"I'd take it back. Can you do that?" His whisper in my ear was like a caress.

I shook my head. "No, it's mine now. Are you okay? It can be draining."

His laugh was not full of mirth, it was more sardonic. "Yes, I'm fine. You're the one who went through that. I've actually never felt better in my life. No wonder they erected a fortress and called it a temple to protect people like you. Sienna, you'd never be left alone."

I held onto him. "You were the one living like that. For so long. I barely touched a fraction of it. We could have gone for hours."

"No." He pulled back to stare at me. "I told you. I'm

here for you. I'm yours. You aren't going to do that again. Do you understand? Not for me, and frankly, I'm not sure I can stomach the idea of you doing that for anyone. That was painful for you. Your whole body was pale, your eyes vague."

I'd never heard that before, but then again, I'd never had exactly that experience. "I'm okay, and it's not avoidable. Sooner or later, by choice or not, I'll have to do it again."

He kissed me. It was such a sweet embrace that I melted into him. Anders stroked the side of my face. "I just want to keep you safe, and it seems like the last thing I'm able to do. Why can't we put an end to these fuckers? You being here helps. Like from the time you woke up from cryo, there were so many things that were just better. Because you exist. I can't explain it. I just knew you were the one for me. And here you are."

Tears flooded my eyes. "In other words, the loneliness might go away?"

He shook his head. "It's always there waiting to surge forward, like when Devil took you away and I wondered if we'd never see you again, it surged back. I thought okay, yeah, this is familiar. It's just part of things, and now, if I gave it to you..."

I cupped his cheeks. "It'll pass in me. I don't keep what I take. Eventually, I shed it like a bad layer of skin on a snake. I'm going to be okay. It's just going to suck for a few days."

He nodded before he leaned over to kiss me. His lips were smooth, warm. I loved the faint smell of sweat on his body, and I roamed my hands over him. I'd helped him. Every second of the discomfort was worth it.

I kissed him back, relishing in getting to do this with him. His hard body hardened even more, and I sighed against him. He moaned, a small sound in his throat, and I was undone. I wrapped my arms around his neck to try to get closer. He dropped his hand and rubbed it between us, cupping my breast. I jolted under his touch, and he smiled against my mouth.

"You like that?" His voice was a whisper.

"I more than like it."

He nodded. "I take great directions. I'll learn to do whatever you like, even though I am so completely new to this. I think the others are probably..."

I put my finger on his mouth to hush him. "I don't want to talk about the others right now, just us. I'm not exactly swimming in experience. But you said I made you less lonely, and that's such a gift to me. You can't know what that means. I couldn't care less about what you know how to do. Let's figure it out together."

"Sienna." He shook his head. "How are you real? When the universe is so completely filled with nothing but sludge and pain?"

I hated that was his life. I didn't want that for any of us anymore. We needed clear skies. No more being lost in the universe, no more not knowing where and how we belonged. Was it possible? We could belong together?

He laid me down on the bed. "You're amazing, you know that, right? What you did, taking those feelings, I didn't know such a thing was possible. Even seeing what you could do, even knowing it. Experiencing it was something else."

I sighed. "It's just something I was born able to do. Don't be over impressed. Nothing I worked at. Nothing I earned. Like I have blue eyes. I just have it."

He kissed my neck, right at the place where my shirt exposed it. "Guess what? I'm impressed with your eyes, too." He winked at me, which seemed such an un-Anders thing to do. "Deeply, deeply impressed with them."

That filled me with so much warmth. It was such a silly thing, but it really did. "Thank you. They're just eyes."

Anders shook his head. "Not to me. They're gateways to your soul. I want to know all their secrets."

"I have no secrets." I really didn't think that I did. Everything they needed to know about me, they knew already.

He let out a long breath. "Yes, you do."

Anders kissed me, and that effectively cut off what I would have asked him next. What were my secrets? By the universe, I'd work that out later. How could I think when his lips were moving down to kiss my neck again? Oh yes, apparently that was a spot I liked.

I squirmed beneath him, which gave me a good feeling for just how hard he was.

Biting down on my lip, I decided exactly what I wanted. "Flip over."

I would have moved him if I could, but this was Anders. I wasn't going to get him to move unless he wanted to. But he'd told me that he wanted to know what I wanted. Well, I *wanted* this.

He did just as I asked. Leaning down, I kissed him and he kissed me back. He sighed, and I ground against him, digging my core into his cock. His sigh quickly changed to a moan as his hips jerked upward, meeting me in how I moved against him.

Soon we were in a rhythm, grinding against each other while our tongues danced in each other's mouths. He moaned, and so did I. My breasts hardened, my nipples aching. Yes, I wanted this. My insides actually throbbed with need.

He was shirtless. I needed to be. Throwing my shirt away, I rid myself of all of the clothes that were in my way from being entirely naked with him. I tugged at his pants, and he ripped them off, throwing them aside.

I stared at him for a second. Yep, that had happened. He'd ripped his pants right off and thrown them to the side. His cock was right there, blocked only by his briefs, and he must have been hurting from the inability to be free.

Touching it on the outside of the cloth, I met his gaze with my own. He was such a beautiful man. Almost like he wasn't quite real. How could he exist? He thought I was beautiful in a place of darkness? Well, this man needed to take a look at himself.

Because he was stunning.

"Are you going to rip them, too?"

His smile was slow. "Would you like me to?"

Giddiness filled me. "Yep. Do it."

We grinned at each other like neither one of us had a care in the world. Anders finally did just what I wanted, he ripped them right off and threw them wherever his discarded clothes went in this room. He was so strong, he could tear into material like it was nothing at all. He'd barely lifted a muscle. It was like he'd barely moved at all.

And it was so fucking hot, I didn't know what to do with myself.

"Well, here we are." I lifted an eyebrow. "You're stunning, Anders. Really, really beautiful."

"Hey, that's my line, gorgeous."

No, it was totally mine.

HE PRESSED INSIDE OF ME, filling me up. How was this my life? I had thought, and it was the last coherent one I'd have for a while. He pulled out and then pressed back. I couldn't believe how good this felt, how complete I was with him between my thighs.

I'd felt so much pain, taking his emotions inside of me. Now I had him actually with me, inside my body, my thighs wrapped around his waist, holding on for dear life. Anders wasn't all pain and suffering. No, he was actually about pleasure, about adoration, about just feeling like everything really might be okay.

He kissed me as he moved, saying things into my mouth, words I could hardly understand. I loved them just the same. Everything in the whole universe was going to be okay, because he existed.

Yes, I was half out of my mind, but it was a wonderful lunacy. I would drown in this, I would live in this, I would... I never got that thought out, he jerked his hips along my clit, and I came, hard. I called out his name on a gasp, knowing that nothing would ever be the same for me. Not ever again.

He came on a sigh, hardly making a sound at all as he kissed all over my face, finally pushing his forehead to mine. He panted, having a hard time catching his breath, which made me smile. I'd made a Super Soldier lose his breath. That really was something.

Anders kissed my nose. "Don't ever disappear on me, okay? I need to know where you are all the time. I just have to."

That was a big ask, but right then, I didn't mind. I wanted to give it to him. "I'll do my very best. Disappearing tends to be something that happens to me, not something I plan. Although, I suppose I participated in it last time. Dev offered it."

He nodded, an amused look on his face. "Blaze made him his second-in-command."

Now that caught my attention and ripped me out of my carefree haze. Reality rushed back in. "Really? Why did he do that?"

"He didn't share his reasons with me, but my guess would be it forces cohesiveness. We're a pretty good team. We need direction from Blaze, but we actually work really well without having to say anything. It's hard to fit someone in with us. Except for you. That was easy. But now that we have to take orders from Devil, it tells the rest of us that Blaze has confidence in him and that we'd all just better get on board."

I sat up, and he adjusted to hold me next to him. "And how is that going for you? And the others?"

"I guess we'll see how it goes. I worked with Devil once. He never gave me a terrible time. I did my job, and he was satisfied with it. He's a scary motherfucker. Oh, sorry. Language."

Waving my hand, I smiled at him. "I don't care about

the cursing."

Something dinged, and Anders grabbed his tablet. "They're about to open the door. Come on, we should be there. They might need me, and we'll all feel better having you with us. Grab Wade's tablet. He needs it. That's who sent the message. The others just started talking, and I could hear them."

Okay. I guessed we were back to it now. Whatever it was, and whatever my role was going to be. If anything. I'd love to know in what ways I could actually do anything.

We dressed fast, and I managed not to forget Wade's tablet on my way out the door. Anders didn't slow down to wait for me, which just showed how focused he was on getting there. Like he'd thought about it, he swung around. "Sorry." He put out his hand. "I forget sometimes."

"It's fine." I let him lead me because truthfully, I had no idea where I was going. I loved this ship, but I didn't know it that well yet.

That was something I could rectify. I didn't have to be totally out of it if I could at least know my way around Artemis. That would be a great first step to not feel quite so much like a lost child.

We arrived just in time for a loud screeching sound to fill the room. I covered my ears, dropping Anders' hand when I did. The noise didn't last long. A big hole appeared where a door had been. It was hot as hell in the room, not that I'd noticed it right away because of the noise, but the heat hit me hard as soon as the loud intrusive screeching stopped.

"And that," Corbin said with a smile, "as they say, is that." He set the machine that had been cutting a hole in Artemis aside.

Kellan scratched his head. "Who says that?"

"People." Corbin grinned. "People say that."

"Which people?"

"Okay," Devil interrupted. "We can figure out who said what later. It's just an expression, Kellan. You don't have to use it if you don't like it. But we need to go out there, and we need to do it systematically to keep Sienna safe. Evander is probably on this planet somewhere, too." He turned toward Blaze. "Orders?"

Blaze rocked forward on his feet. "Omega Zeta Five. Now."

They moved so fast that it was like a whirlwind of activity I couldn't quite follow. Even Wade and Trenton seemed to know what he meant by that. But of course they did. War did that to people, and they'd all battled together.

Kellan jumped through the door. Hold on. How high up was that door? We were on the ground, but this had to be at least...six feet off the ground. I rushed toward him and looked down as a strong hand grabbed my arm.

Dev shook his head as though he thought I might leap after Kellan.

I turned to him. "I wanted to see, not jump."

And I'd been right. It was really, really high up. I didn't even see Kellan. Where had he gone?

Corbin touched my shoulder. "Excuse me, sweetheart." He winked, and as I moved slightly, Corbin leapt down like Kellan had done. This time, I could watch it. He hit the ground and ran left. Where was he going?

"What's going on? I don't know what the things Blaze said mean."

"It's instructions." Blaze walked toward me. "They all know in what direction I want them to scout. Our systems are mostly down. As you know by how hot it is in here. We kept your section cooled while you were knocked out. But now we'll let them up, too. Once the guys have eyed the perimeter, Trenton will get started checking to see what is wrong with Artemis, and we'll go from there."

Well, that made sense. "Blaze, I don't want to make things difficult, but I need something to do. I can't just stand here. I can't."

He nodded. "Well, as soon as the guys clear the area, you can help Trenton. Legitimately, he's going to need it."

Trenton took my hand. "I really will. It's too much for me to get done in the time we need to get it done in."

He lifted my wrist and looked at the number before making eye contact with Wade. "It's five. Unless it's gone up?"

Wade nodded. "It's five. Just up from the last time I saw it. Sorry, we shouldn't do that. It's rude."

I shrugged. "Don't worry about it."

"No, actually, my mother would be really upset I'd just done that." As he spoke, Anders nodded to both of us before jumping out of Artemis. How much time were they taking before each of them left? Trenton kept speaking. "I was raised with manners, even if I haven't used them in years. I should have asked you if it was okay for me to look, and then spoke aloud to you about you. I know better."

I smiled at him. It was sweet he cared this much. "We can just let it go. It's not a big deal."

"Not a big deal, maybe, if I do it once. A big deal if I make a habit out of it. I won't. And I'm grateful for your help."

Blaze stepped up. "I'm going to leave and go on perimeter. See if we can sniff out Evander before they sniff out us. You'll be with Devil, Wade, and Trenton here. They'll keep you safe."

"One of these days, I'd like to keep all of you safe." I

rocked back on my feet. "But yes, for now, that's fine."

I didn't imagine he'd stay if I'd said otherwise. Although I appreciated the courtesy, considering I knew just how awful Blaze could behave when he wanted to. He winked at me before he jumped out of the ship.

Turning to Dev, I asked a stupid question that I really wanted to know the answer to. "Does it hurt even a little when you jump down there?"

Devil shrugged, smiling at me in that way that made my heart beat faster. He really was so handsome in all of his darkness and hardcore glaring. "I guess if you landed on something the wrong way. Like if you were a dipshit and you landed on something sharp, that could hurt."

Wade groaned. "They're all alike when it comes to the macho. They won't tell you if it hurts. That would be admitting weakness, which they only do when they're almost dead."

I was surprised by Devil's laugh. "Well, if you were potentially killed every time you said something hurt as a child, you'd stop saying it, too. Whiners have no place in the program."

Dev lifted his head. "Trenton, it's clear to the east. If you want to get started in that direction."

"What can I do?" Wade voiced the question I felt I was constantly asking. What could I do? Wade was at least useful a lot of the time.

Trenton scratched his head. "Go into the control room. I'm sorry to ask it. It's going to be hot as hell, but I need you to tell me what the readings say, and I don't trust the tablets right now. They're too plugged into the ship, which is malfunctioning. I need to know directly what it says." Trenton pulled out a communicator. "It's not advanced, but it'll do. I trust this more than anything else right now. Oh."

Trenton pulled a laser from his pocket. "Take this. In case we get boarded."

Wade nodded, but didn't take the gun. "I have my own, and I'm comfortable with it. Keep yours. In case they get to you first."

Dev put out his hand. "I'll help you down. It's clear north now, too. Oh and south. Just waiting on Blaze. He's west. It's thicker, harder to get through forest. So keep out of the west until I tell you it's clear."

"Will do." Trenton nodded. "So useful to have you guys around. We never need the communicators. Not when we have you."

Wade scooted backward. "I'm going to get some water and head to the control room. I'll be there, and I'll use the communicator in case Devil is otherwise occupied. And, Devil, thanks for your help."

"I told Blaze that, ah, I'd never have imagined this, but now that I'm with all of you, it feels exactly like what I should be doing with myself. Being here, not just with Sienna, but all of you. Maybe there is room for a lot of redemption. Maybe things have a way of working out the way they always should have."

Trenton laughed. "You spent way too much time in the presence of the Chens. You're starting to sound profound."

"The Z warriors do that to people. They're always thinking about life. It's a good thing."

Trenton finally took his arm, and Devil helped him get off the ship. I guess we couldn't jump it, or at least not easily. We could be hurt on more things than a sharp edge on the ground. With Trenton down, Dev turned to me. "Ready?"

I nodded. "Sure."

I expected him to help me down like he had Trenton,

but instead, he held onto me and jumped. I squealed for a second, but my feet never touched the ground until Dev set them there.

"Scare you?"

I blew a piece of hair out of my face. "Yes, I was startled. I thought you were going to help me down."

"Got us both here at the same time. West is clear."

If that was true, then where were the rest of the guys? "Everyone coming back?"

"No, they'll go on and see if they can find Evander now. We'll get started on fixing this baby up." Dev touched the broken ship. "I don't want to leave her here. The Chens will never forgive me. Their wife saved them on this baby. It's something of a legend."

I ran my hands on her side and walked toward Trenton. "All right, boss. Give me a job."

He handed me his tablet. "I don't trust it to communicate with it right now, but we can record on it. Like you're writing it down."

I nodded. "Okay. I've never written on one, but I'll figure it out." I smiled at him. "And someday, everything won't be new and I won't be lost every time I go to do something. I'll have done it."

Trenton nodded. "That would be frustrating. But if I'd had to step into your life, I'm not sure that I could have done it. I mean, what if I had to try to handle the day in and day out routine of your life with no instruction? If they took away my tech, I don't think I could function. So give yourself a break. If things got turned around, I'd be royally fucked."

I hadn't thought about that. "Well, I promise to be as nice to all of you as you've been to me. I'll make notes and put them on the walls."

Trenton grinned. "A rather brilliant move by Corbin. Not that I love saying that he's brilliant when he can hear me."

"Which would be always."

Trenton nodded. He was really delicious looking all the time, but even more so when he smiled, which wasn't very often. "He's probably not listening now. I find they are super focused when it comes to battle. And this is a different kind of battle. We're hunting them, and they are in turn hunting us. Unless they blew up on landing, which I doubt, they're out here somewhere trying to find us."

I considered that for a second. "Couldn't that be on the other side of the planet? Like nowhere near here. Not capable of even getting here by foot."

He walked over and put his arm around me. "Sure. But I never get that lucky. I should warn you. If you stick with me, you're going to discover that whatever can happen to me, does. Okay. So first things first, we have a big giant hole. Write that down."

"You want me to write big giant hole?"

He laughed. "Yes. Totally specific, engineering words. Big. Giant. Hole."

I wrote down just that. As I ran my finger over the tablet it appeared on the screen. Dev walked over and nodded. "It really is a big giant hole."

We all stared at it for a second. I had to ask. "Can we fix it?"

"We can. It's going to mean rebuilding the entire side of the ship, but yes, I can fix it. It would be better if I had a team of people and say, Thomas Sandler to direct the fixing but yes, I can do it."

That name sounded familiar. "Paloma, right? Her husbands were at the disastrous meeting. Blonds?"

He nodded. "They're actually really good guys. Intense. But good. All of the guys in there are. In their own ways. It wasn't a good meeting, and we discounted you. Not okay. We'll do better."

"I don't need you guys to keep apologizing." I walked around looking at the hole. "We have the equipment to fill that hole?"

Trenton smirked. "Hope so."

He put his head in the hole. From that point on, I was making up spelling. The words that he said to me weren't ones that I'd ever heard before. Sometimes he'd call out what tools he was going to need. Like a water wrench. I knew what that was. We had one of those at home.

Dev leaned against a tree and watched us. If Trenton wanted him to help, he didn't indicate it. I figured out pretty quickly that Dev's job seemed to be to watch us. In case something happened.

The planet was hot. There were a ton of thick trees around us, and as the hours passed, it only got hotter. I fanned myself with the tablet. If either of the guys noticed how uncomfortable the temperature was, they didn't mention it, and I wasn't going to be that person, whining when there was nothing to do about it. Particularly because I was pretty sure they'd bend over backward to try to make me feel better, and their attention was better served elsewhere.

Trenton jumped down a ladder from the wing and picked up his communicator. "Wade? You still with us?"

There was a pause before he answered. "If I wasn't, then it's been a long time since anyone checked. I could be dead."

"Nah." Dev shook his head. "Tell him I'd have heard his heart stop beating."

Trenton repeated that, which made Wade laugh. Finally, Trenton spoke again. "Okay, I'm going to try the systems. As it is, we have to fill a really big hole."

"Scientific term." I leaned against a tree, and Dev jolted.

"Quiet." He rounded on us. "They've spotted Evander. They're not far. Close enough that if they get any closer to us, they'll be able to hear our heartbeats. Kellan's closest to them. He's moving fast to disguise his sounds."

My body went cold. "What do we do?"

Dev took my hand as Trenton pulled out his weapon. "Tell Wade to secure himself and hide in the ship. Trenton take Sienna. And run. That way." He pointed straight ahead of him. "Get as far as you two can get before nightfall. We'll find you."

As Trenton relayed the message, I caught my breath. "What will you do?"

"We're going to battle, sweetness. Try not to worry. I almost always win."

Except when he didn't. There had been one time he'd absolutely not won. I wasn't going to bring that up now. "Okay. Be careful."

"One of us will find you as soon as we can."

Trenton pulled me along with him. "Careful, brother."

Dev widened his eyes. It was the last thing I saw as Trenton pulled me away. He hadn't expected the brother comment. But then, I guess maybe they were all brothers in war. This time, Dev was on the same side as Trenton. I held Trenton's hand and tried to keep up with him as we ran. I was terribly dressed for this and had almost no experience running. Walking was about as fast as I'd ever done anything before I'd woken up from cryogenic sleep.

"I can take care of you." Trenton didn't bother to lower his voice. My guess was that we were either far enough to not be heard, or we weren't. "Even though I'm not a Super Soldier."

It hadn't occurred to me that he couldn't. Panting, I nodded. I wasn't going to be the reason we'd get caught. I could do whatever I had to do. I'd always been able to. We ran hard for I didn't know how long. Finally, he stopped.

"You have to tell me if you need to stop."

I nodded. Talking wasn't something I could do right then. I was too out of breath, but I think I managed to nod.

"We don't have any water." He put his hands on his knees. "And I have no idea of the terrain. To say this was not prepped correctly is an understatement. But I will keep you safe." He looked up at the sun. "I know how long a day is here." Trenton took the tablet from me. I didn't realize I'd still been carrying it. "We have another hour of daylight."

Staring up at the orb in the sky, that seemed really surprising to me. "It's still so bright."

"We'll get ten minutes of sunset and then pitch darkness. I want us somewhere we can hide in the dark. I don't want us to just keep running. The guys will keep them back. I know they will. We'll keep moving in the daylight. I have no idea if people live here or what animals come out at night. These bullets are for Evander. Not shooting unknown wildlife."

That made sense. "I trust you."

His face was hard when he stared at me. "I lost my wife. I wasn't with her. But I swear to you, we're going to have time for you to know who I am and that you can trust me."

The pain he carried. I touched the side of his face. "There are some things I know just because I know them. Trusting you is one of those things. I just have one question."

"What's that?" He took both my hands in his.

"What color is your hair? Is it brown? Is it blond? I can't tell."

He snorted, throwing his head back. "It's brown. I'll do something about the dual color when this is over. Unless you'd rather it be blond."

"I don't care what color your hair is. Dye it pink if you want. I was just curious. You're handsome, end of story."

I put my hands on my knees. With everything happening, I probably should not have been focused on his hair. But that other—the big bad Evander that had been chasing me for so long—I was beyond able to deal with that. I was running for my life, and that was enough of a feat for now.

"You okay?" I asked him. "I mean, I guess neither of us thought we were going to do this today."

His smile surprised me. "I'm always up for a good fight, or in this case, run and hide from Evander. I'd rather it was Sandler Cartel, but someone else beat them. I'm still fighting the good fight, and you feel like...a second chance. I couldn't save someone I loved deeply, but I can save you. I know I can. And in the end, we can all walk away and have a great life. Or at least you can. I don't know what happens to me at the end of this. I just know when I saw those blue eyes of yours that I'd do whatever to make sure they always had life in them."

For the first time in my life, I wanted to take someone's pain. I actually would have killed for it. But Trenton had been clear with me from the beginning. That was his and only is. This wasn't the time nor the place to push on that.

Not on this hot, foreign planet. Who would have terraformed a place like this, and why would anyone live here?

Those were not questions I'd get answers to, I didn't think.

WE WALKED, instead of running, until the sun went down. When darkness hit, so did the rain. It was cold, a stark contrast to the heat on my skin. At first it felt nice—a cool shower after a hot walk—but it quickly changed to just being wet and uncomfortable.

Trenton had been quiet for a long stretch of time. He was looking for somewhere to get us cover, and eventually pulled on my arm to drag me under a stretch of trees. The trees were so grown over each other, the branches and leaves seemed to have created an umbrella. We stood under it for a second before he climbed onto one of the trees and extended his hand so I could take it. Unlike when Dev had jumped out of Artemis, I had to help myself up somewhat. Trenton helped for sure, but I did have to participate in the climbing.

He wrapped his arms around me. "I'm sorry. I wish I had a way to get you dry."

Was he kidding? "You're all soaked because you're taking care of me. I should be apologizing to you."

He shook his head. "You're a light in the universe. I'd

never have met you if we weren't living in hell. But even this, hanging out in this tree, wet, it feels great to be here with you." He took my hand. "If I had a light, I'd ask permission to look at your wrist. Let's just assume that tonight, it's at zero. Okay? You're not sick. We're just having a weird date on this planet in the middle of nowhere where we wanted to get wet and sticky."

I laughed. "Are we safe? Did we get far enough away?"

"I think so. We won't know for sure, but I don't hear any gunfire. I don't hear any fighting. And we have signals worked out from the main fighting days that would tell me if we were in danger. The nothingness is a good sign. They're playing cat and mouse with the other Super Soldiers. It could go on a long time. Trust me on this, if you were in danger, we'd know. They won't let anything happen to you any more than I would."

I shivered, and he held me closer, then he stiffened. "Do you see that?"

I didn't see anything, not really. When the clouds moved occasionally, I could see the moons were bright, but all I could see when they weren't illuminated in the darkness were trees, rain, rocks. Not anything else.

"Stay here. I'm not going far. Do you see that glint on the horizon over there?"

I looked, but I really didn't. "No."

"It's...it's close. Just stay up here. I'll be right back. I'm not leaving you."

I cleared my throat. "Trenton, don't forget I can zap. Anyone comes at me, I'll hurt them."

"I haven't forgotten. But if you do that, you'll get taken down and the next one can knock you out. You're not capable of fighting off an army. Just stay here. Two minutes, I'll be back."

What did he think he saw? I never got to ask him, because just as soon as he said those words, he was gone. He disappeared into the night, and I sucked in a breath. I really wasn't as brave as I was pretending to be. It was just when everyone was so incredibly brave, and all for me, I couldn't be whining and screaming in this wet, hot jungle just because I was scared out of my mind.

I listened to the sounds. In the days I wanted to get away from my life, I couldn't have pictured this. All of these men dedicated to me, and this strange place. In some ways, I was the luckiest person in the world. If I could pretend I didn't have any of my other struggles, I'd never been so happy in my life. Wow. I'd really gotten deranged.

Rubbing my eyes, I also tried to listen to the sounds around me. We hadn't seen any animals, but I could hear sounds in the distance that didn't sound human. Something howled. I had next to no experience with wildlife. We had been sheltered from all things that were too 'real' at the temple. More and more resentment rode me about that. There were things I could have known how to handle, if only I had realized I needed to know those things. They'd kept me like a child. No, it was worse than that. They'd left me feeling like a tool. Oh, don't worry, Sienna, you need no life skills. You'll just be a tool for the rest of your life that other people use to feel better. Sit here and do as you're told. You had the so-called good fortune of being born very powerful in the gene mutation department.

Something snapped, like maybe a branch, and I stiffened. Okay. That was close. Whatever it was and I—

"It's me." Trenton climbed back up to where I sat on the branch. I hadn't seen him. Of course, I hadn't been looking, and maybe he was good at hiding. He held something, a bag, in his hand.

"What did you find?"

"There's a cabin, a metal one, a little ways from here. We're going over there to spend the night. It's not warmer, but it's dryer. Put this on. It'll give you some coverage until we get there."

He handed me a jacket. "They have rain gear?"

"That's what is mostly in the cabin. It's loud in there, too. But I think coverage is the most important thing right now. It must rain here like this all of a sudden. Whoever owns that thing is most concerned with not getting wet. There are a few other tools. No food. It'll do for now."

He wasn't covered in anything as he handed me the rain gear. "Why didn't you grab one for you?"

"I was more focused on getting you dry." He smiled. "Come on. I'll be fine for five more minutes, and then I'll change in the shed. It's really a shed. Don't expect great things."

Spending the night in the tree wet or dry in a shed? I'd take the shed. He helped me get down, and although my legs burned from using them in all kinds of ways, I managed not to stumble. Once we were down, I put the coat on, and it did offer some protection from the rain. It was certainly better than not having it.

We walked in silence to the shed he'd found and stepped inside. If outside was dark, it was even more so when he shut the door and closed us in. Trenton pulled out his tablet, which offered some light, and pulled some clothes from a container in the side of the room. He pulled off his shirt, and I did the same, each of us changing into new tops and then eventually bottoms. They were water resistant outfits, not comfortable, but it was nice to be dryer.

The rain pounded on top of the shed's roof. It was loud,

almost deafeningly so. Trenton pulled me over to him, and we both sank down onto the ground.

He stared down at his tablet and then turned it off. "Nothing from them, but I wouldn't expect it. If they were to lose their tablet, it's too easily hacked."

"Should you have it at all then?"

He shook his head. "No, probably not. But we do. So we'll take good care of it."

Trenton drew me close. He smelled like the rain, and I imagined that I did, too. "I wish I had food for you. I'll try to hunt in the morning. I have the tools in here, which are, I think, more meant to handle chopping up tree branches. But I'm good at repurposing things. I'll see what I can do."

I put my head on his shoulder. Exhaustion was starting to hit me, which must mean the adrenaline was running out. "I'm not hungry, and maybe we won't have to worry in the morning. Like we can get back to Artemis."

"Best case scenario, for sure."

I listened to the pounding some more, but it did nothing to soothe my nerves. It was possible to be tired but too strung out to sleep. "Did you grow up doing all of this? Hunting? Climbing? Running?"

His laugh surprised me. That didn't seem like the right response to that question. "Sorry." He laughed again. "No, I'm very rich. Or my family was. We had lots of people to do whatever we wanted to do. I liked ships, so I learned them, and eventually started to fight on behalf of the rebellion when Sandler became a problem. But I mean, rich. That's how I was able to get a wife. Or to be the sort of person she'd meet and pick. Then when she died, I threw my past away pretty much. I don't know what my family is up to. I still have the credits and the gold in my account. It's paid for us to resupply on occasion but...yeah. I'm not the same as I used to be. Or maybe I was never that way. I just tried to make it work, because I thought it was going to be life."

I nodded. "So you and I are the same in some ways. We have a before and an after. And the two lives are hardly recognizable to each other."

He was so quiet, I wondered if I had said the wrong thing. My heart clenched. Finally, he answered. "I'd never thought about it before, but yes, you're right. A before and an after. I like that. It lends itself to the idea that there can be something substantial in the after." Trenton squeezed my hand. "You should try to sleep. I'm going to stay up, and I'll wake you if we need to move or if the guys are coming. Try to rest."

He expected me to rest? In these circumstances. Even as tired as I was getting, I couldn't see that happening. But eventually, I did doze. It might have been the sound of the rain on the roof, my utter exhaustion, or the fact that Trenton held me tight against him and I trusted him. Or maybe it was that I was sick and my numbers were rising. Or that I'd run for hours when I'd never done anything like that before.

All I knew was that one second, I was wide-awake, and the next, there was blissful darkness.

"Sienna." Trenton shook me gently. Once, then twice. I came awake, all at once, and he placed a hand over my mouth to hush me.

I nodded. Okay. I wouldn't talk. He let go of my mouth and held up his tablet so I could see what he'd typed on it. *Someone is here.*

That someone was obviously not one of our someones. I lifted my head to nod. What were we going to do inside this shed? Trenton got to his feet and pointed at me. He wanted me to stay where I was. I pulled my knees up to my chest. Would making myself smaller and hidden work in this place? There was the slightest sunlight coming through under the door. How did he know we had company?

Trenton grabbed a tool off the wall. If it could strike down branches, it could hurt people. He snuck out the door, closing it behind him silently. I was glad the thing didn't squeak.

I put my head on top of my knees. I had to learn how to fight. That was pivotal. I had to be able to take care of myself if it came down to survival. I had to learn electronics. There were a lot of hads in my life. Right now, I wanted to help Trenton. I didn't want to be a damsel in this shed. But I'd only make things worse by interfering at this juncture. I was incompetent, but not stupid.

A sudden oof followed by a yell sounded outside. A second later, Trenton spoke. "Who are you?"

"Oh, no. Please don't hurt me. Take what you want. Just let me get home to my family."

I jumped to my feet and rushed through the door. A man was on his back on the other side of it. Trenton held the cutting tool to his throat. "I'll ask again. Who are you?"

"My name...my name is Robert Seewald. This is my hunting shed. I... Take it."

Trenton met my gaze and then dropped his weapon, throwing it to the side. "We don't want your shed. Or your stuff. We needed it for the night. We're running from some people who would hurt us."

Robert's color came back slowly, but he still didn't get off the ground. "Wh-what?"

I didn't know for sure, but since Evander was made up of Super Soldiers, I was going to fathom a guess that this poor man, who we'd terrified, was not one of those. He was at least fifteen pounds overweight and smaller in height than me. Unless I was only seeing one kind of Super Soldier, I didn't think this guy would have qualified.

I walked over to him, bent over, and helped him up. "We're on the run from Evander. Do you know who that is? We had to hide in your shed. And borrow your things. We aren't going to keep them. We're going to figure out how to get them back to you."

He finally stood up straight. "Evander? That's awful." Robert shot Trenton a long look. "Maybe I can understand why you knocked me down. Sort of." He pointed to the shed. "Is Evander here again? Because if Evander is here, we need to tell people. And maybe we could help you instead of you hiding in that shed and hurting people."

Trenton cleared his throat. "Sorry about that. I wasn't sure that you weren't here to hurt my girl. I had to be sure."

Robert's jaw hardened. "Come with me. We have people who can help you get away. Why does Evander want you anyway? I thought they were gone. We get such conflicting information out here, which is a good thing and a bad thing. A good thing, because people mostly leave us alone."

I caught Trenton's gaze. What did he want to do here? Did he want to go with this man or stay here in his shed? Or do something else entirely?

"Okay." Trenton nodded. "We'll go with you." He held out his hand, and I took it. Why were we changing our strategy like this? I didn't ask, because Trenton kept speaking to Robert. "You have experience with Evander, then?"

He looked over his shoulder as we followed him. "Does anyone not have experience with Evander? They got all the way out here. I know this is supposed to be the end of the universe, but we still have our bad experiences out here."

I smiled. If only he knew how much farther out in the universe I'd come from. We'd been the last planet they terraformed all those long years ago. Way before I was born. Before my grandparents were born. And here we all were... still on the edge of the galaxy.

"Oh yeah?" Trenton squeezed my fingers. "What did they do to you guys?"

He grumbled. "They took all of our fruit. Every last bit of it. That's what we sell here, mostly. Our fruit is the best in the galaxy."

I suddenly knew where we were. Yes, the McGrintaugh Cluster—as the three planets were jointly known, even though people only lived on one—was famous for fruit. We really weren't that far into the Dark Planets. This was practically the Earth Zone.

"It is really good fruit," I said. "I miss it. Our local grown fruit doesn't compare. We don't get it that often because of pirates, but when we do, oh my gosh, it's the best."

This seemed to tickle Robert's happy button. He grinned. "Mine is the best, too. These are my woods. Well, you've figured that. We'll be lucky if we manage enough of a crop to deal with next year. It might be two years." He sighed. "I'm so glad they ran them out. Those people from Mars and their ilk."

Trenton smirked. I bet he liked that description. Those people from Mars. Were any of them actually from Mars?

"We'll take your thanks. And they're not totally gone yet. Soon. We're getting rid of them."

Robert whirled around. "Really? You're one of them?"

"Yes, I was part of that crew. Frankly, we only got as far as we did because some of Evander turned on Evander. Do you have food where we're going? I'm happy to pay for it. I just need to get food for my girl."

I loved how he called me that. His girl.

"We'll get you squared up. I'll forgive you now that I know you're one of those people from Mars."

Trenton's smile was huge. When he grinned that big, he had a dimple I hardly ever got to see. "My wife, sorry, my late wife, she was from Mars. Originally. But I'm from Earth. Born and raised in the Canyon District."

Now Robert seemed even more impressed. He was practically bouncing. "Earth? Really?"

We came through a clearing, and there was a small town ahead. I'd had no idea we were so close to civilization. It had felt like we were in the middle of nowhere. Trenton pulled out his tablet. There was a message on it. He quickly put it away. I nudged him. "All okay?"

"Wade's checking in. I'll shoot him a message when I'm sure it's safe." He spoke low. "That's right. I'm from Earth."

"It's you," someone shouted from the distance, and we all turned. "You're from the temple."

A woman rushed toward me, her husband in tow. I blinked. It had been a long time since I'd seen them. They'd moved off world a long time ago. Almost no one did, so it had caused something of a stir at the time.

"Hello." I stiffened my back. "I'm sorry. I don't remember your names." I rarely did. Just their struggles. I still had Anders' pain running around inside of me. I'd gotten used to it, but it was there. These two had been anxious about the future and...

She opened her arms wide. Oh. She wanted a hug.

Trenton put his arm around me. "I'm sorry. She's not doing that right now. Sienna's not feeling well. Mostly because Evander tried to hurt her. It's been an ordeal. You wouldn't want to hurt her, right? I mean...you're so excited to see her. So you must care. Right?"

His words were a challenge, but those two couldn't feel how tense he was next to me. If they made a move for the hug I didn't want to give right then, he might physically hurt them. Robert cleared his throat. He knew how Trenton could react to things.

"You know her?" he asked between them. "I found them in the shed. They're hiding from Evander."

The crowd that was slowly forming behind us started to whisper to each other. Finally, someone shouted. "Evander is here?"

I nodded. "Unfortunately, they are. We have...friends who were on our ship with us. Haven't seen them in a while, but they're trying to take care of the Evander problem."

"We spent the night in a shed, and Sienna's not feeling well. Is there someplace we can pay to stay?" Trenton asked, but no one was paying attention to him.

Instead, the woman whose name I still couldn't remember leaned forward. "This woman has powers to make others feel better. She lived in a temple, sort of like a priestess." I wouldn't have put it like that, but no one was asking me as they turned toward the storyteller. "We need to protect her. She's very important. Hide her until it's safe."

"Um..." I wasn't sure what to say to this. "I'm not interested in getting anyone hurt on my behalf. I'm just a person like any other person."

"I insist." She grabbed my arm. "Come along. And no more talk about paying anything. This is our pleasure to do this. People have to know what's happening. They have to protect you. Evander can't be allowed to just take what they like."

We were rushed into a building, then out the back door of it and eventually into another house that was further into the woods. Food was put out in front of us, and I was separated from Trenton when they insisted I had to have a shower. I took advantage of the time. What were the chances that I'd run into someone here? Or maybe the chances were quite high. My planet's people were scattered. They were probably everywhere.

Trenton stood outside the door, waiting for me when I'd come out. He was changed, too. I walked up to him, breathing in his clean scent. "Do you think this is okay? I don't want Evander to hurt them."

"Doubtful they'll hurt them if they don't get in the way. I messaged Wade back. He's on his way. If it's safe. He's had no contact either." Trenton had a good poker face, but something about the way he twisted his bottom lip told me he was concerned about that fact.

I nodded. "This is off protocol, right? All of it? Them not making any contact. No sign of any of them, and Wade leaving Artemis?"

"It is. I'm concerned. But if these people can help us—starting by getting you fed—then maybe they can help me fix Artemis. Then I'm getting you off this planet while I figure out what to do for the others. That's what's happening."

I shook my head. "We're not leaving them here."

"Yes we are. That's what's happening. Your safety, Evander not getting you, it comes first. They would agree. They would insist on it."

I put my arms around his neck. "Trenton, I can't stop caring that people are getting hurt for me."

"They're not. They're getting hurt because Evander has an agenda that includes using you. Think about it this way, and if no one has told you this or if they have and you just can't roll around with it, try again. If Evander takes you, they will figure out a way to hurt a lot of people using you. Or using your abilities. I don't know how or why yet, but that's what's going to happen."

The truth of that settled on my shoulders like lead bricks. It was a lot to carry. "Trenton..."

"Your father thought it was important to keep you safe. He was right. We think that, too. These strangers here think it as well. It's time for you to decide it's true. Do you understand?" He kissed the end of my nose. "If we want to keep you safe, that's what we're doing. And you need to stop feeling badly about it. Do you understand? Just do your best to help us do that. Someday, you can try really hard to keep me alive or something."

My nose tingled where he'd kissed me. "Okay."

"Let's get you fed."

I nodded. I wanted to agree with everything that he'd said to me. The trouble was that I'd looked at the number on my arm when I'd been in the shower. I was up to seven. There were some things they couldn't protect me from.

THEY WERE INCREDIBLY gracious with us, feeding us and not letting Trenton pay, even though he kept trying to do that. We sat at a table, listening to the others talk about the terrible time they'd had with Evander. They'd really been raided.

"I hate to tell you that you guys were lucky." Trenton cleared his throat. "Most of the time, when Evander takes on a planet, they don't leave anything. Not even the people." A knock sounded, and everyone jumped. Trenton held up his hand. "Don't panic. That's Wade. He can actually attest to what Evander does to planets."

Julia—I'd finally remembered the name of the woman who was helping us—looked around. "Who is Wade?"

"He's with us." Trenton went to the door and opened it. Sure enough, Wade stood there. He looked worse for wear. He had a night's worth of hair growth on his face. His eyes were bloodshot, and he was still in the same clothes he'd been in before, except that he'd clearly sweated through them.

"Hey, everyone." Wade smiled, and after a visible

breath, stepped inside. "I didn't realize there were so many people."

I rose and strode toward him. "I'm glad that you're here." I took his hand. "And not happy that the guys have all vanished."

Wade ran a hand through his hair. "I don't love it either, but I trust that they know what they're doing. I promise you, they're not dead or taken. There would be an explosion or something before that happened. If they're all silent, and they're not contacting us, then all I can say is that we just have to trust they know what they're doing." He motioned toward the table. "Would it be okay if I poured myself some water?"

Everyone jumped to their feet and scrambled to make Wade a plate. He sat down quietly. I could really see the tired in his eyes. I'd dozed on Trenton, who seemed okay, but Wade had been all on his own. I sat down next to him, Trenton taking my other side.

"Did you do okay in the ship?"

He gave me a small smile. "It was very, very hot."

"Drink more water."

He lifted the cup to his mouth. "On it. Gladly. I was glad to get Trenton's message and directions to get here from the tablet. Not protocol, but I wasn't spending another night on that ship. I'd never have made it. Not with the water down."

"The water was down?" Trenton shouted, and then grimaced. "Sorry. That's a change."

"It went out halfway through the night."

I winced. "That's awful. I'm sorry."

Trenton leaned back in his chair. "We have to abandon Artemis. We have to buy a ship and get off this planet before we hurt these people by being here, and we have to get Sienna away."

Wade nodded. "Agreed."

One of the men at the end of the table, whose name escaped me, leaned forward. "We can keep her safe for you until you get back, if that's what you want."

My heart sank into my stomach. "Shouldn't we wait for Blaze? I mean...wouldn't this be a discussion he would want to be a part of."

Julia smiled at me. "Are you in one of those plural marriages so popular on Earth? The ones with multiple men?"

I hadn't expected that question, and suddenly, sitting in this place with its yellow walls and bright fixtures was exposing. I didn't really know what we were doing, and marriage had certainly never been discussed, not even a topic of conversation. Things were just getting started.

"We're very serious about her," Wade answered. "But we haven't had those conversations yet. Ultimately, it's what Sienna wants. It will be what we want. Is there a place I can shower? I hate to keep having to rely on all of you."

Trenton answered my question I'd asked earlier. "We'll wait till tomorrow morning to make any decisions. By then, I think we'll have heard from them. And if we haven't, that is its own answer. I need you to trust Wade and me on this. We've been with these guys a long time. If we haven't had some contact by tomorrow, then we have to get out of here."

I did trust him. I just hated this.

"Shower is through there," Julia indicated.

"I got a message out to reinforcements before we landed. But who knows if they got it and how long it'll take them to get here if they did." Trenton rubbed his eyes. "We'll figure it out tomorrow." He got to his feet. "I'll show you where the bathroom is, Wade. Don't want you getting lost."

They were tired. Maybe that was why Trenton wanted to show Wade, even though it had been shown to him before. I could see the exhaustion in every move they both made, and if I was worried, they had to be doubly so. They actually understood how weird this was that they'd been so out of touch. I walked into the kitchen to help clean up, and after a while, it was just Julia and me there.

She stopped the water and turned to me. "Is it weird to be here? To be out of the temple?"

A fair question. "This place is more like the temple than where I was on the ship. I couldn't even make the lights work."

Julia crossed her arms. "You sound like that bothers you, like you're embarrassed. That's what I hear in your voice."

I swallowed. All the women from our planet had some abilities with emotions, even if none of them were me. The right word for it might be empathic. There was always a certain amount of empaths in any population. Or at least, that was what I'd learned. Our planet had something unique with the female line.

I had to answer her, as uncomfortable as it was to do so. "It does. I felt like a baby, and there have been parts of me every day that continue to feel that way. Like I never know exactly what to do in any situation. How am I supposed to help if I'm constantly lost?"

"Sienna, you've helped people your whole life. It isn't too much to have to ask others help you for a while as you find your feet. And as for the technology, I was a little lost with it too. Once you settle someplace safe, you'll learn your own tech, and eventually, it won't feel so weird."

I supposed that made sense. "Feels ridiculous to worry

about any of it when there are five guys out there in potential harm for me."

"I doubt their fight with Evander started or ends with you. I think you've just found yourself in the middle of the story. Take a breath, healer. You're allowed time to adjust. You're not lost in the universe. If anything, you needed help, and I was here. What are the chances of that? Someone who knows who you are? Maybe you're right where you're supposed to be."

She was turning out to be a lot nicer than I'd have thought she would. Maybe I had overreacted to the hug she'd wanted. It was just so...invasive.

"Thanks. That does help me look at it slightly differently. I've been a fish out of water for a long time."

Trenton rushed into the room, followed by Wade, whose shoes were untied. He must have been getting ready to sleep. His hair was wet. What was happening?

"Got to go. Julia, can we use your shuttle?"

Her eyes widened. "Of course. What's wrong?"

Rather than answer her, Trenton passed his tablet to me. It had one word on it from Blaze. I stared down at it as though I'd never read words before.

Blaze had texted the word *Run*.

Trenton pulled me up against him. "We'll pay you for your shuttle. More than it's worth. Thank you for helping us. Come on."

Wade nodded. "No time to lose."

Yes, but where were we going to run to? "Guys, where will we go?"

Trenton pointed up at the sky. That was right. The other Super Soldiers could maybe hear us if they were getting close. We couldn't talk. I swallowed. We were going to space. This time, without Artemis and any Super Soldiers to guide our way.

I nodded. I might never find my feet in this war, in this world, in this madness. But I'd be damned if I let Evander make me scared for even one second more. I could control nothing but my reactions, and it was time for me to be angry, not scared.

I had a feeling I'd much prefer that emotion.

Dear Reader,

Please don't worry. You can grab Pointed Arrow (Wings of Artemis 12) the last book in Wings of Artemis here: https://amzn.to/2K69SpB . I hope you liked reading Sienna's first book as much as I did writing it and don't worry, their adventure and love story continues right where this one left off.

Please turn the page for the complete list of my books and to see where to find me online.

Regards

Rebecca Royce

As a teenager, I would hide in my room to read my favorite romance novels when I was supposed to be doing my homework.

I am the mother of three adorable boys and I am fortunate to be married to my best friend. I live in Austin Texas where I am determined to eat all the barbecue in town.

I am in love with science fiction, fantasy, and the paranormal and try to use all of these elements in my writing. I've been told I'm a little bloodthirsty so I hope that when you read my work you'll enjoy the action packed ride that always ends in romance. I love to write series because I love to see characters develop over time and it always makes me happy to see my favorite characters make guest appearances in other books.

In my world anything is possible, anything can happen, and you should suspect that it will.

I'd love to hear from you! Please visit my website at www.rebeccaroyce.com to sign up for my newsletter and learn about my books!

Here's where you can find me online:

Rebecca's Randomness Reading Group https://www.facebook.com/groups/RebeccasRandomness/

https://www.rebeccaroyce.com

https://www.facebook.com/authorrebeccaroyce/

www.twitter.com/rebeccaroyce

Instagram: rebeccaroyce79
Cheers!!
Rebecca

OTHER BOOKS BY REBECCA ROYCE...

Wings of Artemis

Kidnapped By Her Husbands https://amzn.to/2BQdUxy

Rescued by Their Wife https://amzn.to/2Rr9as4

Crashing Into Destiny https://amzn.to/2VkyXRL

Meeting Them https://amzn.to/2BLPaXm

Reclaiming Their Love https://amzn.to/2GKAw8E

Loving Them https://amzn.to/2BKDmEK

Ship Called Malice https://amzn.to/2BNputj

Saving Them https://amzn.to/2SsrBtH

Dark Demise https://amzn.to/2VidXv3

Light Unfolding https://amzn.to/2GO6Yqr

Still Waters https://amzn.to/2CFePT8

Rising Tides https://amzn.to/2MCdTlM

Lost Star https://amzn.to/2X8hcZA

Pointed Arrow https://amzn.to/2K69SpB

Last Hope (completed series)

Tradition Be Damned

Past Be Damned

Destiny Be Damned

Compassion Be Damned

Future Be Damned

Dragon Wars (completed series)

Forever

Eternal

Always

Evermore

Endless

Wards and Wands (completed series)

Hexed and Vexed

Curse Reversed

Meow, Baby (novella, co-written with Ripley Proserpina)

Tragic Magic

Safe Haven

Everywhere and Nowhere

Dimension X (coming soon)

More coming soon....

Soul Bound

Prisoner of the Dragons

More coming soon....

Shadow Promised

Strange Days

Weird Nights

Bizarre Years

More coming soon...

The Warrior (completed series)

Initiation

Driven

Subversive

Redemption

Justice

Warrior World (spin off of The Warrior, completed series)

Deacon

Micah

Jason

The Westervelt Wolves (completed series)

Her Wolf

Summer's Wolf

Wolf Reborn

Wolf's Valentine

Wolf's Magic

Alpha Wolf

Angel's Wolf

Darkest Wolf

Lone Wolf

Fallen Alpha

Alpha Rising

Alpha's Strength

Alpha's Sacrifice

Alpha's Truth

Alpha Enticing

Hidden Alpha (coming soon)

The Capes (completed series)

Seductive Powers

Adrenaline Rush

Last Ascension

Illicit Minds

Illicit Senses

Illicit Connections

Illicit Alliance (coming soon)

The Outsiders

Love Beyond Time

Love Beyond Sanity

Love Beyond Loyalty

Love Beyond Sight

Love Beyond Expectations

Love Beyond Oceans

Love Beyond Flames

Love Beyond Lies

Love Beyond Death (coming soon)

Cascade (completed series)

Haunted Redemption

Phoenix Everlasting

Fragility Unearthed

Persuasion Enraptured

Reverse Harem Story (completed series)

Unconventional

Unexpected

Undeniable

Kiss Her Goodbye (completed series)

Hard Truths

Dark Truths

Deadly Truths

Shifter World

Planet Bear

Planet Wolf (coming soon)

The Swamp

Hidden

Pursued

Caught (coming soon)

Stand Alone Titles

Under The Lights

No Quitting Allowed

Mr. Wrong

Bite Marks

Bitten Surrender

The Vampire and The Virgin

Demon Within

Crimson Lust

Call Me Crazy

The Men of Elite Metal

The Storm (writing with Ripley Proserpina) **completed series.**

Lightning Strikes

Thunder Rolling

The Deluge

Heart of the Nebula (writing with Heather Long) **completed series**

Queenmaker

Deal Breaker

Throne Taker

Stupid Boys (writing with C.R. Jane)

Stupid Boys

Dumb Girl

Crazy Love

Through the Gates (writing with Skye MacKinnon)

Purgatory City

Infernal Land (coming soon)

The Coveted (writing with Ripley Proserpina)

Eyes in the Darkness

Voices in the Darkness

Return to the Darkness (coming soon)

Prison Princess (part of the Nightmare Penitentiary world, writing with CoraLee June)